Elizabeth Rolls lives in the Adelaide Hills of South Australia, with her husband, two sons, several dogs and cats and a number of chickens. She has a well-known love of tea and coffee, far too many books and an overgrown garden. Currently Elizabeth is wondering if she should train the dogs to put her sons' dishes in the dishwasher rather than continuing to ask the boys. She can be found on Facebook, and readers are invited to contact her at books@elizabethrolls.com.

THE SCANDALOUS WIDOW

Elizabeth Rolls

MILLS & BOON

First published in Great Britain 2024
by Mills & Boon, an imprint of HarperCollins*Publishers* Ltd,
1 London Bridge Street, London, SE1 9GF

www.harpercollins.co.uk

HarperCollins*Publishers*, Macken House, 39/40 Mayor Street Upper, Dublin 1, D01 C9W8, Ireland

ISBN: 978-0-263-32093-0

10/24

For Gabby and Anna.

This is for all the friendship and laughter
in the Hawks' Nest kitchen over so many years.

And huge thanks for letting me make you
ladies of 'ill-repute' in the last book!

Prologue

Early March

Althea Hartleigh held the letter her manservant had handed her between thumb and forefinger and considered it carefully. Yes, that was her name and style, set out correctly in a neat, businesslike script. On the reverse—no need to look again, it was engraved on her memory—was the name, style and address of her brother's solicitor. No postmark.

'This was hand-delivered, John?'

She hadn't meant to sound snappish. The whiskery nose of her small scruffy terrier emerged from under her desk in hopes of a walk, but retreated immediately.

'Yes, ma'am. Chap's waiting in case you wish to send a reply.'

She hardly ever lost her temper now. There was so rarely anyone with whom to lose it. For the past several years she had deliberately lived her life free of familial entanglements and obligations. Who the hell needed them?

But now memory rose up, flooding through her in a scalding torrent—memories she preferred to forget. Everything she had lost, and decided she no longer needed or wanted, spilled over in a fury of hurt. Her fingers opened, and the letter fluttered into the fire. Satisfaction burned darkly as the letter flared. No doubt Frederick's solicitor, the hapless Mr Hugh Guthrie, was really a very nice old man. She knew he had delivered Frederick's last communiqué some years ago under duress, and she had felt sorry for his obvious discomfort, but if Frederick wished to speak to her, he could find the intestinal fortitude to face her.

'Ma'am? Is that your reply?'

She stared at the merrily burning letter a moment longer. The wax of the unbroken seal went up with a hiss. She clenched her fists, then forced them to relax, and reached for calm.

'You could say that.' Poor Mr Guthrie didn't deserve her venom. 'Please inform the messenger that, while I have no personal animus towards his master, my brother Frederick may burn in hell along with all his works for all I care.'

'Yes, my lady.'

As the door closed behind him, Althea reflected that she must have shocked John to his boots for him to fall back on calling her *my lady*. For a moment she wondered if burning the letter unread had been the best decision she could have made. She dismissed that. It was done now. Time to gather her thoughts. She sat back at her untidy desk, picked up her pen and dipped it in the ink. Back to work. This letter was important.

Ten minutes later she was still staring at a blank page, the thoughts she actually *wanted* ungathered. The ink upon the quill went dry as thoughts she very definitely didn't want churned through her.

Damn.

Words eluded her. She wished her thoughts would do likewise. Had she done the right thing?

'Too late if I haven't, Puck.'

A tail, attached to the dog beneath her desk, thumped.

'Damn.' Saying it aloud didn't help either.

She looked under the desk, met hopeful brown eyes. 'We'll walk down to the bookshop.'

She bent down and changed into her outdoor shoes, conveniently located under her desk.

The tail increased its activity and Puck, correctly interpreting the shoe change and the word *walk*, trotted over to the door where his leash hung. Althea rose. One of the many nice things about living alone was that no one cared if your bonnet and cloak hung on the back of the parlour door with the dog's leash, or that your outdoor shoes lived under your desk. It wasn't slovenly. It was *convenient*. Your shoes and cloak were exactly where you needed them if you decided on impulse to go out, and no one cared or fussed at you over it. She retrieved a pair of gloves from her desk drawer and drew them on. Her house, her home, her life and her choices. No one told you that, no, you might not have a dog under any circumstances. Having a dog and keeping a pair of gloves in the drawer of your desk might not be very important choices, but they were *her* choices.

Her finished library books were already on the hall table. Selbourne's Antiquarian Books a few streets away had a circulating library attached. By rights she should finish her letter before going for a walk. Instead she'd change her books and take some fresh air—well, as fresh as London air ever got—and settle her mind. She could negotiate better afterwards.

Her stomach was still knotted twenty minutes later when she pushed open the door of Selbourne's, despite the brisk walk. Why should she feel guilty about burning a letter from Frederick's solicitor? Whatever social crimes her not-so-beloved brother was laying at her door now, she didn't need to see them set out in his solicitor's elegant script.

Smiling at the proprietress as she rose from her desk, Althea asked, 'Have you anything suitable for mentally consigning uncongenial relatives to a place of great heat?'

Miss Selbourne, a lady some years older than herself, raised her brows as she took a dog biscuit from some fastness in her desk. 'I believe I can accommodate you with a nice translation of *The Divine Comedy*. Puck?'

The dog sat immediately, and Miss Selbourne tossed the biscuit to him. He snatched it from the air, trotted to the fireplace where Miss Selbourne's much larger, if equally scruffy dog opened a tolerant eye in greeting, and then Puck settled down to enjoy it.

Althea smiled, some of her restless irritation melting away. She liked this shop, and she liked its owner. She had no idea how Miss Selbourne, whose married name was Lady Martin Lacy, managed to balance marriage, family and owning a business in practical terms, let alone the legal quagmire for a married woman running a business. Sometimes she wanted to ask, but that would require a greater intimacy than she was prepared to accept. Relationships, most of them, were too wretchedly complicated.

One week later

Hugo Guthrie spent as little time as possible hanging around inn yards. Especially on cold March days, and extra-especially the Bolt-in-Tun on Fleet Street. In his admittedly theoretical experience, inn yards were an excellent place to have your pockets picked whatever the weather. They were also excellent places to find a whore for the night. Often you could have both for the price of one, with your choice of whore slipping a little something extra into your drink and making off with your possessions. Including your clothes.

Or so he had been told. He was not interested in learning such things from his own experience.

The Bolt had a particularly well-earned reputation for drunken sprees and otherwise riotous gatherings. Again, this was second-hand knowledge.

With these dubious delights in mind, he kept close to the wall of the inn, making sure his wallet was secure along with his watch. For good measure he added a forbidding frown for any suspect female who thought to approach him.

It wouldn't do his reputation in the legal fraternity any good if his partner had to rescue him naked from some stew near the Bolt. He glanced at his watch for the umpteenth time—the stagecoach was now officially late.

Probably not unusual. Indeed, when he'd come down a couple of days ago, to ask the landlord what time the coach was due in from Hastings, he'd been told as much. But he hadn't dared risk being late. Not for this particular coach. So he'd arrived early, whiling away the first hour in the tap with a quiet pint of ale.

The pint a pleasant memory, he'd decided to wait in the yard despite the light drizzle. He stiffened as a respectable looking female sauntered in. It was possible she *was* as completely respectable as her garb implied. That she'd merely come to meet a relative off the stage…or it was possible that she was a brothel-keeper, looking not for clients, but for new girls. And, if the latter—he noted her speak briefly to a much younger, prettily dressed female—it was also likely she was keeping an eye on the current girls.

Men and horses came and went through the narrow tunnel leading out to Fleet Street. Two young bucks rode in a hired gig with a dappled cob between the shafts. Errand boys scurried in and out, doubtless with a sprinkling of pickpockets amongst them. A stray dog nosed about, but made off when an ostler threatened it with a broom. All sorts made their living around an inn.

He idly wondered, if he took all due precautions, it might be interesting to spend more time in places like this, watching the bustle from a safe distance. With his back firmly to the wall.

A small ginger cat strutted across the yard, a large rat dangling from its jaws, and disappeared into the stables. From the plush state of the cat's fur, Hugo surmised that the creature more than earned its keep. He pulled his cloak a little closer against the rain and the wind that whipped against it even in the sheltered yard. He'd wear his muffler if he did this again.

'Here she comes!'

The yell from a man by the gate heralded a clatter of hooves and rumble of wheels, magnified by the confines of the tunnel, as the stagecoach lumbered in.

Hugo stepped forward as soon as the vehicle drew

to a halt, taking care to stay out of the way of the os-
tlers managing the four sturdy, sweating horses who
looked as though they needed a feed and a rest.

The doors opened and passengers alighted. None
of them, he saw at a glance, were the pair he was supposed to meet. Worry gnawed in his belly. What if
they'd got off too early? What if—

'Sorry, guv. 'Scuse me.'

He turned, moving aside for the ostler. 'My apologies.'

'No problem. Just got to help this little lass down.'

Little lass? Down?

Hugo looked up at the dark-haired child, no more
than eight, which the guard was helping down from
the roof. Another girl, several years older, started to
scramble after her. Her hood tumbled back to reveal
a pale face and honey-gold curls.

'Now, hold on, missy.' The ostler set the little girl
down and held up his hand for the older girl, who
clutched a valise. As soon as she was down the girl
hurried to the smaller child who clung to her hand.

Hugo didn't believe it. Didn't want to believe it. The
bastard hadn't even paid for inside seats?

He swallowed. What the devil did he know of young
girls? What was he supposed to say to them? Sometimes the obvious was best.

He cleared his throat. 'Miss Price? Miss Sarah
Price?' He wondered at the croaky sound of his own
voice.

The girl, her knuckles white on the valise, looked at him. The little girl, eyes reddened and swollen, shrank against her. Hugo's stomach knotted.

'Yes. Who…who are you?'

The defiance in her voice and lifted chin told him everything he didn't want to know. And everything Sarah Price didn't want him to know—that she was terrified.

'I'm Mr Guthrie, Mr Hugh Guthrie. Your father's lawyer. I'm here to meet you and your sister.' He smiled at the little girl, who practically disappeared into her sister's shadow. 'Did no one accompany you?'

Why was he even asking? The man who had refused to look after these children, had put them on the stagecoach in outside seats, wasn't going to waste a return fare on a servant to accompany them.

The older girl shook her head. Suspicious green eyes looked him up and down. 'How do we know you're who you say you are?'

Hugo took out the letter he'd been sent. It was the last thing he wanted to show the poor child, but he couldn't expect her to trust him without question. 'This was sent to me by your cousin, Mr Price-Babbington. Asking me to meet you today.'

Still the child hesitated. Beside her the smaller girl began to shiver.

'Sarah?' The voice was a mere whisper, as though the poor little scrap scarcely dared speak. 'Did he know Papa?'

Hugo tried again. 'Sarah, your sister—Kate, isn't it?—is cold. Why don't you come into the inn with me? I... I can secure a private parlour. Perhaps some dinner.'

The little girl looked hopeful. 'Dinner? Really? The driver shared his food with us, but we didn't have enough money at the last stage for anything.'

The rage Hugo had been tamping down since receiving Price-Babbington's instructions for these girls flared up all over again. Damn the bastard to hell and back. No. Not back. Price-Babbington could stay in hell where he belonged.

'Dinner, then.'

Sarah Price's expression still spat defiance. 'Are you taking us to the orphanage after that?'

He clenched his fists. 'No.'

He'd spent the last week tracking down as many members of their family as he possibly could. While he didn't hold out any hope for their father's estranged—not to mention impecunious and disgraced—sister, Lady Hartleigh, to take them in—apparently she hadn't even bothered to read his letter—there were plenty of other relatives who could. He'd hoped that by now one of those relatives would have replied in the affirmative.

The next words out of his mouth burned every bridge there had ever been. 'There won't be any orphanage.'

He'd write to the entire family again. They couldn't

not respond, surely. Meanwhile, Hugo contemplated the wreck of his own neatly ordered world while he waited for them to do so.

Chapter One

Two weeks later

Althea set her pen down, and sprinkled sand on her completed columns of figures with pardonable pride. After four years of hard work and stringent economy she was solvent and looked like she would remain so. She even had a nice little nest egg. Money, safely invested, that brought an income she could live on comfortably. Not extravagantly as she once had, but comfortably. She was safe. Well, as safe as she had ever been. Certainly safer than she had been during her marriage, let alone the first two years of her widowhood.

Because she'd made herself look at figures.

She *hated* figures. As a very small child she had got into trouble for praying to God to 'uninvent arithmetic' so she wouldn't have to do it. Nanny had thought it was funny and told the other servants so that it got back to her governess.

Miss Fairley had informed her small charge that she was both ignorant and irreligious. Extra sums for a month was the penance.

Althea stuck her tongue out at the defeated figures. She *loathed* doing the household accounts, but adults often had to do things that they hated and found boring, and do them properly. Responsible adults that was—those who wished to understand how much money they had to live on and thereby remain out of a debtors' prison. She might hate the household accounts, but she liked managing for herself and not being dependent on anyone.

Now that she had finished the thrice cursed accounts she could get back to the new people strolling around in her head. She needed to get them out of her head and onto paper so she could find out what they were going to do. At least she was reasonably sure that Miss Parker... Sarah? Sarah Parker? She liked that. It was a decently plain name. Nothing outlandish—no Esmeraldas, thank you very much—and she'd always liked the name Sarah. Hmm. Hopefully if she got Sarah onto the page a gentleman would show up to annoy her in due course. She pulled out a piece of paper and picked up a pencil.

This was another way she could be in charge. In theory at least, the people in her head did what she wanted them to do. In theory. The reality was that they were as stubborn and uncooperative as any other people.

Sarah Parker...

She could work with that for now. If it wasn't right she'd know soon enough, because Miss Parker would freeze solid on the page and decline to budge. Mr Annoying wouldn't show up either.

She stretched, wriggling her tight shoulders. Beneath her feet there was an instant upheaval and Puck's greyish, brownish nose poked out from under the desk. Hopeful brown eyes smiled up at her—she knew that under the desk a decidedly scrappy tail would be blurred. The flyaway ear twitched and the droopy one did its very best to stand up. It failed.

She rolled her shoulders and sighed. 'You're quite correct. It is time to go out. I've been at this desk far too long. We can discuss Miss Sarah and her potential swain on our walk.'

Head cocked to one side, Puck uttered a whine.

'I'll point out to you that it was raining until quite recently. And I was doing my accounts. Seeing how much it costs to feed you.'

Puck whined again, emphasised with a paw on her knee, and she grinned. 'Oh, very well. Leash. Where's your leash?'

The dog shot across the room, his tail a paean to the heavens, and grabbed his leash that hung from the doorknob. He trotted back, dropped it at her feet and sat expectantly.

Althea laughed outright as she stood up. 'Good boy. Give me a moment to change my shoes and—blast!'

The doorbell jangled loudly.

She wasn't expecting anyone. No one called much anyway, and the one person who might call unexpectedly at this hour—her friend, Lady Rutherford—was not currently in London. John would send the unwelcome caller away. He knew better than to admit anyone when she was dealing with the accounts.

She sat down again. Best not to go out into the front hall while John was lying through his teeth, telling whoever it was that she wasn't home.

The door opened and John came in. 'I'm sorry, ma'am. A gentleman to see you.'

She knew better than to think John would have accepted a bribe to make the attempt, but some gentlemen she knew could be unpleasantly insistent. 'I'm not at home, John. You may tell him I said so.' It had been a while since any gentlemen had thought it worth their while to call on her. She'd hoped they had given up.

John hesitated. 'Ah, it's that lawyer, my lady.'

She stared. 'A lawyer? Mr Brimley?'

John held out a salver with a card on it. 'The one who wrote to you, ma'am.'

She took the card in disbelief.

Hugh Guthrie Esq
Guthrie & Randall Attorneys at Law.
Lincoln's Inn Fields.

Not her own lawyer then, but her brother's lawyer. Her stomach twisted into icy knots as she read the name on the card. Hadn't her deliberately rude response to that letter a couple of weeks ago—or was it three weeks?—been sufficient? She remembered Mr Guthrie well enough, although the debacle of his last visit had hardly been *his* fault. He was a nice enough old man and he had only been doing his job. However—'I'm definitely not at home. Ever.'

John nodded awkwardly. 'The thing is, my lady—' He broke off.

'Oh, spit it out, John.' It wasn't his fault either.

'He's got two little girls with him.'

Had she misheard? 'Two *what*?'

'Little girls.' He elaborated. 'Well, one's not so very little. About twelve or so I'd guess. T'other's the little one. They look proper done up, my lady. Got caught in the rain, I daresay.'

She gritted her teeth. That was nothing to do with her. Only…what could Frederick's lawyer possibly want this time? And why had he brought two girls? She'd only find out by seeing him. It wasn't as if she could drop a whole lawyer, not to mention two young girls, into the fire.

'Very well. Show them in.' Whatever Mr Guthrie wanted, she'd settle this for once and for all. Her conscience delivered a solid, if unwelcome nudge on behalf of two damp, possibly cold children. 'And ask Mrs

Cable to heat some milk. I suppose there is cake? And biscuits?' As a child she'd preferred biscuits to cake.

'Yes, my lady.' John bowed and removed himself.

Althea looked at Puck. 'Sorry.' The dog's tail drooped along with his whiskers. 'Burning the letter didn't work. I'll get this done and we'll go. Goodness knows why he'd want to see me again anyway. Surely you can only be disowned once?'

That had been…she frowned, calculated dates… six years ago.

Catching a glimpse of herself in the mirror, Althea cursed. Of course Frederick's solicitor had to call when she'd been doing her accounts, wasn't expecting visitors and had bundled her hair up all anyhow. With another curse, she snatched off the eyeglasses she used for reading and writing.

She looked around to make sure the room was tidy. Why give any ammunition for the family's view of her as an impecunious slut?

The room was tidy except for the overflowing bookcase. Not grand, but comfortable and clean. And hers.

She glanced at Puck. 'We'll see what he wants, then send him on his way. Maybe you could find a nice growl?'

Puck waved his tail agreeably, not looking in the least like a dog who could find a growl. Even a nice one.

The door opened.

'Mr Guthrie,' John announced.

* * *

Her breath jolted in. It wasn't the same Mr Guthrie. Not unless Time itself had reversed when she wasn't looking. This man was much younger. Although she thought there might be a resemblance in the tall, spare frame. Even in the neat, utterly respectable black suit.

The other Mr Guthrie must have been seventy at least. This one looked to be in his forties. Cool grey eyes skewered her from under heavy brows. Two girls—she assumed John was correct, and there were girls under those damp cloaks—trailed in behind him.

'Lady Hartleigh? Née Miss Althea Price?'

She stiffened at the icy tones that oozed disapproval—who the hell was he to look down his nose at her?—and donned the grand lady mask she rarely bothered with nowadays. 'The same. This is quite a surprise, Mr Guthrie. Either you have discovered the Fountain of Youth—and if so you might be so good as to furnish me with its direction—or it was some other Mr Hugh Guthrie who called upon me several years back.'

'My late father, ma'am.'

She hid the wince. 'Ah. My sincere condolences then.' Drat it! Now the fellow was looking at her as if she were a bedbug. Worse, she deserved it.

'Thank you, ma'am. I found your direction amongst his files.'

'You amaze me.' She had changed address since the previous Mr Guthrie's visit. Finally accepting that the mansion in fashionable Mayfair was far beyond her extremely limited income, she had moved to this far more modest house in Soho. Possibly one of the best decisions she had ever made.

He acknowledged that with a nod. 'I may say that it was no mean feat finding you.'

'I'm surprised you bothered. I hope Frederick is paying you handsomely.' She didn't bother to sweeten her voice.

'Papa is dead.' The taller of the two girls pushed back the hood of her cloak and lifted her chin.

Althea choked back a gasp.

It was as though she stared into the mirror of her childhood. Bright, honey-gold hair, a perfect—if she did say so herself—heart-shaped face and, most disconcerting of all, her own green eyes.

Dead. Frederick was dead? So that letter, the letter she had burned unread… Oh, *hell.*

'You're Frederick's daughter.' Who else could the child be, with the same hair and eyes she and Frederick had inherited from their mother?

'And Kate.' The girl put a protective arm around her sister.

'Kate.' She supposed she'd known there were two of them. Hadn't she? 'And you're…' She floundered, searching for the name. She didn't even know her nieces' names. And Frederick was *dead.* How was she supposed to feel about that? And what did it have to do with her? Frederick, dutifully followed by the rest of the family, had disowned her six years ago and made quite sure the entire world knew it.

'Sarah. I'm Sarah.' The green eyes were defiant.

Sarah? Oh, damn. Miss Sarah Parker's nascent literary existence flickered, guttered...

'Sarah.' At Guthrie's gentle but firm voice, some of the defiance ebbed, or at least was banked.

'Yes, sir.'

'May they sit down, Lady Hartleigh? It's been a difficult time for them.'

'What?' She pulled her scattered wits together. She had been living alone too long if she couldn't think to offer a seat to a pair of damp, exhausted children. 'Yes. Yes, of course. Come near the fire, girls, and take off those damp cloaks. Puck! In your bed.'

He was sniffing at the smaller girl's ankle with enthusiasm, but looked up with his *Must I?* expression.

The girl—Kate—looked up. 'Can we pet him? We like dogs. Only we weren't allowed to have one.'

Althea found a smile, even as memory reared up. 'If he isn't bothering you.'

She had never been allowed to have a dog either. Her father had disapproved of house dogs—*'women mollycoddling animals'*—and her husband had flatly refused her request. *'Have some revolting lapdog all over the house? Certainly not.'* She clenched her fist. She made her own decisions now and she had a dog. Then she returned her mind to the real problem: What were Frederick's daughters doing here?

Kate didn't bother with a chair. She dropped straight down on the hearth and Puck, viewing this as an invitation, got as much of himself as possible into her lap. Small arms closed about him, and the child buried her face in his rough coat.

Sarah stood, her expression uncertain.

'Sit down, Sarah.' Guthrie spoke again. Steady, reassuring. The sort of voice that could ease you into doing things you weren't entirely sure about.

Althea nodded. 'Yes. Please, sit down. John is bringing hot milk and cake. Or biscuits. Possibly both.' Good God! She was wittering. 'Mr Guthrie, I am at a loss as to why you have brought the girls here. Surely—'

'No one wants us. You probably don't either. Mr Guthrie's office clerk said you burned the letter he sent you.'

'Sarah.' The gentle reproof in Guthrie's voice had the girl—her *niece*—flushing scarlet.

'It's *true!*'

'But not a conversation you were supposed to be listening to, Sarah.'

Althea stared in shock at her elder niece. That might have been her own voice. Hard and cold, stating an unpalatable fact before someone could stuff it back down her throat.

'I'm sorry, sir. I didn't *mean* to listen. I just heard.'

'And if you do *just hear* something not meant for you, Sarah, then you do not blurt it out.'

'No, sir.'

Kate looked up as Puck licked her face. 'Mama died two years ago. And we couldn't live at Wellings any longer.'

Althea stared at them, a cold certainty growing in her. 'Your mother, too?' No, this couldn't possibly be happening... And why on earth hadn't Frederick re-married? If she knew anything about the man he had become, it was that he had been desperate to sire an heir.

Sarah sat down on a chair beside her sister. 'She won't care about that, Kate. Why should she? No one else does. And even if she did, you're telling it all backwards.'

Again that hard, bitter voice lashed at Althea.

The door opened and John came in with the maid, Milly, each bearing a tray.

Althea breathed a sigh of relief at the distraction. 'Thank you. John, the milk and cake—oh, and the biscuits for the young ladies. Milly, please set the tea tray on my desk.' She moved her account books out of the way.

'Does Puck like cake?'

Althea smiled, quelling the panic that threatened to explode. 'He does, but the cake is for you and your sister. Here.' She took several small, dry biscuits from her desk drawer. 'These are his.' She gave some to each girl. Kate took them eagerly, Sarah with a scowl.

Ignoring the scowl, Althea walked back to her desk and sat down. 'Please sit, Mr Guthrie.'

Guthrie seated himself.

'Milk, sir? Sugar?'

'Neither, thank you.'

Tea dispensed, the niceties dealt with—and her nieces occupied with Puck, hot milk and cake—Althea spoke very quietly. 'Why are you here, sir? And what did my niece mean by that extraordinary statement?'

'That no one wants them?' The lawyer sipped his tea. 'Precisely what she said. No one in either family will take them in. I wrote to everyone I could think of.' He shot her a cool glance over the teacup. 'Including yourself.'

Ignoring that last comment, she set her own cup down sharply. That wasn't how things were supposed to work. 'Surely Frederick made provision for them, appointed a guardian?' The estate had been entailed on the nearest male heir. Since Frederick had died without a son that meant the estate had gone to their cousin Wilfrid. But he *must* have provided for his children... And the last thing he would have wanted was for *her* to take them in!

'Your brother named his heir—your cousin, Wilfrid Price-Babbington, as the girls' guardian. As Kate said, their mother died two years ago. Childbirth. You... ah...remember Price-Babbington?'

'I do.' Only too well. A boastful sort of boy, very full of his own self-consequence and always tale-bearing. Perhaps she was being uncharitable; people did grow up. Witness the change in Frederick from the adored brother of her childhood to the man who had— no, she wasn't going to think about what Frederick had done. But if Wilfrid had improved on her memories, why was her brother's solicitor here with her nieces?

Guthrie frowned. 'Lady Hartleigh, your brother died two months ago. Were you not aware?'

She favoured him with a glittering smile. 'Mr Guthrie, I am the family's skeleton. Very much *persona non grata*. They prefer me to rattle safely in my closet, and they certainly don't furnish me with the latest news.'

Disapproval wafted from him. 'Hardly the latest. You make no effort to stay in touch?'

She snorted, sharply aware of a little spurt of anger. Who was he to question her decision? 'If you found my old address in your father's files—and I truly am sorry he is dead, I liked him—then you probably found a copy of the letter, notarised no less, that my brother ordered him to deliver and read out to me. It was very explicit about *why* I was *persona non grata*.'

His mouth flattened. 'I did read that. In fact, I read it at the time.'

She sipped her tea. 'I'm sure you were enthralled.'

'Disgusted would be closer to the mark.'

She stiffened, but leaned back with her best supercilious smile. 'Really? Well, don't let me keep you.'

He glared at her. 'I meant that I was disgusted with your brother for sending such a letter. Especially that he used my father to deliver it. I'll withhold judgement on the rest. Lady Hartleigh, those children deserve better of us than this sniping.'

She clenched a fist, then drew a careful breath. 'You're right. My apologies. If Frederick named Wilfrid guardian, then why—'

'He refused to act and instructed me to enter the girls in *some charitable institution*.' He hesitated. 'Lady Hartleigh, if you didn't know your brother had died, then you can't know the circumstances. He had gambled away the bulk of his fortune.'

'Oh, good God! The idiot! Then—'

'What little was left he bequeathed to his heir. Along with a request that Price-Babbington take responsibility for the girls.'

'A *request*?' Althea didn't bother to hide the derision. 'Would that be a *gentleman's honour* sort of request?'

A small cynical smile curled his mouth. 'Precisely.'

She should show him out now. Every instinct screamed it. 'And how do you come into this, sir?'

'When Price-Babbington refused to act as guardian I wrote to the girls' other relatives. On their mother's side as well as your family. No one was prepared to take them.'

'So, they're homeless and penniless.' She let out a breath. Why the hell hadn't she refused to see him? 'When you say, *no one*—'

'I mean *no one*.' He was speaking softly, but lowered his voice further so that she had to lean forward. 'I have made enquiries. I did that before the girls reached London. Sarah is of an age where she will be accepted by the Adult Orphan Institution.'

Adult? She was a *child*!

'How frightfully charitable of them. And Kate?'

'She is not old enough. She may go to the Female Orphan Asylum at Lambeth.'

Althea gritted her teeth. 'I see. So why are you here?' She didn't need this. She didn't *want* this. She *liked* her life now. It was *her* life. The life she had built for herself. The one with no blasted family.

Only…they were children. Not the adults who had turned on her.

'The rest of your relatives replied in no uncertain terms declining to take the girls,' he said. 'Since your response was to consign your brother quite literally, I understand, to hell—'

She winced. He knew she'd burned the letter, then.

He went on. 'I suspected that you wouldn't read any other letter I might send you.' He shot her a cool glance. 'I thought it wiser to call on you myself.'

Althea gritted her teeth She was *not* going to bare her soul to this man and explain precisely *why* she'd burned that letter.

He spoke carefully. 'I thought after my father's last visit that your response was at least understandable.'

His forbearance positively grated on her. Althea grasped at what felt like the last straw of her patience.

'If you want me to write to their—my, *our* relations, I can assure you that—'

'They need a home, Lady Hartleigh. You're their nearest relation. Their aunt. The only person who hasn't given an outright refusal. They need you.'

'You want *me* to take them.'

'You're their only hope, Lady Hartleigh.' He scowled at her. 'And, despite that letter my father was forced to deliver, he said he thought you...had much to recommend you.'

Half an hour ago she had been so proud of her nest egg. That enormous—*hah!*—buffer of a few thousand pounds. She looked over to the fireplace where the girls drank their milk and munched on cake. Kate still sat on the floor with her arm around Puck, who leaned on her like a dog starved of all affection, and kept his focus on the cake.

Adding two young girls to her household, extra food, clothes, shoes—good Lord, they were growing, and they'd need a governess eventually—was impossible. It would stretch her budget to the limit and beyond. She couldn't do it. She wasn't *going* to do it.

As if her gaze were a tangible weight, Sarah looked up, her mouth a flat, hostile line, her eyes blazing with *don't care* defiance.

Althea knew that gaze, knew the hurt hiding behind it. She'd seen it in her own mirror often enough. Yet despite the defiance, Sarah leaned closer to the smaller girl, her hand creeping to her little sister's shoulder.

They'll be separated. Alone.

She might be used to being alone. Damn it, she *liked* being alone. She didn't want to be saddled with children. Not now. Refusal was the only sane response.

She reached out and rang the bell.

Blast you, Frederick.

John reappeared so fast she suspected he'd been waiting in the hall.

'Yes, my lady.'

'Please help Milly prepare the spare bedchamber for the young ladies.' Ignoring Guthrie's startled intake of breath, she looked straight at Sarah, and spoke the final words to nail her decision shut. 'They will be living with us now.'

Hugo felt he had due cause for wondering if he'd been catapulted into a different universe.

'You'll…you'll take them.' He'd have sworn she was going to refuse. That she was ringing to have them shown out.

Those green eyes narrowed, firing chips of ice.

'Yes, Mr Guthrie, I will.' Her voice matched the cold fury in her eyes. Who was that fury for? And on whom would it spill out? Should he leave the girls with her after all?

She turned back to the servant and her voice softened. 'Soup for the young ladies, too, please, John.'

Relief sighed out of him. Whoever was the focus of her icy rage it would not spill over the girls. Not if she could think of hot soup for a pair of frightened children and keep calling them *young ladies*.

He'd come here because… Why the devil *had* he come? Not because he had expected Lady Hartleigh— by all accounts self-absorbed and heedless, not to mention impecunious—to take Sarah and Kate. That letter from her brother, disowning her…it had been damning.

He shoved all that away. He'd come because Althea Hartleigh had been the girls' last chance, and there were things he needed to say to her, tell her. Only not in front of the girls. If she hadn't known about Frederick's death, then obviously she couldn't know the circumstances.

He had to get the girls out of the room. 'Ah, Sarah, perhaps you and Kate might like to look at your room? Take your valises up and unpack.' Please God, Lady Hartleigh would understand and back him up.

Sarah gave him a suspicious glance, and who could blame her? They had been kicked out of the only home they knew and all their relatives, except this one, had refused to take them in. For the last fortnight they had been living in two-roomed lodgings that, while perfectly adequate for a single man, were cramped for that man and two lively young girls. His landlady had been deeply unimpressed.

'What if we don't *want* to stay? What if Aunt Hartleigh doesn't like us? What if *we* don't like *her*?'

Kate tugged at her sister's hand. 'Don't, Sarah.'

Her voice shook. 'Please! I don't want to go to an orphanage!'

'I'll wager you don't.' Lady Hartleigh's voice was brisk, matter of fact. 'I suggest you at least look at the room, Sarah. Which room did you have at home?'

'Home?'

'Yes. At Wellings Park. I grew up there, remember.'

'Oh. It…it was at the back. Two down from the schoolroom.'

'Ah. The big room. That was your father's when we were children.' She smiled at Kate. 'Did you have the little one next to the schoolroom?'

Kate bit her lip. 'Yes.'

'That was mine. I'm afraid you'll have to share here.'

Kate nodded. 'We don't mind. We've been sharing Mr Guthrie's bed.'

Hugo shut his eyes. *Oh, Lord!*

'Er… I've been sleeping on the sofa. My lodgings are only two rooms.'

Lady Hartleigh blinked. 'Most uncomfortable, I should think. The sofa, that is.'

His shoulders and neck agreed.

Lady Hartleigh turned to the girls. 'Take your things up and unpack. You have my word of honour that unless you request it, you will *not* be going to an orphanage.' She smiled at Kate. 'Take Puck along with you.'

Kate beamed. 'May we? Thank you. What sort of dog is he, Aunt Hartleigh?'

Hugo considered the scruffy rough-coated little creature, with its mismatched ears and bedraggled tail. *Good question.*

Puck's owner looked amused. 'One with a tail. In polite company we call him a terrier and leave it at that. And perhaps you might call me Aunt Althea. A little less stuffy and formal, I think. Off you go.'

Kate trotted out—happily enough, he thought—the dog at her heels.

Sarah lingered, her gaze hard and suspicious. 'Why?'

Hugo opened his mouth to reprove her, but shut it again. Best if they sorted it out. He wasn't going to be here to mediate, after all.

Lady Hartleigh met that direct gaze, seemed to consider her answer. 'How old are you, Sarah?'

'Nearly fourteen.'

Hugo cleared his throat, hid a grin. The child was a solid six months short of that.

Lady Hartleigh, despite flicking him a glance, appeared to accept the reply at face value.

She nodded. 'There's no mystery, Sarah. Quite simply, when the news gets out that you are living with me it will annoy the rest of the family greatly.'

Sarah looked at her uncertainly. 'Annoy them? You want to annoy them?'

'Good God, yes. Don't you?'

Hugo choked on a laugh.

'Kate's only *eight*.' Sarah bit her lip. 'I want to *kick* them!'

Lady Hartleigh nodded her approval. 'Very reasonable. For the moment, however, we shall content ourselves with annoying them. Now, go and unpack.'

Chapter Two

Hugo took a deep breath, preparing to speak…

Lady Hartleigh rose abruptly and walked over to a side table. 'I believe I need something rather stronger than tea, before you tell me whatever it is you did not wish to say in front of Sarah and Kate. Brandy, sir?'

She had understood then. 'Yes, please. I understand this must be a shock to you.'

She shot him an amused glance as she picked up a decanter. 'Just a little. There I was, contemplating my most excellent household economy, and lo! I have two nieces to fit in.'

She poured two glasses of brandy.

'Will they be an imposition, ma'am?' Was he doing the right thing in leaving the girls with her? The house looked comfortable enough, the lady dressed plainly but with elegance, even if her glorious honied hair was a little dishevelled. He'd noted what he thought was an apron stuffed under a cushion. Had she been at some household task? He knew she was far from wealthy.

She frowned, passing him a glass. 'I don't like that word. At least not for children. My accounts, on the other hand, are always an imposition.'

'There is no money with them.' He hated saying it, but he had to spell everything out clearly. He sipped the brandy. It was excellent.

She snorted. 'If there were, Mr Guthrie, one of their loving relatives would have snatched them up instantly.'

He blinked at this brutal summation. He strove for truth at all times, thinking of it as a clear flame— Lady Hartleigh wielded it like a burning sword.

'You don't think much of your relatives, do you?'

Her laugh was bitter. 'No, sir, I do not. And I can think of at least two members of my sister-in-law's family who could have provided a home for them. While as for Wilfrid—' her free hand balled into a fist '—best not to let me start on Wilfrid.'

He sipped his brandy again, enjoyed the fiery burn as much as the controlled blaze of her temper. 'There was a reason, beyond the lack of money, your family declined to take the girls. You haven't asked how your brother died.'

She sat down. 'No. I became distracted with the girls, but I assumed an illness, an accident perhaps?' She let out a breath. 'That's not it, is it? You'd better tell me.'

No gentle way to put it. 'He shot himself.'

Her glass rattled as she set it down. 'The gambling debts.'

Lord, she was quick. 'Yes.'

A careful pause. 'He really gambled *everything* away?' A bitter laugh. 'How ironic.'

He didn't understand. 'Ma'am?'

'My apologies.' She waved it away. 'I was speaking to myself. It's not relevant. Are you telling me that, apart from the lack of money, the family abandoned those children because of Frederick's suicide? They feared the taint?'

He nodded and sipped his brandy. 'Yes. Exactly the word they used. Several family members said they did not care to have "that" in their homes. It was covered up, fortunately—an accident as he was cleaning a pistol—but the family knows. Price-Babbington was particularly vocal on the matter. How he could not possibly have that "weakness"—that was how he put it—in his home, with his impressionable sons.'

Not an unusual response. An unvarnished verdict of suicide could see the victim's entire property sequestered by the law. If the coroner were sympathetic enough not to want the family's property sequestered, the usual verdict of *suicide while of unsound mind* was still a disaster. In that case they might have the property, but they were tainted with the label of insanity.

Lady Hartleigh made a rude noise. 'Apparently Wilfrid hasn't looked in the mirror recently if he's worried about *weakness*. So he brought them up to London and left them for you to dispose of.'

'Not quite.' He deliberately kept his voice even, emotionless. 'He wrote to request that I make the arrangements to enter them in *"appropriate charitable institutions"* and informed me that they would be on the stagecoach a week later. I met them at the Bolt-in-Tun.' Even now he felt sick at the thought of what might have happened to the girls if he had not received the letter in time, if he had not met that stagecoach.

'Good God!'

Hugo watched, fascinated, as she brought herself under control. Those white knuckles slowly relaxing, the careful breaths. There was silence, as if she did not trust herself to speak further, but he had the impression that she knew as well as he what might have happened if he had not been there. Possibly even knew the Bolt's reputation.

'And you've been looking after them ever since.' She met his eyes. 'Thank you.'

The frank gratitude in her face made him squirm. 'No decent man could have done otherwise.'

Her mouth flattened. 'A pity Wilfrid does not comprehend that. Do the girls know how Frederick died? Please don't tell me one of them found him!'

'No, thank God. The servants did. They heard the shot in the library.'

She snorted. 'The very place a man would clean a pistol, of course. Why not somewhere logical like the gun room?' She shook her head. 'I'm glad for the girls' sakes that it was covered up and they don't know. You may rest assured I won't inform them. At least not until they are very much older.'

He breathed a sigh of relief. 'You'll still take them?'

Her brows lifted. 'Mr Guthrie, I am far from being the mercenary, cold-hearted bitch that letter made me out to be, thank you very much.'

He opened his mouth. Shut it again. Informing her that she might not be a—*that word*—but that she certainly had teeth, did not present itself as the course of wisdom.

'Obviously not.' A second thought occurred. One that gave him a very great deal of pleasure. 'Should you like me to write polite notes to your relatives? Apprising them that the girls are safe with you?'

Her brandy stopped an inch from her lips. 'How much will that cost me?' She cleared her throat. 'My accounts, you know. Which reminds me, you will be out of pocket already, so—'

'Stop right there.' He fought to suppress the flare of annoyance. She was only trying to be fair. 'I won't take a penny for helping those girls. And as for the letters, annoying your relatives will burden neither my pocket nor my conscience.'

She sipped her brandy as a smile glimmered, Titania plotting mischief. 'Full of unintelligible, lawyerly language?'

He kept a straight face. 'Not too unintelligible. We want them to understand they've been insulted.'

She raised her brows. 'Of course. Do be sure to stress my Christian charity, won't you? Especially to that insufferable prig Wilfrid!'

Apparently eyes really could dance. He found himself smiling in response. 'I thought you weren't going to start on him?'

She rubbed her nose. 'I did say that, didn't I? Oh, well. *Tant pis.*'

His pent-up laughter escaped. 'We'll consider the letters pro bono. Especially the letter to dear Wilfrid.'

Those elfin green eyes regarded him much as he thought Titania might have considered a mortal.

'You don't like Wilfrid either.'

He definitely wasn't going to start on Wilfrid. What he thought of Price-Babbington was beyond unprintable. Although he had a sneaking suspicion that Althea Hartleigh would only roar with laughter. 'Insufferable prig is the least of it!'

Laughter rippled. 'How very restrained of you, sir.'

He found himself laughing back into that dancing green, and he had the distinct impression that she knew exactly the words he had refrained from using. Which, much to his surprise, did not shock or disgust him in the least.

Walking back alone through Soho Square an hour later, Hugo shook his head. He'd considered visiting

Althea Hartleigh a waste of time. So much so that he nearly hadn't bothered.

Thank God he had.

The lady—and she *was* a lady, whatever her fool of a brother had thought—had been a surprise all round.

When the girls had come back down, Kate bubbling and Sarah subdued, she had provided them with soup and toast. She had been calm and matter of fact with them, allowing them to settle and have their meal. She hadn't bothered with overtures, hadn't gushed, hadn't assured them she was delighted to have them.

An intelligent female. Sarah would have repelled any overtures and disbelieved any reassurances.

He let out a breath as he walked down towards the cab stand outside St Anne's church. Sarah had asked when they would see him again and Lady Hartleigh had said nothing either for or against when he had explained, gently, that they had someone to take care of them now. They didn't need him.

Kate's mouth had wobbled.

Sarah's mouth had set like granite, and she'd given a sharp nod, addressing herself to her soup. Just one more person who had abandoned them.

He wanted to see the girls again. While his conscience had refused to allow him to dump them in orphanages, he had also become fond of them. His lodgings, although cramped, had been brighter and cheerier with their company.

What would you have done if she had refused to take them?

Hell's teeth! He confronted the truth he had refused to admit until Althea Hartleigh had shocked him witless—he would be looking for new lodgings, lodgings that could accommodate two young girls. He would have willingly moved back into a house very like the one he had left in his grief ten years ago.

And what the hell would you have done with them? Schooling? Providing a dowry?

While it hadn't happened yet, and he still couldn't imagine it, he might marry again one day. What would a wife think of a pair of orphans with no claim of kinship? The thought slid across his mind that a woman who would consider two orphaned girls an imposition—*I don't like that word...not for children*—was not a woman he would care to marry anyway.

Still, taking on the girls would have been difficult, if not downright impossible, and since when had he become so damned impulsive that he'd been prepared to keep them? Thank God Althea Hartleigh had confounded all his expectations and proven herself to have a heart.

How had his father described her? He remembered the old man coming back from that last visit, shaking his head over what he had described as a family spat turned vicious.

'She was always a pretty child, not that I saw her often, but now? A walking, breathing temptation, my

boy. Aphrodite and Helen rolled into one. But I think her brother is a fool for all that. I very much doubt she's the whore he's painted her.'

The pater had been right about Frederick Price being a fool. And yes, Althea Hartleigh was…beautiful, without a doubt. Aphrodite? Perhaps. But still, Aphrodite never seemed to have much of a sense of humour. Titania was more like it, for his money. Wicked mischief glimmering in green eyes that could lure a mortal man to glorious, abject folly.

Easy to believe what Frederick Price's letter had claimed—that she'd had a blazingly indiscreet affair with the Earl of Rutherford. Not to mention several others prior to the Earl. The family had considered itself disgraced, and she might consider herself cast off. According to rumour, she had disappeared largely from society not long after the Earl's marriage. Yet, despite the fact that she was clearly living in reduced circumstances, away from the fashionable world she had married into, she had been the only one willing to take in a pair of orphans.

Perhaps Price had got it wrong, and had listened to unfounded gossip.

No. He didn't think so. Something about Lady Hartleigh told him that she probably *had* earned that reputation.

For being female? Because while he had made enquiries about her before his visit, he had found nothing that would have even raised an eyebrow had she been a man. Of course, the tale of her sins had been embellished with speculations on her deviousness, and her cunning plan to ensnare Rutherford into marriage.

Odd though. It was pretty universally known that she had run through all her money. A little circumspect investigation had garnered that information. But while she wasn't living in luxury, she was living very comfortably. He'd seen no sign that she was in dire financial straits, nor had his recent enquiries turned up any disgruntled tradesmen. It seemed Lady Hartleigh paid all her bills on time and lived within her income.

Still, he nearly hadn't gone to see her because of her very dubious reputation. And even when he had decided to call on her, he'd expected a beautiful harpy. Instead he'd found a charming siren. One who could probably lure an unwary man to his grave, watery or otherwise, let alone her bed. Or even a wary man.

He took a steadying breath.

Sirens were dangerous. And he was mixing his metaphors to boot. She wasn't a harpy, but she couldn't be both siren and Titania. Could she? Somehow the woman had repaired her finances, at least to some degree. And, if she *had* conducted a series of affairs with wealthy gentlemen, that was one way she could have done so.

That or her circumstances had never been quite as dire as they'd been painted. He hoped that he hadn't done the wrong thing in leaving the girls with her.

Either way, he would have to keep an eye on things

from a discreet distance at least for a short time and pray she never realised. He was no Oberon, and he didn't fancy a pair of ass's ears, that—if Shakespeare were to be believed—was the fate of mortals who flirted with faeries.

Later that evening, her nieces safely in bed, and her dog missing in action—she suspected that Puck, having deserted her, might be curled up on Kate's feet—Althea stirred up the fire before settling down to her desk again.

She adjusted the lamp. Miss Sarah Parker was fictionally dead before she'd made it as far as the page. Having a Sarah in the house, as well as one instigating mayhem in her head, was just impossible. Far too confusing. She needed a new name for the wretched girl.

She jotted down name after name, finally underlining *Lydia*. Lydia Parker. The clock chimed ten. Althea ignored it. If she wanted to add to her capital, and thus her income—even more important now she had added two extra people to her household—she needed to get this book properly started.

Half an hour later Althea still only had Lydia. That was the problem with finishing the proofs of one book. Your ungrateful publisher immediately began badgering you for another. Which, she freely admitted, was better than being told never to darken their doorway again. But she still had to start the wretched thing.

This afternoon she'd had ideas aplenty rattling

around in her imagination, distracting her from her accounts. With the explosion into her life of Sarah and Kate, every idea had fizzled out like so many damp firecrackers. Lydia. She had Lydia. A girl—no, a woman—of decided opinions. The hero unfortunately had yet to make an appearance on the stage of her imagination. Not even a name. Perhaps she should consider allowing Lydia to enjoy an existence of blessed singleness and have a cat instead of a husband?

'Or a dog.' She scowled. Leaving Lydia happily single at the end of the book, with a couple of cats or a dog for company, would not please her publisher. But really, the poor girl did not *need* to marry. She had a perfectly adequate fortune, enough interests to keep her occupied, and unless the right man for her turned up...

Women find their highest purpose and joy in being a wife and mother.

She snorted. How often had she heard that? But right now she had a character who appeared utterly uninterested in such things. Rather like herself.

What would you do if the right man turned up for you?

Althea scowled at her page of notes, refusing to contemplate a slightly ascetic face with heavy brows over direct grey eyes. She neither needed nor wanted a man, right or wrong. Men complicated everything. Especially since they always thought *they* were right. She nudged her mind back to creating complications for Lydia.

*You could take away her fortune. Or at least re-
duce it vastly.*

Then Lydia would be forced to consider marriage
to save herself and her younger sister. *Younger sister?*
Althea blinked at that revelation. Noted down *younger
sister. Name?* Plenty of drama and conflict in that.
Except she didn't want the wretched girl forced into
marriage for those reasons alone. She needed a better story than that.

*Better not to think of Lydia as 'the wretched girl' if
you don't want your readers to think of her like that!*

With a muttered curse, Althea dipped her pen in the
ink and started scribbling in earnest. Sometimes you
had to start writing and see what someone did when
you let them loose on the page...

An hour later she had discovered Lydia's aversion
to seed cake—*why?*—and one Sir Edwin Jamison had
strolled into her head and out onto the page. Since he
was sniffing around her younger sister, Sophie, Lydia
had taken him in extreme dislike, which suited her
creator perfectly. He didn't like cats either, and Lydia's cat had taken that as a challenge.

Sometime after the clock chimed midnight, Althea shuffled her pages together and locked them in
her desk drawer. Her shoulders ached, and she covered a yawn. She hoped Sir Edwin had annoyed Lydia
enough for one evening to have the words coming easily again tomorrow.

Chapter Three

Late April—
Lincoln's Inn Fields

'Lady Hartleigh.' Hugo rose from the chair behind his desk. 'This is quite a surprise.'

He'd taken a full half minute to recover from the shock after his office clerk had told him she was there, requesting a moment of his time. Shock was one thing. The leap of his heart, the sheer delight bouncing through him at the sight of her, was positively frightening.

Had she somehow divined that he was having her watched? So far the reports had been completely benign. No gentlemen had called. At all. Her three servants thought the world of her, and she had only left the house for walks with the girls and the dog, to pay bills, or for very local social engagements, so innocent as to beggar belief.

Her ladyship visited the circulating library at Sel-

bourne's Antiquarian Books. A gentleman opened the door for her and the young ladies.

That was as close to any sort of encounter with a gentleman as Althea Hartleigh had come.

She bought flowers from a street seller.

And that was the closest she had come to extravagance. She paid her bills either on receipt or on a monthly basis.

He pulled himself together, came around the desk and placed the visitor's chair for her. 'Will you be seated? I... I hope all is well with the girls? How do you go on?' Lord! What had happened to his lungs? And his brain—he was babbling for God's sake!

She sat, arranged her skirts. 'Oh, we're all well enough. They wished to come with me, but I thought it better not.'

His heart sank—all the delight at seeing her died as disappointment bit deep. 'You regret your impulse then?' He couldn't keep the chill from his voice, didn't even want to.

She looked up sharply. 'What? No, not in the least. I need to make a new will, Mr Guthrie.'

'Oh.' Commendable, responsible and utterly unexpected.

'As it stands, bar a couple of personal bequests, ensuring that my dog is looked after and annuities to my servants, everything goes to charity. Which is all very admirable, but not when I have family dependent on me.'

He sat down again. 'If you have a will, then you already have a solicitor. Why are you here?'

She smiled, an amused twinkle in her eyes. 'I did have a solicitor. He has taken a sudden fancy to grow roses.'

'I—he what?'

'Mr Brimley has retired. He has purchased a small villa at Richmond and intends to grow roses.'

'Ah. That would be Mr Harold Brimley.' He grinned. 'I believe *his* father retired to Reading to breed dogs. Spaniels, if I remember correctly.'

She stared at him. 'Are you serious? Spaniels?'

'Oh, yes. He was a contemporary of my grandfather's.'

'And what did *he* breed?'

'Grandfather? Books,' he said gravely, enjoying the tart humour in her voice. 'My father did the same. And birds. He liked watching birds.'

A peal of laughter escaped her. 'How very conventional.'

He grinned. 'I daresay I'll do the same one day. Books and birds. We're a boring lot, we Guthries.'

Still laughing, she said, 'Oh, I doubt that very much. Not the books and birds. The boring part. Now, about this will. I have given it some thought, and—'

'What about my colleague Mark Brimley?' He forced himself back to the matter at hand, and from the worrying delight that Althea Hartleigh did not consider him boring. The firm of Brimley, Brimley &

Whittaker was still running, albeit minus one Brimley. He didn't like to think he might be poaching a client. Mark Brimley was more than competent to draw up a will. Although he could imagine him muttering over clauses to protect a dog.

She grimaced. 'Mr Brimley's son? If you must know, he didn't like my, er, thoughts. Or me for that matter.'

Ah. There was that, too. His undoubted competence aside, Mark Brimley was the sort to believe women shouldn't have thoughts at all. He would disapprove mightily of a woman like Althea Hartleigh.

He took a deep breath. 'Perhaps you might outline these thoughts?'

He listened, made careful notes, asked a couple of questions for clarification.

When she had finished, he set down his pencil carefully. 'The choice of trustees for something like this will be of the utmost importance. There isn't a great deal of money involved, but still.' How the deuce was she so beforehand with the world? 'Do you have anyone in mind? I should recommend three. Then if one dies or is unable to act, there is time to appoint another.'

She nodded. 'Yes. Two of the three I have already written to, and they have agreed.'

He picked up his pencil. 'And they are?'

'The Earl of Rutherford.'

His pencil hovered over the paper. 'Rutherford.'

'Yes. The countess is a friend of mine.'

He met her cool, clear gaze directly. 'You amaze me.'

Nothing in her faltered that he could observe. Instead an amused smile flickered. 'Mr Guthrie, if Meg Rutherford were to eschew the company of every woman in London that Rutherford bedded before he married her, she would lead a very solitary existence.'

Society gossip didn't come his way. But once he'd realised Althea Hartleigh was all that stood between the girls and an orphanage—barring his own insane and illogical impulses—he'd dug up every scrap of information he could on the lady and her previous affairs. And if everything he'd discovered about the earl were true, she had a fair point. Still.

'And the other?'

'Mr Jack Hamilton.'

He blinked. 'Hamilton? Member of the Commons, pushing for reform and the complete abolition of slavery? That Jack Hamilton? Is his wife also a "friend"?' Hamilton's name, as far as he knew, had never been linked with hers. Possibly he had missed something, but Hamilton appeared to have led a positively blameless existence. As had Rutherford since his marriage several years ago.

She smiled. 'She is, although Hamilton was never my lover. And she has agreed that, should something happen to me, she will take Puck.'

He always appreciated openness in a client, but this

was—he struggled for the right word. There was no suggestion of boasting. Just a statement of fact.

Rutherford had been her lover. Hamilton had not. And his wife had agreed to take the dog.

He would have considered this attitude perfectly normal in a man, particularly an aristocrat. In a woman? Shameless.

And yet, she was not shameless. Not that she appeared to mind what he might think of her. She was speaking to him as an equal. He wasn't quite sure how he felt about that.

He frowned, looking over his notes. 'I should tell you that tying Kate and Sarah's money up so tightly in trusts will make most men think twice about marriage to them.'

'Good.' Gloved hands clenched to fists in her lap. 'A woman should not be dependent on her husband *doing the right thing.*' He blinked at the viciously soft tone as she went on. 'If they are to marry, I want them to be safe.'

As I was not.

She barely stopped herself saying it aloud.

And even with that left unsaid, she'd said too much. It was a gauntlet flung down. She didn't care. Better to know at once if she'd misjudged him. If he disapproved of her personally it didn't matter, as long as he was prepared to act for her. For the girls. All that mattered was getting her will and the trusts in place.

She said simply, 'A decent man should understand

that. If he cannot, then a woman is better off without him.'

Guthrie raised his eyes from his notes. 'Is that what the younger Brimley choked on?'

She snorted. 'My unholy attitude to husbands? We didn't progress that far. Your learned colleague choked when we reached Rutherford as one of the trustees. His not so delicate remarks about *my* indelicacy got my back up.'

'Fancy that.' He made a few more notes. 'Right.' He looked up again. 'Who is the third trustee?'

Despite herself, she snorted out a laugh. 'You don't disapprove?'

He raised his eyebrows. 'Of what? Your affair with Rutherford? It's none of my business. Of protecting Sarah and Kate from—' he scowled—'fools like their father, not to mention the insufferable prig who tossed them to the wolves? That you made provision for your dog? No. Now, stop distracting me. Who is your choice for the third trustee?'

'You.'

'Me?' He looked as shocked as if she'd tipped a bucket of water over him. 'You want *me* to act as trustee?'

'Yes, of course.'

'Of course? Damn it, Lady Hartleigh, how the hell do you know you can trust me?'

'Althea.'

'What?'

'My name. You must know it's Althea.' Amusement at his stunned expression—the dropped jaw and slightly wild eyes—danced in her. Who knew solicitors could be so very charming? 'I think if you've progressed to swearing at me, you can use my Christian name.'

She continued as he stared at her. 'As for how I know I can trust you? You brought the girls to me. Instead of entering them in orphanages, you tried to find them a home while you gave them your bed and slept on the sofa.' She took a deep breath. 'You kept them safe. That's how.'

There was more she could have said. Things she had only discovered just now. His calm acceptance of her as…as a *person*, as someone with flaws and foibles, but who didn't need to be lectured like a child on the perceived folly of her previous choices. Her initial instinct had been spurred by his kindness and care for the girls. He had looked after them from the start— she could trust that he would continue to do so.

And she did not believe that, had she refused to take the girls in, he would have dumped them in those orphanages.

'Lady Hartleigh—?'

'Althea.'

He grimaced. 'Althea. There is something else that puzzles me. I have to say I am more than a little surprised at how…beforehand you are with the world. I was under the impression that your own inheritance was gone and that your husband left you very badly off.'

She stiffened her spine. 'Correct.' They were going there, were they?

'Then you found a way to repair your finances.'

His tone remained even, uninflected. But she could *hear* the questions seething underneath. Like a swan gliding on still water while the feet must paddle madly underneath. Two could play at that game. 'Also correct.'

'Are you able to tell me *how*?'

'No. At least, I don't choose to do so. Beyond telling you that I found something to sell. And *not* myself.'

'That's…good to know.'

The slight hesitation made her wonder if his mind had gone precisely there. And that stung, but she didn't dare tell him the truth. If news of her authorship got out it was perfectly possible that her reputation, deserved or otherwise, would destroy sales of any future books. It was doubly important now that she had the girls to provide for. It wasn't that she didn't trust *him*, but secrets were safer the fewer people who knew about them.

What was the saying? *Three may keep a secret if two of them be dead.*

'Do you need to know in order to act for me? I can assure you that I have done nothing illegal nor immoral to alleviate my finances.' And why the devil was she feeling so hurt and angry that he might believe she had whored herself to survive? You had to care about someone for their opinion of you to hurt. And she'd been close enough to disaster that she wouldn't have judged any woman forced into that choice.

Keeping her voice light, she said, 'Do I understand you would rather not act? Or be on Christian name terms with me?'

His mouth opened. Shut again. Then—'Hugh. Hugo.' He leaned forward, held out his hand across the desk. 'And... I apologise for my unseemly and disrespectful suspicions.'

She took his hand, felt the reassuring grip of strong fingers, wondered at the flicker of awareness that shot through her along with a wave of relief. *Good Lord!*

She managed a smile, despite the speeding of her heart, her leaping pulse. 'Delighted to meet you, Hugo.'

Over the following hour they thrashed out the details. Or most of them.

He'd never drawn up anything quite this stringent, and said so. 'I'll need to ask a few questions of my partner before you sign anything. He's had more experience with this sort of trust than I have.'

She nodded. 'Good. Thank you.'

'You don't mind?'

'That you can admit when you are unsure, and be willing to ask for advice? Of course not. I'd mind if you made a mull of this. In fact, I'd come back to haunt you.'

Laughter welled up. 'You'd make an interesting ghost. Very well, I'll ask my questions, get these documents drafted and have them sent over to you.'

She fiddled with her reticule.

'Something more?' He hadn't thought she was capable of uncertainty.

'I mentioned that the girls wished to come with me this morning.'

Her gaze was firmly in her lap. Was Titania ever shy?

'You did.'

'I hoped perhaps you might deliver the documents yourself. If you have time?' She looked up and, to his disbelief, there was the faintest tinge of colour staining her cheeks. 'We—the girls, that is—would like very much to see you. Even when you don't have documents to deliver.'

Something in him leapt. 'You would not object if I visited them occasionally?'

She shook her head. 'No. If not for you, Sarah and Kate would have disappeared into orphanages without me ever being aware of their fate. And, the thing is, they took a liking to you over and above that. They... they would like to see you from time to time. I believe it would reassure them. And if you are to be one of their trustees it would not be at all inappropriate.'

He nodded slowly, thinking. At least, he hoped he

was thinking, because he didn't give a damn about appropriate. 'Then perhaps you might care to meet me at Gunter's with the girls on Saturday afternoon. They will enjoy ice creams while we sip tea.'

She raised her brows. 'Sip tea? You may please yourself, of course, but I assure you I will enjoy an ice at least as much as the girls.'

He grinned at the return of confidence. 'I will enjoy an ice myself.'

A few moments after Lady Hartleigh's departure, Hugo's senior partner strolled in. A portly gentlemen some fifteen years older than Hugo's forty-two, Jacob Randall exuded good nature and a sort of guileless benevolence that was deceptive in the extreme.

'That's set hearts aflutter in the office. Your new client tipped Jem a sixpence for opening the door for her, and it appears her smile has slain even that confirmed old bachelor Blainey.' Jacob sat down, stretched out his legs and crossed them. 'I was going to talk about the idea of taking on another partner next year, but your recent visitor seems a far more interesting topic.'

The bright blue eyes gleamed with curiosity.

Hugo nudged his notes across the desk. 'Possibly. You tell me.'

Jacob read them through, his eyes widening as he read. 'That's something to get your teeth into all right and tight.' He looked at Hugo hopefully. 'May I stick my nose in?'

Hugo grinned. 'By all means. I was intending to consult you. This isn't quite my area, you know.'

Jacob snorted. 'The hell it isn't. I'm sticking my nose in because tying money up like this is just plain fun, not because I think you can't handle it.' He reached for a pencil. 'Right. The first thing you need to consider—'

They scribbled notes, argued points of law and generally enjoyed themselves until the silence from the outer office and the clock chiming six brought them back to reality.

Jacob winced. 'I need to go home now, or I'll be late for dinner. Again. And Alice will claim justifiable homicide.' He gave Hugo a hopeful smile. 'Care to come home with me?'

'And be justifiably murdered when we talk law over dinner?'

Jacob grinned comfortably. 'We'll leave the law here.'

Hugo very much doubted that. They never did, and Alice nearly always told them to stop. 'I'll come, and thank you very much.' Alice Randall was a kindly woman who never seemed to mind an extra and unexpected guest at her dinner table. And what else did he have to do this evening? He would otherwise read his book over his dinner in the tavern and then retire to his very empty lodgings.

Jacob clapped him on the back. 'Good. You've been a little out of sorts recently. You should get out more.'

Hugo tidied away his papers. 'Then no doubt you'll be delighted to know that I'm taking three females to Gunter's Tea Rooms for ices on Saturday afternoon.'

Jacob stared. 'Three? You dog! Nothing like making up for lost time, I always say.'

'Since I'm entertaining my new client and her nieces I thought to take the expense out of petty cash.'

Althea, Sarah and Kate walked from Soho to Berkeley Square on Saturday afternoon. Puck trotted beside them, Kate holding his leash. The child chattered brightly, full of questions about everything and everyone she saw.

Useful, because it took Althea's mind off the ordeal ahead. She had controlled her instinctive recoil when Hugo Guthrie suggested taking them to Gunter's, but oh, good Lord!

Gunter's Tea Shop in Berkeley Square. Where all society liked to be seen. Where she would probably be cut dead by people she had once considered friends. Her stomach executed an ungainly roll, but she made herself respond to Kate's excited questions. The child gasped as they walked into Berkeley Square. So many grand houses! Did Aunt Althea know people who lived here? She did. And what about that grand lady waving at them? Did Aunt Althea know her?

Aunt Althea did, and waved back to the Countess of Rutherford, who was descending the steps of the Earl and Countess of Jersey's house, accompanied by her husband. She had not realised that the Rutherfords had returned to town.

'Lady Rutherford. A friend of mine.' She had said nothing so far to the girls about the arrangements she was making. No doubt Meg would call very soon, quite possibly accompanied by Rutherford to discuss the trusteeship.

'She looks nice,' said Kate.

Althea glanced down with a smile. 'She is. Very nice. They both are.'

And right now she wouldn't have minded in the least if they were walking into Gunter's with her.

Althea stiffened her spine, ignoring the squirming in her stomach. Did it matter if people cut her? She wasn't going to see *them*. She was taking her nieces for a treat with the man who had cared enough to ensure they had a home.

'Come along, girls. Gunter's is over there.' She pointed to the east side of the square. 'We mustn't keep Mr Guthrie waiting.'

Sarah's steps faltered. She had been very quiet on the way from Soho, although to be fair, her little sister had chattered enough for both of them. But this was different.

For the first week after arriving in Althea's life, Sarah had been full of sulky silences. She did as she was asked, completing her lessons, eating her meals mechanically even as she glowered. Then she had seemed to settle. She spoke voluntarily, laughed and commented on a favoured dish. She seemed to enjoy the lessons Althea gave them. French, mathematics, history. She had arranged music lessons for them with the daughter of a friend in Compton Street not far from Selbourne's Books.

Althea had relaxed. Kate was easy to manage, a delight, affectionate and eager to please. Sarah, she thought, was a great deal like herself. Cynical, suspicious and far less willing to accept things at face value. She liked Sarah very much indeed.

But after Althea's visit to Lincoln's Inn, Sarah had retreated into herself again. She was not rude, far from it. She couldn't even be said to sulk, going through her days with an almost painful obedience. She was, Althea thought, plain miserable.

Last night the child had crept down to the parlour long after midnight. Althea had heard the creak of the stairs as she was readying herself for bed and gone out to look. Following her down quietly, she had heard muffled sobs from behind the door and yet she had hesitated to walk in and ask what was wrong. Surely the child deserved some privacy? If Sarah wished to confide, then she would… What did *she* know about young girls and their needs? Plus, she was tired. Her writing now had to be done in the very early mornings before the girls woke up, or in the evenings after they were in bed. Sometimes she excused herself from their daily walk and sent them with John to squeeze out a few more pages.

Perhaps she could mention Sarah's unhappiness to Mr Guthrie? Or Sarah might confide in him herself if she were given a chance. Walking into Gunter's and seeing Hugo Guthrie rising from his seat, Althea admitted that she had been a complete coward.

She was going to have to confront Sarah with or without his help.

Chapter Four

From his seat inside Gunter's, Hugo saw them cross the street and his heart—stupid organ!—leapt. Lord, if Alice Randall knew about that he'd never hear the end of it from Jacob. They'd both chuckled over his *assignation* the other night. And now Lady Hartleigh was laughing at something Kate was saying, the child almost dancing as she chattered, and his heart was dancing right along with her. The dog trotted beside them, ridiculous tail waving, and he smiled. God only knew what had gone into the creature's ancestry, but it had a tail to wag and that seemed to be enough for his mistress.

Then he saw Sarah's face. Utterly blank. Something wrong there. And Althea—were those shadows under her eyes? She looked as though she were not getting enough sleep. He rose as they entered the shop.

'Ladies.'

Kate bounced forward. 'Good afternoon, Mr Guthrie. Are we really to have ices? I've never had one! Do you have them all the time?'

He laughed. 'I don't have them very often, no. So it's a treat all round. Good day, Sarah.'

'Sir.'

She sat down as he imagined one might sit in a tumbril. If there were seats in a tumbril. Perhaps not.

Hugo turned to Althea with raised brows.

She shook her head very slightly. 'Good day, Mr Guthrie. I hope we are not late?'

He grinned. 'Not at all. I believe ladies arrive neither late nor early, but when they are meant to arrive.'

A ripple of laughter.

'Very tactful. I must remember that.' Althea sat down with a swish of her skirts.

The tea room was full, but he had secured a table by dint of arriving very early and enjoying two cups of coffee while he waited.

Carriages were lined up all along the square under the trees, and waitstaff dashed back and forth with orders so that, if ladies wished, they might enjoy their ices in the privacy and comfort of their carriages.

In order to get business out of the way he handed Althea the drafted documents, safely sealed. 'You will wish to examine those. If you are satisfied, I can have them ready for signing next Saturday.'

She nodded. 'Thank you. This will take a great deal off my mind.'

'Do you wish to look at them now?'

She smiled. 'No, Mr Guthrie. That can wait. Let us examine the menu. It's years since I've been here.'

Even looking at the menu and discussing with Kate the merits of vanilla versus strawberry or even toasted almond, Hugo noticed the way people, particularly the ladies, were reacting to Althea.

It was obvious that many of them knew her. Startled glances when she walked in turned swiftly to sneers and backs turned. Not one person came up to greet her. Fleeting glances, followed by whispered conversations. That annoyed him, but it was the so-called gentleman who eyed her as if assessing a likely filly, trying to catch her gaze, that had his metaphorical hackles rising. He suspected that it was only his own presence that kept the fellow at bay.

With Kate and Sarah hotly debating their choices, he leaned over, speaking softly. 'Lady Hartleigh— Althea, I had not thought that this might be awkward for you. Would you rather—'

'Miss out on an ice cream? Absolutely not.' She gave him a glittering smile. 'Think what a public service I am doing, sir. They have something to talk about for a change.'

Several heads turned sharply, and he hid a grin. She'd said it loudly enough to be heard.

He reached out and gripped her gloved hand. 'Well done.'

Utter stillness as she raised her eyes to his face. And yes, there were shadows under her eyes. His hand tightened on hers. Her eyes, those fairy-green eyes, widened. His heart quickened as her fingers returned his clasp. Had he lost his mind? What was he thinking to behave in such a familiar fashion? She was his client, a titled lady, not a woman he could—

'Althea! How nice to see you here!'

Hugo looked up with Althea at the lovely, musical voice. A tall woman and even taller gentleman stood there smiling. The lady's eyes of deep blue grey held pleasure, and her hand was extended to Althea. Hugo forced himself to release her.

Althea rose to shake the woman's hand. 'I had no idea you were returned from the country. May I present my solicitor? This is Mr Guthrie, Lady Rutherford. Mr Guthrie, the Earl and Countess of Rutherford.'

Hugo rose to shake hands, and Lady Rutherford's smile deepened. 'A pleasure, sir. And these must be your nieces, Althea. Rutherford read your letters to me. Don't get up, girls. We don't mean to intrude.'

As his countess chatted to Althea, Rutherford stepped a little closer to Hugo. 'I understand we have some business to conduct, Guthrie.'

'We do, my lord.' For the life of him he couldn't keep the chill out of his voice as he rose.

Rutherford raised his eyebrows. 'Should I call at your offices? Or is it easier for you to call at our home in Berkeley Square? I would like to see those documents before Lady Hartleigh signs anything.'

'Oh?' Again he couldn't help the chill.

Rutherford grimaced. 'Yes.' He studied Hugo for a moment and seemed to reach a conclusion. 'Let's put it this way, Guthrie.' He shot a glance at the ladies and lowered his voice. 'Althea Hartleigh has been appallingly treated by too many men. Myself not least of them. This is one way to make amends. Are the documents ready?'

'They are.' Hugo considered a moment. He had an extra set of the drafted documents. Rutherford's house would be a great deal more private than the office. 'When is a convenient time for me to call on you, my lord?'

Rutherford took out his card case and a pencil, scrawled a brief note on the back of a visiting card, and handed it to him. 'Tomorrow afternoon? Any time after five o'clock. Give that to my butler.'

Hugo tucked the card in his pocket. 'Very well, my lord.'

Rutherford nodded. 'Thank you. I'll say this. I'm glad to see that she has found someone to look after her interests. Good day to you, Guthrie. We won't impose ourselves on your party.'

He was as good as his word, gathering up his countess and taking his leave without the least appearance of any snub. Indeed, the countess's suggestion that Althea should 'bring your nieces to stay with us this summer' was seconded by Rutherford immediately.

Althea smiled, said that was very kind, but gave no indication of acceptance or refusal.

Why had he wanted to hear her decline? Did he want to reassure himself she was not wearing the willow for the earl? It was none of his business either way.

Still puzzling over it, he smiled at the girls. 'Have you made your choices?'

They had. At the countess's recommendation Kate had decided on raspberry and chocolate, Sarah thought toasted almond and vanilla. Althea, perhaps not surprisingly, had chosen ginger ice cream.

Althea wasn't quite sure what to think when Hugo insisted on walking back to Soho with them. On the one hand it looked very peculiar. On the other hand it meant she could walk home without the complication of telling any importunate gentleman to go to hell in front of the girls. She had noticed the interest of Mr Mainwaring in Gunter's.

Not even the brief interlude with Meg and Rutherford had sufficed to quell the leers he sent her way.

For most of the way the two girls walked on ahead with Puck. Sarah had brightened over the ice creams and pot of tea they had shared with Hugo. Kate had wrinkled her nose at tea and asked if she might have lemonade.

Sarah dropped back to walk with them as they turned into Wardour Street. 'May I...may I speak to you, Aunt Althea? Privately?' She cast an apologetic look at Hugo. 'It will take only a moment, sir, and it's the only way Kate won't hear. I've told her I want to ask about more arithmetic lessons.'

Althea choked back a laugh at the expression on his face.

He patted her shoulder. 'Of course. I'll walk on and distract her.' He lengthened his stride and left them together.

Althea said nothing. Best to wait, let Sarah speak when she was ready.

'I... I'm sorry!' Sarah blurted out, the threat of tears in her shaking voice.

Without further hesitation, Althea put an arm about her shoulders. 'Oh? What have you done that I don't know about?'

'I... I didn't trust you.' Her voice shook. 'When you went to see Mr Guthrie the other day and wouldn't take us, I thought... I thought—' She hung her head.

Althea could have kicked herself. She tightened her arm. 'You thought I went to tell him I didn't want you after all.' Hugo had thought the same for a moment. 'Has this anything to do with your visit to the parlour last night?'

'You knew?'

Althea nodded.

'I... I didn't want to frighten Kate, but—' Sarah broke off, dragged in a breath. 'I knew I was going to cry and if she woke up she'd want to know what was wrong, so I sneaked out. I thought that—'

'That I was going to hand you over after lulling your suspicions with ice cream?'

She could have kicked herself again. If she'd had the courage and compassion to walk into her own parlour last night and *ask* the child what was wrong—or even days ago when she had noticed Sarah's change in behaviour.

Sarah looked up, her eyes damp. 'I thought you might not bother with the ice creams.'

Althea hugged her close. 'It's all right, Sarah. It's my fault. I should have told you what I was about. And I should have asked you what was wrong.'

She had not wanted to alarm the girls by raising the spectre of yet another death—her own—turning their world topsy turvy all over again. Perhaps that had been the right decision for Kate. Apparently not for Sarah.

She held up the folder of documents. 'I went to see Mr Guthrie to have him make a new will for me, and to ensure that if something happened to me you and Kate would be safe and provided for. These are the drafts.'

Sarah stared at her. 'You mean a last will and testament?'

'Yes. And I have appointed trustees to look after you. Guardians. Mr Guthrie is one of them. Lord Rutherford is another. So you're both safe. You don't have to worry about landing in an orphanage ever again.'

Sarah stopped dead. 'You did that for us? You asked an *earl* to be our guardian? And Mr Guthrie?'

'Yes, and—'

The hug smothered her. Sarah flung her arms around her and clung. Slowly Althea's arms closed about her niece. When last had anyone held her, hugged her like this? She couldn't remember. Her throat closed on an aching lump.

Finally Sarah let go. 'I... I don't know how to thank you.' A tear slipped down her cheek.

Althea patted her cheek, brushing the tear away and praying that the heat pressing behind her own eyes wouldn't spill over. 'I think you just did. Let's catch up with Mr Guthrie and Kate, before she comes back to find out what maggot you've got in your head that you'd ask for more arithmetic.'

'You aren't going to tell her?'

Althea shook her head. 'You asked to speak to me privately. So no. It's between us, unless you choose otherwise.'

Sarah let out an audible breath. 'You can give me more arithmetic if it helps. I should have asked you, shouldn't I? But it felt like if I asked, I'd *make* it happen.'

Althea considered. 'I can understand why you didn't. I wasn't raised to question adults either. But yes, in future if something is worrying you, tell me. And—' she fixed Sarah with a stern glare '—I fail to see why I should come up with an extra arithmetic lesson that I will then have to correct!'

They caught up with Kate and Hugo as they drew level with Gifford's Music Emporium and something slid into Althea's mind. Above the shop there was a small concert hall—she had been planning to attend a concert there next Saturday evening.

'Are you enjoying your music lessons, Sarah?'

Sarah turned a careful gaze on her. 'I *am* enjoying them.' She sounded as though that surprised her. 'Miss Barclay is nice, too.'

Althea laughed. 'So would you enjoy attending a concert with me? This is not extra arithmetic.'

'Oh.' Sarah giggled. 'I might.' She tugged at the end of her little sister's plait. 'Kate would. She used to slip off and play for fun at home, not because our governess Miss Burford said we had to practise.'

'I *like* music,' Kate said. 'It makes me feel happy when I play.'

Althea gestured to Gifford's. 'There's a concert upstairs next Saturday. Would you like to go?' It wasn't only the music. She had avoided most social entanglements for years, but now she had the girls to think of. Living like a particularly reclusive hermit was no longer an option. Even if her stomach turned over at the thought, she was going to have to rejoin society.

Kate stared. '*Can* we? I mean, are children allowed?'

'If you promise to be very still and quiet. And I have a further suggestion to make. I'll explain over supper.'

Hugo left them very properly at the door. He walked away perhaps even more bemused than the first time he had left this house. Whatever had been bothering Sarah enough to risk extra sums was clearly resolved. He rather thought a few tears might have been shed, but she was radiant as he left, teasing her little sister as the door closed behind them.

And Althea? Her eyes remained shadowed and tired, but after that little *tête-à-tête* with Sarah, something seemed to have lifted from her mind. Apparently by interfering, and becoming personally involved, something Jacob had warned him against, he had done the right thing.

Later that evening as he ate dinner at the inn near his lodgings, he wondered idly what suggestion Althea might be making to the girls. He suspected that supper in the Soho Square house was not nearly as peaceful as his solitary meal. Oh, there were diners at the other tables, including a group of half-sprung young gentlemen who were becoming very boisterous over their steaks and tankards. But Hugo had long ago cultivated the ability to remove himself mentally from his physical surroundings.

A good book at dinner, the newspapers at breakfast, and he could banish a near riot from his mental space. Only sometimes he looked up from his book and tankard of ale, and wondered if life was sliding past while he sat in his usual corner. Regulars might stop briefly to speak, but for the most part he maintained a slight distance—people had accepted that.

He stared at his pint. It hadn't always been this way. Once upon a time he had gone home for dinner, had gone home to a house that held everything of joy, all the potential and expectations of a nascent family. And it had all ended in screams of agony followed by a shattering finality of silence, all the potential and expectations snuffed out when his Louisa died in childbirth. All his joy extinguished, and grief an endless ache in his heart.

That joyful home seemed as unreal as a fairy tale. He had left it in the past years ago, and had achieved a measure of contentment. Jacob's wife Alice, thank God, had given up producing possible brides for him, as had the wives of other friends. He was comfortable enough as he was. The even tenor of his life suited him. Calm, logical and steady. One day he would retire to the villa by the river at Petersham, which his father had left him and where his Aunt Sue currently resided. He'd breed books. He might have a dog, too. A companion for walks along the river looking for birds to note in the journal he and his father had kept.

He frowned at the ale. Was it possible he had allowed his life to become regimented? Or even deliberately cultivated a certain boredom?

He shrugged off the thought. Tomorrow he would

be calling on an earl. A glimpse into that world would be a rarified treat for him. None of the firm's clients were aristocratic. His partner and his father before him had preferred to confine their dealings to the upper gentry.

His father's reasoning had been succinct. *'They pay their bills.'*

The following Monday morning Hugo looked curiously at the two notes proffered by his clerk. 'What have we here, Timms?' More surprises? He was still getting over the shock of being invited to dine with the Earl and Countess of Rutherford the previous evening. And the further surprise, despite his reluctance, of liking the earl very much.

There was something to be said for a man who so clearly loved his wife and showed it in a dozen tiny ways. Hugo suspected the man didn't even realise. He shoved away the ache in his own memories and returned his attention to his clerk.

Timms grinned. 'Chap—footman, I'd say, although he's not wearing livery—says you need to read this one first.' He handed over a missive with Hugo's name set out in large, careful script. Hugo couldn't help smiling as he noted the single, very small splotch of ink marring the penmanship. He thought he knew who had written that...

'Very well. And the other?'

Timms handed it over. Hugo's hand shook, and he

fancied that a subtle faery scent clung to the paper, that the blob of wax sealing it, once broken, might release an irreversible enchantment. The handwriting, also setting out his name and style, was as lovely and feminine as Althea herself.

Devil take it, what was wrong with him?

'Is the footman waiting for a reply?'

'He said if you wished to reply at once he could wait. Up to you, sir.'

He nodded slowly. 'Ask him to wait.'

He broke open the first note. Read the contents and stared. The concert Althea had mentioned to the girls. An invitation from Sarah and Kate to attend with them. To thank him for the ices and everything else he had done for them. At once open, and utterly prim. He found himself swallowing a lump as he remembered the tiny, doomed daughter who had lain in his arms for that one short day before joining her mother in the silence of death.

Lucy, he had had her baptised, summoning the priest urgently when the doctor and midwife had warned him the baby was unlikely to survive. To him Lucy had been a gift. Given—and swiftly, cruelly taken away.

He tucked the letter safely away in the small drawer where he kept notes from his father. What the hell had the rest of their family been thinking that they would have let Kate and Sarah be swallowed up by orphanages?

He opened Althea's note. A simple confirmation of the invitation. A suggestion that he might care to come to the house early and escort them to the concert after partaking of refreshments...

Which should give me sufficient time to sign all the copies of the various documents, assuming the final copies are ready. I had a note from Rutherford this morning that you and he had gone over them and he thought they were more than adequate to protect Sarah and Kate's interests. If this does not suit you, please say so.

There was no question that he wanted to see her again. And it wasn't because she was beautiful, or he hoped it wasn't. He had called off the watch he had set on the house in Soho Square first thing that morning. He couldn't settle it with his conscience to spy on her any longer. Either he trusted her with the girls, or he didn't. And if he didn't, then he should never have left them with her in the first place.

The woman who had changed her will, set up trusts at some expense to herself and persuaded two powerful men to protect her nieces, should it ever be necessary, was a woman he could admire.

Admiration was not a problem.

Staring at the note, he thought he knew exactly what

advice Jacob would give him. After dinner the other night Jacob had walked him to the door.

'Ragging on you aside, I'm a little concerned about this outing with Lady Hartleigh and her nieces, Hugo. No good can come of too close an association with a client. You know that as well as I do. Cannot this meeting take place in the offices? A little more formally?'

This? Accepting an invitation to a concert? Saying that the girls had invited him would have Jacob's eyebrows disappearing into his fast-receding hair. Damn it. His own father would be frowning over it.

It would be easier if he had never met her.

But he *had* met her. The problem was that he *liked* her. Of course it behoved him to maintain a relationship with the girls, since he was about to become one of their trustees. But still, some part of him wondered what he was getting himself into pursuing a—pursuing a *what*? Relationship? Friendship?

If this does not suit you...

It suited him only too well, because the real problem was that he desired her. And possibly not just desired her.

Ten years. He had been alone for ten years, and in that time, while he had occasionally felt a mild interest in a woman, it had been precisely that. Mild. Yes, he had liked women. He *did* like women. But the thought of pursuing any relationship had not interested him.

He had loved Louisa. He loved her still, and the tiny daughter he had held so briefly. He had assumed that part of his life was over. Once he had wondered if he might love again one day, but in ten years it hadn't happened.

And now he had discovered in himself a burning desire for a client, coupled with that nagging under-current of *feeling*. A woman with a dubious past, and one moreover to whose nieces he stood, he supposed, as a sort of father figure. A future guardian, should something happen to their aunt.

Surely a sensible man could ignore that fierce at-traction and pursue a disinterested friendship with a woman, couldn't he? They had a common interest in the girls' welfare, and—who was he trying to con-vince? He wasn't at all interested in being disinter-ested. Or sensible.

And yet. They were from different worlds. His fam-ily had been solidly middle class, professional. Althea had been born into the upper gentry and had married into the aristocracy. She might have withdrawn from that gilded circle due to her straitened finances, but she still had friends within that world. It had been clear last night that, while Rutherford himself might maintain a discreet distance, both he and the countess considered Althea Hartleigh a close friend.

It was also clear that if she ever chose to step back into aristocratic circles, they would help her. And there was a puzzle. For some reason, and he didn't think it was guilt, the countess insisted on maintaining a friendship with Althea.

Last night they had dined in Rutherford's library. Something, he understood, the pair of them did routinely when they were alone or had family with them. Friendly, intimate. The conversation had been mostly about the girls and the arrangements that were in place for them.

Lady Rutherford was thinking further ahead. Potentially to marriage. She was prepared to bring them out, give them a season.

'If that is what they and Althea want. A London season, or somewhere else if Althea thinks it more appropriate.'

He let out a breath. Where could he possibly fit into that scenario? He was comfortably off, yes. More than comfortably off. But he did not delude himself that he would be welcomed into aristocratic company, except in a very private capacity. And it seemed to him that Althea had no desire to step back into the world of the aristocracy. She maintained those friendships, but refused to use them to her own advantage. What if she wished to use them to ensure good marriages for Sarah and Kate? That would be another matter altogether.

He knew what Jacob would advise. He knew what his own father would have advised. But he didn't even know what *he* wanted yet. Except that he wanted to keep on seeing Althea. And the girls. Those wants were each independent of the other. And somehow he had to maintain a professional relationship with all of them, when he wasn't feeling even remotely professional about Althea Hartleigh.

He blew out a frustrated breath. It ought to be simple enough. If ever his personal feelings for Althea and his professional judgement came into conflict, he had to err on the side of being professional. That was the logical and rational thing to do.

Escorting a woman and her nieces to a concert was hardly a breach of professional conduct.

He picked up his pen, dipped it in the ink pot and penned his acceptance to Sarah and Kate's invitation. Then he folded Althea's letter up and slipped it into the inner breast pocket of his coat.

Chapter Five

Althea wondered if anyone had ever looked forward to one of Mr Gifford's concerts with quite so much anticipation. The girls had been in a buzz of excitement all week about this evening's concert. She glanced at the shining heads, bent over their schoolbooks, and then at the clock. Ten minutes and she'd be sending them upstairs to change their shoes and put on coats for their walk with John and Puck.

She cast a disgusted glance out of the window. In the middle of the square, King Charles II sneered down at the flower bed beneath him, despite the bright, sunny day. No walk for her. Since they had the concert this evening, she needed to work this afternoon. Not that she had explained any of that to Sarah and Kate. The fewer people who knew how she augmented her income, the better.

Not even her newfound friends could know— Kit Selbourne at the bookshop and Psyché Barclay who ran the tea and coffee shop, the Phoenix Rising. To her surprise, the moment she had dropped her self-imposed reserve, she had discovered them to be friendly and willing to take her into their tight little circle. She had known of their connections to the world she had left behind. It had never occurred to her that they might have deliberately put that world behind them, too.

In approaching Kit for advice on where to find a music teacher, and perhaps some sort of governess or tutor for the girls, she had discovered an odd world where people simply *were*. No one cared that Psyché was Black, or that Kit used her own name rather than her aristocratic husband's to run her business. No one even cared that she, Althea, had been ostracised by society after conducting an affair with the Earl of Rutherford.

And they knew. When, at the first friendly invitation, she had dropped the information at Kit Selbourne's feet rather like a bomb, Kit had shrugged.

'Yes. We're aware of all that. And that no one, least of all his countess, is drumming Rutherford out of society.' A small smile. *'It would be another matter if you attempted to seduce one of* our *husbands.'*

'Or they attempted to seduce me?' Despite society's prejudice, it was not always the woman's fault.

The smile had taken on a glint. *'Oh, we'd slice the idiot up for the dog's dinner in that case.'*

And just like that she had friends again. A social circle, who, between the demands of their work and families, visited each other and closed around each other when help was needed.

Psyché's daughter taught the girls music, and the tutor who taught Kit's boys took Sarah for Latin and mathematics. And in between it all there was somehow time for cups of tea and an occasional supper.

Odd, though. Now, when she had so many restrictions on her time, it was as though she worked better, despite being so tired from working late into the evening last night. Rather than staring out the window daydreaming this afternoon, having the deadline of the girls' return focused her mind most wonderfully.

Her mind already sliding into the next scene—wherein Miss Lydia Parker was spoiling to give Sir Edwin the set down of his life—Althea cursed silently as she heard the doorbell.

The girls looked up.

'Are you expecting someone, Aunt Althea?'

'No.' Both Kit and Psyché would be working. 'John will see who it is.' And hopefully send them away.

A wonderful thing having a servant you could depend upon to distinguish between welcome and unwelcome visitors, and get rid of the unwanted ones without a fuss.

The door opened and John came in with the salver kept for receiving visiting cards. His expression was apologetic as he extended it to her.

Althea picked up the card with foreboding. Read it.

'Did you happen to notice the sky, John?'

He looked at her enquiringly. 'The sky, ma'am?'

'Yes. You know. Up there.' She pointed upwards. 'Blue stuff, or grey as the case maybe. Was it all still up there? Or are there bits of it littered about the square?'

He grinned. 'Far as I noticed it was all up where it's supposed to be, ma'am.'

'Hmm. Perhaps it will fall down later. Show my aunt in—no. Wait.'

She turned to the avidly watching girls. 'You may go upstairs and get ready for your walk.' She absolutely did not need to expose her nieces to the nosiness of Miss Elinor Price, whose reputation in the family hovered between that of Basilisk and Gorgon.

Sarah tilted her head questioningly and Althea sighed. Best to be open with her. 'My great-aunt, Miss Elinor Price.'

Kate looked impressed. 'So she's sort of like our *great*-great-aunt? Is she frightfully old?'

'Frightfully. I'm surprised she's still alive. Now off you go.'

John cleared his throat. 'Ah, Miss Price said she'd like to see the young ladies—'

'What I said, my good man, was that I'd see Frederick's brats, too. And I'm still alive, Althea, because the devil won't have me.'

Althea met her aunt's hard, bright glare with an affable smile, as her affronted relative stalked into the room.

'I've always suspected that the devil had a great deal of good sense about him. Do come in, Aunt—since you are in already. Thank you, John.'

The servant retreated as Elinor Price advanced, leaning heavily on her stick.

'If someone told you *this* was an eligible address, Althea, they lied.' Elinor glanced around, her expression scornful. 'And what the devil is *that*?'

Puck had emerged from under the desk.

'A dog, Aunt Elinor. *My* dog.'

Elinor subjected Puck to a gimlet-eyed stare. 'If you say so.'

Althea shrugged, beyond caring how rude it was. 'I do. And as for the address, I was assured that it was far enough out of the way that no one would bother calling on me here. But as you say, they lied. Apart from your carriage, Elinor, what brings you here?'

After Hartleigh's death, Elinor had been very quick to join the rest of the family in blaming her for the parlous state of her finances, and condemning her supposed lack of morals.

'Going to ask me to sit down?'

Althea eyed her thoughtfully. For all the old lady's belligerence she struck Althea as frail, and a quick mental calculation told her that Elinor must be verging on ninety by now. 'Very well. Do sit down, Elinor. To what do I owe the honour of this visit?'

The old woman sat, glared. 'An impertinent letter

from some solicitor! I came to see if it was true. That you'd taken in Frederick's daughters.'

Althea's temper slipped a notch. 'As you see. They are living with me now.'

'Why?'

'Is it any business of yours?'

'Hoping for some money with them, were you? You ran through your own fortune fast enough, didn't you? After you ran through Hartleigh's!' She thumped the stick on the ground.

The hell she had. 'I had no idea you had such a taste for unfounded gossip, Elinor.'

A snort greeted that. 'Unfounded? Hah!'

A little more temper slipped its restraints. 'Did no one mention the ten thousand pounds' worth of gambling debts that Hartleigh's executors saw fit to pay out?'

Audible gasps came from Sarah and Kate.

Elinor Price gripped the top of her cane harder. 'Fustian! He gambled no more than was genteel! Frederick told me that.'

Elinor had always thought the sun shone brighter when Frederick rose from a chair. The temptation to set her right, to tell her the truth about what Frederick and Hartleigh had done, burned inside Althea, but she quenched it. Sarah and Kate were right there.

Instead, Althea took a death grip on her temper and shook her head with a pitying smile 'You really ought to get out more, Elinor. Someone might tell you the truth.'

However, it wasn't going to be her. At least, not all of it.

Mentally editing, she said, 'Ten thousand pounds was the figure, which I think you'll agree was a little more than can be considered genteel.' Fury scorched through her. 'And that was after he had persuaded my trustees to release the bulk of *my* fortune at various times to pay off earlier gaming debts.' And for other *expenses* that, if possible, had stung even more.

She took a sharp breath. This was verging on the subjects Sarah and Kate definitely did not need to know about.

'So.' She favoured Elinor with a brilliant smile. 'May I offer you a cup of tea, Aunt Elinor? Since the truth doesn't sit comfortably with you?'

Elinor heaved to her feet. 'Why, you impertinent baggage! How dare—?'

'She's *not*!'

Sarah was up, too, fists clenched and her face red.

Althea turned. 'Sarah, sit down, sweetheart.' For the life of her she couldn't bring herself to reprove the child.

'No! She's being horrid to you, and you were the only one who'd take us in after Papa died and Cousin Wilfrid said we couldn't stay. Even though you haven't got nearly as much money as some of our other relatives!' She turned on Elinor. 'Like you! I know you were on Mr Guthrie's list. And you're as rich as Midas! So go away!'

'Charming!' Elinor glared at Sarah. 'Do you imagine she took you without there being something in it for her, child? I've no doubt your cousin Wilfrid gave her something for taking you off his hands.'

Sarah snorted. 'I don't think so. Since we were going to orphanages otherwise! He didn't even give us enough money to buy our dinner on the way to London. What would *you* know about it anyway? No wonder the devil doesn't want you! You'd put him out of a job!'

'Orphanages? *Frederick's* daughters? What nonsense is this?'

Seeing Elinor's jaw drop, and not entirely convinced the old lady couldn't throw actual lightning bolts or at least spit venom, Althea stepped between them. 'There you have it, Elinor. Good day to you. I'll see you out. Sarah, dear,' she turned to the child, 'ring for John. A pot of tea for me—' tempting to lace it with brandy! '—cake and milk for you and Kate before your walk. You may give Puck a biscuit.'

She strode to the door, opened it. 'After you, Elinor.'

'Kicking me out, are you?'

'Well spotted.'

She shut the door behind them with something perilously close to a bang and stalked to the front door.

Elinor looked at her, scowling. 'You think I can't and won't ask questions? Find out the truth?'

'Have at it, Elinor. With my blessing. But think about *who* you ask. And whatever you find out, do not bring it back here to distress my girls.'

The old lady snorted. 'Don't think I don't know who your principal trustee was after your father died, girl! And what did that chit mean, that Wilfrid wouldn't let them stay? He was supposed to be their guardian. What was he thinking giving them over to *you*? And what was all that nonsense about orphanages?'

Althea opened the front door. 'Elinor, mind your own business. If you came to assure yourself that Frederick's daughters are safe, you may rest assured they are as safe as I can make them, and that's no thanks to either their father or Wilfrid. Good day to you. Happy gossiping. But please, don't bring what you find back here to those girls!' She softened her voice. 'Whatever you do, please don't do that. They don't deserve it.'

A footman hurried across the pavement towards them from Elinor's waiting carriage.

The old lady's scowl deepened as she waved the footman off. 'That letter. From the solicitor telling me they were with you. First thing I knew about Frederick's girls being homeless.'

Althea snorted, and realised that she sounded for all the world like Elinor herself. 'Mr Guthrie assured me he had contacted all the other possible relations before coming to me. I had assumed you were on his list. Sarah certainly seems to think so.'

The thin old mouth flattened. 'Apparently I was. Servants didn't tell me because I've been ill. Doctor had me near buried. So there's that.'

Althea softened a little. 'Oh. I'm sorry you've been unwell, Aunt.'

The old lady gave a sniff. 'I daresay. I'll get to the bottom of this. Don't think I won't.' She beckoned to her footman. 'I'll bid you good day.'

Althea watched as the footman handed the old lady down the steps and into the carriage.

Elinor put down the window and leaned out. 'That girl's got a nasty tongue in her head. The same as you always had.'

Althea inclined her head. 'Thank you, Elinor.'

Impossible to know if the answering snort betokened amusement or irritation. With Elinor it could have been either, or both at once. As the vehicle rattled off Althea closed the front door behind her and leaned back on it. If Elinor poked around there was every likelihood she'd stir up a veritable hornets' nest. She took a deep breath, hoping she could send the girls out for their walk without too many questions.

Something had upset Althea. Hugo had noticed almost immediately on arriving at the house. On the surface she appeared her usual self during their light meal. Bright, cheerful, a little cynical—although never the latter with the girls. But there was *something*. A little more reserve perhaps. She had been a little short with him, her brow furrowed, although she had relaxed during the concert, clearly enjoying the music. The quartet was excellent, starting with Mozart, then Haydn and finishing with Beethoven.

Sarah, unsurprisingly, had fidgeted a little. Kate, to his amazement, had sat enthralled, leaning forward in her seat in utter silence. At the gathering for refreshments, she was still very quiet, her eyes dreamy.

'You enjoyed the concert, Kate?' He passed her a small plate with cake on it.

She nodded. 'I'm going to practise the piano more.'

Hugo blinked. 'Practise? Where do you do that?' He hadn't noticed any sort of instrument, let alone a piano at the house.

Kate smiled. 'Miss Barclay teaches me, and I am allowed to go to their house to practise. Mrs Barclay runs the Phoenix. It used to be a coffee house for gentlemen, but now anyone can go. We have tea there after changing our library books.'

He had been introduced to Miss Barclay, the daughter of Mr and Mrs William Barclay. He had met them before the concert. Mrs Barclay was the owner and proprietor of the Phoenix Rising. He wasn't quite sure how that had come about, but the teashop had been one of the establishments that had provided a great deal of information about Althea's household. Barclay, he understood, was employed as a steward for the Marquess of Huntercombe.

The mix of guests was interesting to say the least.

Mrs Barclay, a tall, elegant Black woman, was not the only female business owner present. There was also Miss Selbourne who, confusingly, was also Lady Martin Lacy, married to the youngest son of the Duke of Keswick. She ran Selbourne's Antiquarian Books across the road from the Phoenix. He wasn't entirely sure if he should call her Miss Selbourne or Lady Martin. She answered to both with seeming equanimity.

'Did you enjoy it, Mr Guthrie?'

He smiled at Kate. 'Very much. Although I wondered if I had offended your aunt.'

She scowled, bit into her cake. 'I think she's still cross about Great-Great-Aunt Price.'

Hugo realised too late that he shouldn't have raised such a topic with the child. 'Oh. Well, never mind.' Great-Great-Aunt Price, he assumed, must be Miss Elinor Price.

'She called before our walk and said the horridest things to Aunt Althea. And then Sarah said rude things to *her* and Aunt Althea kicked her out.'

Fascinated despite himself, he asked, 'Kicked who out? Not Sarah, surely?'

Kate swallowed. 'Kicked Great-Aunt Price out, I mean. Then we had cake and milk and went for our walk.'

'Was it a nice walk?' A desperate attempt to change the subject if ever there was one.

'Oh, yes. But Aunt Althea was still out of sorts when we came home. She came with us after all. And

I think she was going to work, but Aunt Price annoyed her so much she said she needed to clear her head instead.'

What work? Her accounts? Needlework? But why would Kate say *going to work*?

He tried again to change the subject. 'Why don't we speak to Miss Barclay and her mother about extra practice for you?'

Kate's smile glowed. 'Can we? I don't think they'll mind, but I have to *ask*, not expect.'

Relieved, he nodded. 'Of course. Come along.' He'd confess and apologise to Althea for his accidental prying later.

Chapter Six

'I owe you an apology.'

The girls were walking ahead a little and he had offered Althea his arm. He liked the feel of her hand resting there. Clear through her evening gloves, the layers of his shirt and coat, it burned like a brand. His heart beat that little bit harder in response. And somehow at the same time it felt right. Comfortable. As if it were exactly where it was meant to be. In the same way that the whole evening had felt right.

She gave him a sideways smile that kicked his heartbeat up yet another notch. 'Whatever for?'

He caught at his scattered thoughts. 'I…er…understand you had an unwelcome visitor today.'

Her fingers tightened sharply on his arm, then eased.

'Oh. That.' She wrinkled her nose. 'Not exactly a visitor. And not entirely unwelcome. She didn't stay long enough for either.'

Hugo had the impression she was choosing her words carefully.

'My great-aunt. She disapproves of me. How did you… Ah, Kate.'

'Yes, hence the apology. I didn't mean to pump her. Exactly. I thought perhaps *I* had offended you.'

'You? How?'

'I had no idea. Stupidly, I mentioned it to Kate. She told me all about Miss Price. Is it Sarah's rudeness that annoyed you?'

Her soft chuckle reassured him a little. 'No. Not at all. Elinor infuriated me. She received your letter of course and came to see for herself. Apparently it was the first she knew of the business. She said she had been unwell, but she does like to poke her nose into anything she considers family business. I shouldn't have permitted her to set my back up. Sarah reacted to that.'

'She's very loyal.'

Althea smiled. 'Yes. I'm not sure what I've done to deserve her partisanship though.'

'Giving them a home, perhaps?'

She waved that away. 'Little enough.'

He begged to differ. What she had done was life changing for those girls. And he still did not understand where her money came from.

Althea Hartleigh had been left the most impecunious of widows. Her own fortune had been dissipated.

And, given that dissipation, how had she learned to manage her now straitened finances?

She had turned her financial affairs over to him and, looking through her accounts, he had seen there were occasional lump sums being paid to her. At irregular times, and in increasing amounts. Over the past few years those sums came to around six thousand pounds, much of which she had invested safely in government funds.

His first assumption, that she had sold some jewellery, he now doubted. Surely if she had decided to sell jewellery she would have done it all at once? Unless she had concluded that she would get better prices if she did it bit by bit. And from all he could see Althea hadn't been *forced* to the sale of anything. Her accounts had been in order when each of those sums had appeared. Except for the very first payment, five years ago, the money had not been used to keep her above hatches, to pay off debts or to keep her household running. Significantly, she had told him what that first payment had been for—the sale of her very expensive mansion in Mayfair. After that, the unexplained money was invested, adding to her financial security, and she lived off the income of her investments, not the payments themselves.

He knew she lived frugally. Only the one manservant, her cook/housekeeper and the maid. No horse or carriage. She walked most places, or very occasionally took a hackney. Her gowns were elegant, but far from modish or expensive, and she didn't have many as far as he could tell. She didn't entertain—no dinner parties or card parties. She had a limited circle of friends and accepted occasional invitations to dine.

It still niggled at him that she might have an extraordinarily discreet lover. One who managed never to be seen? Surely no one was that discreet? Further than that, he knew beyond doubt that she would not conduct herself in that way with the girls in the house. If it had been just the one payment, it might have been a single payment from a former lover.

Rutherford, perhaps. But apart from the sale of her Mayfair house, the first of those unexplained payments had been over a year after Rutherford's marriage and the end of their affair. And the payments had continued, the most recent a few months ago. He didn't see Rutherford doing that or, for that matter, Althea accepting.

Besides, she had told him straight out that she had found something to sell apart from herself. He knew her well enough to know that not only was she *not* lying about this, but that she wouldn't lie to him. Logically, if she'd wanted to lie, selling jewellery was the obvious one. He would have believed it.

But when he had first met Althea, he had not noticed dark shadows under her eyes. He'd noticed them when she called at his chambers, as if she were not getting enough sleep, and they were only becoming deeper.

And Kate had said *work*.

It was none of his business unless she chose to tell him. And he didn't care to look too closely at the reasons he was determined not to believe she had a lover.

They had reached the house, and for the first time in years Althea was unsure of what to do with a man. She could invite him in, offer him tea or coffee. Slightly improper, but who cared? She was a widow, not a marriageable young lady. No one was going to worry about her reputation, and she was perfectly sure he wasn't going to make a nuisance of himself.

On the other hand, *his* reputation might suffer if he was thought to be consorting with a notorious widow.

When in doubt, ask.

'Will it sink your reputation straight into the gutter if I invite you in for tea or coffee?'

He gave her a sideways glance. 'A mere invitation won't sink me. Even accepting your invitation—if that was an invitation and not a hypothetical query—won't render me damaged goods. It's what might accompany the tea and coffee that could be construed as damaging.'

She snorted out a laugh. 'Ginger biscuits?'

'I think my virtue is safe then,' he said gravely. 'Except possibly for indulging in the sin of gluttony, I see little danger in ginger biscuits.'

To her surprise he took the key from her and opened the door, gesturing them in.

'After you.'

Kate gave Hugo her most innocent yet impish smile. 'Are you coming in, sir? I'm not in the least tired. Are we having biscuits?'

Before he could step into the trap, Althea fixed Kate with a mild look. 'It's so far past your bedtime, you'll probably need early bed tomorrow night if you don't hurry. Or even an afternoon nap instead of a walk.'

Kate pouted, but Sarah gave her a poke in the back. 'Don't be a brat, Kate. It's after ten. You heard the church bell walking home as clearly as I did. Come on.'

For an instant, Althea wondered if Kate would argue, but she gave a sigh instead. 'Oh, very well. Goodnight, Aunt. Goodnight, sir. Thank you for the concert. It was lovely.'

'You're very welcome.' Althea bent to kiss her. 'Milly will bring up your milk and biscuits. Make sure you clean your teeth properly.'

Sarah kissed her. 'We will. Goodnight.' She dropped Hugo a little curtsy. 'Goodnight, sir.'

John popped into the hall. 'Tea, ma'am?'

'Yes, please. And milk and biscuits upstairs for the young ladies.'

The parlour fire had nearly gone out and Hugo, seeing her bend to stir it up and add coals, nudged her aside.

'May I?'

'Thank you.'

Oddly, it didn't seem as if he were suggesting she couldn't do it, it was more offering to do something for her. Because he wanted to, because he could. She sat down with a little sigh. She needed to work for another hour this evening. Perhaps she shouldn't have invited him in. But it was so nice to sit down and let someone else stir up the fire for a change. She refused to call a servant every time something needed doing. And that would not be the same as watching Hugo add coals to the fire, simply because he wanted to do it for her.

A little warning voice sounded. *Don't start wanting a man to do things for you. For any reason.*

She pushed it away. This was friendship, kindness. She had made herself forget how pleasant it could be to have friends you saw regularly, who could be part of your life.

'Should I sign those papers now?'

He looked up with a frown. 'Absolutely not. You should read them over first, check them against the drafts you and Rutherford approved.'

She knew he was right. And she wanted to see him again…

Are you mad? What are you doing?

'Very well. I'll do that tomorrow and bring them to your office. Leave them with your clerk. Or…' She hesitated, unsure of herself.

He sat down opposite her, nodded slowly. 'You could do that. Or…?'

'Or you might like to come to supper next Friday night.' Hurriedly, she added, 'I have asked the Barclays and Lord Martin and Kit if they would like to come. And their families.'

He looked surprised. 'That's unusual for you.'

She stared. 'Is it?' How the hell did he know that?

He flushed. 'I mean, I had the impression you preferred to avoid society.' He shifted in his seat. 'That you didn't accept invitations or issue them.'

She thought about that. 'True. But they're not "society" precisely. They're friends. I think.'

She thought a little more, watching him. Was the chair uncomfortable? She had never found it so, but he was shifting in it rather... He might have correctly divined her preference to keep largely to herself, but how had he known something so specific, that she rarely issued invitations?

Irritation stirred, then fury uncoiled, hissing, raising its head. 'You've been watching me.'

His cheeks, even the tips of his ears, burned. If she hadn't been so annoyed it would have been endearing.

'I'm sorry.'

Most of her rising anger dissipated at that simple apology. No attempt at evasion. Not even an attempt at justification. She forced herself to think a little further.

'The girls.' He knew her reputation. Perhaps even suspected how close she had been to a different solution for her lack of funds. 'You wanted to be sure they were safe, that I really was a fit and proper person to have charge of them.'

It stung. More than a little. But she had to admit, she had probably earned a little scrutiny from a man who only wanted to protect those children. They had already been put through hell.

She scowled, then forced out the words that had to be said. 'Thank you.'

He looked stunned. *'Thank you?'* Now *he* looked annoyed. 'For what? Insulting you comprehensively?'

The rest of her anger vanished as if it had never been. 'For caring enough about the girls to risk insulting me. For being someone I can trust, always, to have their best interests at heart.'

'If it matters, I withdrew the watch after you called at my office.'

'Oh?' The blush was endearing, and that he still looked ashamed.

'I reasoned that a woman so determined on protecting the girls from the world in general, and men in particular, would hardly behave in a way likely to cause them harm.' That faint smile flickered. 'Your own logic really. I like it.'

At that moment, a slight scratch at the door heralded John with the tea tray. Althea took the reprieve and busied herself pouring tea, as she attempted to bring her thoughts under some semblance of control.

She handed Hugo his cup and a biscuit, as something far more disturbing than anger flickered inside her. A growing interest in a man who liked a woman as a logical, rational being? Rather than a pretty doll to be admired for her beauty, a prize to make other men envious of your luck in possessing her?

She *knew* such men existed. She was neither stupid nor unobservant, and she had seen those relationships for herself.

But for her? She sipped her tea.

Very few men ever seemed to look past her beauty. She knew she was beautiful. There was no point in pretending otherwise, and from her sixteenth year she had considered it a penance. Other girls had either viewed her as competition in the quest for a wealthy husband, or attached themselves to her in the hopes that proximity would bring them to the attention of men. The mothers of those girls had murmured little slights—that it was a shame her eyes were that odd shade of green, or that she thought far too much of herself.

The men had courted her for her beauty and fortune. Not one of them had been interested in Althea Price. The girl who actually enjoyed playing the piano. The girl who covered page after page in a carefully hidden journal with her imaginings.

'Those thoughts are going to be worth a great deal more than a penny.' He set down his cup and the half-eaten biscuit.

She blinked. 'My apologies. I don't think I have ever received a nicer compliment.'

* * *

Hugo stared at her. Was every other man in London blind? He started to say so, but thought a little further. *A nicer compliment.*

He didn't think he had ever seen a lovelier woman. He would be lying if he pretended not to see it, not to appreciate it. But her beauty wasn't why he liked her. He picked up his cup again, absent-mindedly dipped his biscuit in it. How many people bothered to look past that lovely façade? How many of them saw the woman he saw?

He thought Rutherford did. Belatedly. And the countess saw her. The people he had met tonight? Barclay, Lord Martin and their wives? Who did they see when they looked at Althea Hartleigh?

Ah. She had invited them to supper next Friday. She would not have invited them into her home if she were not comfortable with them. And from all he had learned of her, she had never done so before. Which meant...

'You have lived here, what? Five years? And you have only recently become friends with the Barclays and Lacy and his wife.'

She gave him a wry smile. 'And how do you know that?'

'Because this is the first time you have ever invited people to supper as far as I can make out.'

She sighed. 'My reputation. When I moved here... let's say I was raw. Tired of people cutting me, gossiping about me. I decided to keep myself to myself, and the hell with the rest of the world. I wasn't going to give anyone an excuse to accuse me of casting lascivious eyes on her husband, or whatever other nonsense they could invent.'

He could understand that, hiding away to lick your wounds. Hadn't he done much the same, moving back into lodgings that didn't constantly remind him of everything he had lost?

'And the girls changed that.' They had changed things for him, too.

She laughed. 'You really do know me.' Dipping her own biscuit, she said, 'All very well for me to adopt the habits of a medieval anchorite, but that is no life for children.' She ate the biscuit and sipped her tea. 'They need to be educated. They need to know people. How can they navigate the world if they do not live in it?'

He nodded. 'So you took the risk and emerged from your cell to meet your neighbours.'

'I suppose so.' She smiled. 'Not much of a risk, as it turned out. I always liked them, and it turned out they knew all about me and didn't care in the least.'

Others, he knew, had cared. The people in Gunter's tea shop, whispering and sneering behind their hands. Some of them, no doubt, had once called Althea their friend. The so-called gentleman whose greedy eyes had slithered all over her. He could imagine the sort of compliments that type would offer, and thanked

God that Althea was intelligent enough to discount such dross.

'Supper,' he said. 'I would like that very much. However.'

She raised her brows. 'However? That sounds as though there is a caveat coming.'

'Not a caveat precisely,' he said. 'But before I accept, and you cannot rescind your invitation—'

Laughter rippled. 'Don't wager too much on that, Hugo.'

He smiled. 'In the interests of honesty and full disclosure, I should tell you that you are beautiful. Possibly the most beautiful woman I have ever seen. I would have to be blind and six months dead not to notice that.'

'You do seem to be breathing.'

'And plan to keep doing so.' He smiled at her. 'Your beauty is a distraction though. People don't see past it, I suppose.'

She stared. Shook her head slowly. 'They see beautiful, destructive Lady Hartleigh who made a play for an earl, failed and retired from society ruined and humiliated.'

He scowled. 'Is that how you saw yourself?'

She shrugged. 'It's true enough.'

'The hell it is. I see a woman who tried to extricate herself from an impossible situation not of her own making, in the only way she could.'

He leaned forward and gripped her hands. 'Do not

tell me that those women who cut your acquaintance and gossiped behind their hands at Gunter's would not have done exactly the same.' How had she put it once? 'Were you truly the—and I quote—mercenary bitch people like to see, you would hardly have retained Rutherford's friendship and respect, let alone gained that of Lady Rutherford.'

She could hardly breathe—her heart tripped. He still held her hands, at once steely and gentle, as if he sheltered her from everything, yet would release her in an instant should she wish it.

She did not wish it. What she wanted—

He raised first one, then the other hand to his lips and brushed a kiss over her fingers.

The world tilted and whirled around her as her pulse leapt and fizzed like the fine champagne she had once enjoyed. In the past five years her pulse had not so much as flickered over a man. Oh, she had seen plenty of men she considered attractive, but that had been a theoretical thing. She had merely observed their attractiveness. She had not felt any tug of interest, and considered it far less of a loss in her life than champagne.

This was a great deal more than a tug. What she wanted was insane, impossible and far more dangerous than anything else she had ever wanted in her life.

For a moment she stared at her fingers where his

mouth had touched, wondering that her hands looked much the same. Slowly she raised her eyes and found his waiting.

So serious that deep, peaceful grey. Well, usually peaceful. Now they were not peaceful at all. A storm lurked in the depths. A storm she could call or banish.

Her breathing hitched. 'Hugo?'

He leaned forward, still holding her hands, but stopped a heartbeat away.

Her choice. Call or banish.

She leaned forward the last heartbeat and their lips met.

Not the storm, not yet. It was there, but this kiss was gentle, sweet. Almost shy. There was no demand as their mouths moved together. Desire was there, but banked. There to be stirred up should one of them choose it, but this was lovely. A courtship in and of itself. This was a kiss she had never known before. She was not sure she had known it existed.

Someone deepened the kiss. Perhaps it was both of them. Mouths opened, tongues quested and touched. Someone sighed in pleasure and another sigh answered. And still the desire remained simmering, dancing in the wings, waiting for the storm.

She was ready to call it.

Somewhere a bell chimed. And kept chiming.

Hugo forced himself to break the kiss, and felt as though something had ripped inside him. Her lips clung now, and he didn't want to stop kissing her. But the damn clock reminded him that, like Cinderella, he couldn't stay for the entire night.

She sat back a little, her eyes questioning, *wanting*, and his resolve wavered. Those faerie eyes were a little dazed, her lips soft from their kisses. Temptation, he realised, was the absence of all thought. He forced himself to sit up and think. *His* reputation could remove itself to hell and back, but if he remained here kissing Althea, it would not stop with kisses. And that would do very real damage to her reputation.

His lungs were tight and he had an aching erection. They had kissed and held hands, and he was burning for her.

Slow down. This is not something to gulp.

He summoned a smile. 'I'd look a fool running down your front steps with one shoe, wouldn't I?'

She frowned. 'One—oh!' Something of her wicked smile dawned. 'You'd make an odd sort of Cinderella.'

He touched her cheek, felt her quiver. 'We aren't going to rush into this, Princess Charming.'

'Rush into what?'

He let out a breath. 'I suppose when we know that we might move a little faster.' He rose. 'I should leave. Before I do something irreparably stupid.'

She saw him out. He didn't risk kissing her again, but waited on the step to hear the key turn and the bolts shoot home. There were moments when doing something irreparably stupid—like banging on her door and asking to come back in—seemed like an excellent idea.

Chapter Seven

In Althea's former life, the supper parties she held had been formal, elegant affairs. Silks and satins had rustled, the food and wine had been of the finest, and the musical entertainment had been sophisticated. None of the guests would have dreamed of arriving with a bottle of wine or a pie to add to the table, and no one would have brought a fiddle to play.

Those formal, elegant affairs had been worked out and planned down to the last lobster patty. Champagne had flowed, and the bill afterwards had been eyewatering. In addition, Althea had been obliged to send invitations to a great many people she *knew* disliked her, and would gossip the next day about who *hadn't* attended. Even if the supposed absentee had been there visibly enjoying him or herself.

She never had a chance to converse with the people she really wanted to, because Hartleigh had insisted that she be seen with the *right* people. And then, while she pinned a false smile to her face, he lost money in the card room.

Once, when he had criticised her poor household management skills in general, and the bill for a recent supper party in particular, she had suggested that using the music room for dancing rather than cards would be cheaper. She had kept to her room for three days until the mark of his slap faded.

An unusual loss of temper on his part. Mostly he remembered to hit her where the bruises wouldn't show.

In short? She loathed everything about supper parties.

Attending a supper at Selbourne's Books a few weeks ago had given her an entirely fresh perspective. Supper parties, when you only invited people you actually wished to spend time with, could be a great deal of fun. Children and dogs—and one cat—gave a certain measure of unpredictability, but that only added to the fun.

Her own supper party ran along similar lines. A hearty soup, full of meat, vegetables and barley was set out in her rarely used dining parlour, along with a ham, a large pat of butter, freshly baked bread, fruit, a decent cheese and two apple pies. There was not a lobster patty in sight, and champagne had been conspicuous by its absence.

The company was refreshingly informal. Miss Barclay brought her fiddle to play after supper. Kit Selbourne and Lord Martin's sons—fifteen and seventeen—bore Kate and Sarah off to the parlour to play cards.

'It's quite safe.' Kit smiled reassuringly at Althea. 'We don't even permit them to gamble for pins from my sewing box.'

'A good thing, too.' Lord Martin grinned at his wife. 'For all the use those pins get, they must be nearly rusted away.'

'I hear you're sewing your own buttons on now, Lacy.' Will Barclay helped himself to more cheese and poured a glass of wine for his wife.

Althea laughed along with the rest and wondered where this sort of party had been all her life. She had friends, people who liked her for herself, and hosted a party because of that. Not for whatever social cachet they might gain. And Hugo had come. He had, without ever overstepping, acted almost as a host, helping her to ensure that everyone enjoyed themselves. She wished… She put that wish, the wish brought into being with that kiss a week ago, away. It was not possible. For so many reasons, nothing was possible between them but friendship. And in the end, that friendship would be longer lived than an affair anyway.

'It's our turn next,' Psyché Barclay said at the end of the evening as they gathered up their belongings. 'Perhaps in three weeks?' She smiled at Althea. 'Bring the girls. And Puck.' She turned to Hugo with another smile. 'You should come, too, Mr Guthrie. I know

Martin and Will want to pick your brains about the law. I'll let Althea know.'

Althea rose. 'I'll see you out.' And when she came back, after the girls had gone up to bed, she would have to tell Hugo what she had decided, and apologise for leading him to believe something other than friendship had been possible.

Hugo considered that friendly, almost casual invitation as Althea saw her other guests out. Courtesy of Althea, he'd stumbled into a new circle of friends.

'Did you enjoy it, Mr Guthrie?' Kate barely smothered a yawn.

He smiled. 'I did. So much so that I'm nearly as ready for my bed as you are.'

Her eyes widened. 'Oh, I'm not tired!' This time the yawn escaped entirely.

'Well, if you aren't, I am.' Althea came back into the parlour. They had all ended up in there with coffee and tea, with anyone under twenty consigned to sitting on the floor.

'I'm going up,' Sarah announced. 'Goodnight, sir. Come along, Kate. No one wants to carry you up when you fall asleep in that chair.'

Kate sighed. 'Goodnight, Aunt. Thank you for letting me stay up. Goodnight, sir.'

She trailed out after Sarah, covering another yawn, and the door closed behind them.

All evening he had waited for this moment, when

he could have Althea all to himself and speak to her privately. It had been a revelation seeing her like this, with the neighbours she had only approached to give the girls as normal a life as she could.

His parents had held similar family suppers through his boyhood. Friends and neighbours gathering on a Saturday evening to talk and often dance. As had happened this evening, the younger people had gone off to play games. Later they had joined in the dancing. He smiled to himself. He had kissed a girl for the first time at one of those parties, and fallen in love with Louisa.

Even after they had married, he and Louisa had gone to his parents' supper parties.

With Louisa's death everything had changed. The supper parties had stopped while they were in mourning, and it had been easier to withdraw a little. Otherwise he had to contend with his friends' endless sympathy, and later, their gentle attempts at matchmaking. He hadn't been interested.

He'd found a solace moving back into his parents' house, and then removing to bachelor lodgings when his father retired and they moved to Petersham. He'd achieved a balance, a steadiness that he had been unwilling to disturb for a conveniently comfortable marriage. He had loved Louisa deeply and irrevocably. He had never been able to imagine loving another, nor did he wish to offer a woman the insult of being a consolation prize.

But now he smiled at Althea, and she smiled back. Damned if he could say what it was that drew him to her. Oh, she was beautiful. And sharp-tongued, wasp-ish and fiercely independent.

He was going to kiss her again.

She flung up her hand, and took a step back. 'No.'

She had thought about that kiss all week. Thought about more than the kiss. Curse it, she had fantasised about having an affair with Hugo. And in a week of thinking, and fantasising, she had forced herself to confront reality. Over the course of a sleepless night— last night—she had decided that it wasn't going to happen.

He stopped, a faint frown creasing his brow. 'No? To what are you saying *no*?'

'No, you can't stay.'

His brow cleared. 'Of course not. I was going to kiss you goodnight.'

He took another step, smiling, and her resolve shook. She wanted his kiss as much as her next breath.

'No. I've been thinking. We can't do this. We mustn't.'

'Kiss?'

Did he have to be so ridiculously appealing? She let out a shaky breath. 'Have an affair.'

His eyes widened. 'An affair. Right.'

No. It would be wrong. Oh, not for her, but—

He sat down on the sofa.

'What are you doing?' He should be leaving. Annoyed, but leaving.

'I'm sitting down for this conversation.'

'What conversation?'

'The one we're having instead of kissing each other goodnight.'

Why couldn't he behave like a normal man and try to kiss her anyway? Then she could be angry and kick him out. Instead he was being logical and rational about it. Which meant *she* had to be logical and rational, too.

She took a deep breath. 'It's not that I don't *want* to kiss you…' Even though she worried that it would end up being a great deal more than a goodnight kiss. 'Or even have an affair with you. But…'

'What?'

Oh, Lord, she was making a mull of this!

He shook his head. 'Now I'm completely confused. Are you saying that you *do* want to kiss me, and eventually, at some point, have an affair with me?'

She nodded. 'Yes. I would like that. But we can't. It's not possible. So we shouldn't be making everything harder with goodnight kisses.'

'Very well.' He took off his glasses, polished them on a pristine handkerchief. 'Would you care to tell me what brought you to this conclusion?'

Trying to order her thoughts, Althea sat down herself. 'I'm not sure where to start.'

'Anywhere will do.' There was a decidedly snippy tone in his voice.

She glared at him. 'We're friends.' Doubt struck. 'Aren't we?'

His smile came. 'Yes. We are. Is that in the credit or debit column?'

'Both,' she admitted. 'The thing is, if we had an affair, we might not be friends after it ended.'

'Then you envision our hypothetical affair having an end?'

She refrained from snorting. 'Hugo, affairs *always* end. That's part of the definition of an affair, it's finite. I don't think it's a good idea to risk our friendship on something finite.'

'Anything else?'

'The girls.' Even if she had been prepared to risk their friendship, she couldn't risk the girls.

'Go on.'

He was going to make her spell it out?

'Hugo, you know what the world is like. If we have an affair, inevitably people will know. It would damage their reputations.' He said nothing and she rushed on. 'It's ridiculous, and unfair, but I have to contend with the world as it is for their sakes.'

'Ah.' He nodded. 'That, at least, is a valid reason for not risking an affair.' He set his tea aside, rose and walked across to her.

'What are you doing?'

'Guess.' He reached down, took her hands, and brought her unresisting to her feet.

'This is not at all a good idea.'

He smiled and her resolve cracked. 'Probably not. I'm full of all sorts of bad ideas these days. You're an appalling influence. But you're forgetting one thing.'

Just one? With his mouth barely a breath from hers, his strength and scent enclosing her, she was in danger of forgetting her own name. Despite her misgivings—the ones she was struggling to remember—her foolish arms were around him.

If it couldn't be an affair, could it be tonight? One night, nothing more, and afterwards pretend it had never happened? Or at least act as if it had not. She wasn't that forgetful. Which reminded her...

'What am I forgetting?'

'I suppose it's not exactly forgetting. More like misinterpreting.' His mouth brushed hers. 'I don't want an affair.'

And his mouth was on hers, or hers was on his. A meeting of equal desires, with no pretence of coyness. She gave and took, pleasure upon pleasure, a dance of tongues, beating hearts and mingled breaths.

The fire glowed, illuminating his face in flickering shadows as they drew apart slowly, and Althea strove to gather her scrambled wits. Oh, God. It was worse than she'd thought. She was falling—

No. She mustn't even *think* that.

She swallowed. 'If you don't want an affair, then seducing me into—'

He stopped her mouth with another brief kiss. Then, 'Althea, you idiot, I want to *court* you, not seduce you!'

For a moment her wits continued to scramble. 'Court—seduce—*court me*?'

His eyes remained steady on hers. 'Yes.'

'No!' She blurted it out. 'I mean, you can't.'

He went very still. 'You'd have an affair with me, if not for the girls, but you refuse, categorically, even to consider the possibility of marrying me?'

'Yes, no. I mean, it's not you, it's—'

'Me? There's something about me that renders me suitable for an affair, but unthinkable as a husband?'

Oh, God, she'd insulted him, and she was going to destroy their friendship anyway. Panic tumbled around inside her, tying knots in her belly as she fought for the words she needed. 'It's marriage, Hugo, not you. It's marriage and what it means for a woman that I don't want.'

Hugo stared at her. How in Hades had he not foreseen this difficulty? He was a lawyer, for pity's sake. He knew the law as it pertained to married women. They could not own property unless it was tied up in trust. They could not sign a contract, or make a will, without their husband's consent. They had no right to guardianship of their own children. The list went on, offset by the protection a husband was honour-bound to provide.

But honour could not be legally enforced. He already knew that Althea's first marriage had somehow left her ruined financially, as well as socially. She had firsthand experience of how marriage could leave a woman exposed. Vulnerable.

And he knew the usual arguments. Women were not capable of managing their financial affairs. They were too flighty, too emotional. Their intellects were unsuited for anything beyond the domestic sphere, and should they attempt it they would destroy all that was nurturing and maternal within them. In short, they would be unnatural.

He let out a breath. 'I cannot say that you are entirely wrong. But.'

She looked utterly miserable, and that tore at him. 'I'm sorry, Hugo.'

'You haven't heard my but.'

A smile flickered. 'Continue then.'

'Courtship goes both ways. We continue our friendship, but with marriage as a possibility. I will say nothing more on the subject until you give me leave.'

'Until I give you leave?' She stared. 'But what if—'

'You never trust me enough to risk it?'

Because that's what it came down to. Trust. He suspected if she didn't care for him enough to marry him, she would have said so outright.

'That's my risk, isn't it?' He took her hand, felt it

tremble in his. 'We don't need to discuss it until you wish to. Until you've had time to think it through. And we remain friends.'

'Have you considered my reputation?' She drew her hand away. 'What it might do to your career?'

'Yes.' He honestly didn't care. He would be financially secure even if he stopped work immediately.

She frowned. 'Then you must know my reputation could ruin you. I can't believe you would risk that!'

'I did think of it,' he told her. 'And I decided that I didn't much care.'

He rose. 'I'll bid you goodnight, sweetheart. Trust me. I've thought it through. I honestly can't think of anything that would make me regret asking you to marry me.'

Chapter Eight

The following Monday morning Hugo saw several clients and, after the last of them took his leave, began drafting a will. His attention on the will, he ignored the bell on the outer door of the offices. He had no further appointments, so it was none of his concern.

A moment later Timms appeared at the open door.

'A Miss Price to see you, sir?'

Hugo frowned at the clerk. *Sarah?* What on earth—

'An elderly lady, sir,' said Timms. 'With Mr James Montague.'

'Montague…?'

'Am I to be kept waiting all day?'

Hugo rose instinctively at the acerbic tones. 'Thank you, Timms. Close the door please.' He came forward. 'Miss Elinor Price, I presume?' He nodded to Montague, an older solicitor he knew by sight and reputation. 'Sir.'

The old lady glared at him as the clerk made his

escape and shut the door. 'The same. You, my good man, have some explaining to do!'

Montague coughed. 'Miss Price, as I said, it would be best to permit me to—'

He broke off under the force of the lady's steely glare and Hugo knew a fellow feeling for the chap.

Clearing his throat, he gestured to chairs. 'Please be seated, Miss Price, Montague.' And braced himself.

Half an hour later, Hugo felt as though he had been trampled by a team of plough horses. Miss Elinor Price was a force to be reckoned with. She had accepted his flat refusal to discuss Althea's private business with either herself or Montague, but he had confirmed the truth of what she'd pried out of several relatives about Frederick's death. And Wilfrid Price-Babbington's refusal to act as guardian, or provide for the girls.

She sat in silence for a moment. 'Mr Guthrie, what would you have done had my niece *not* given those girls a home?'

'What do you imagine I would have done?' he parried. 'I had my instructions.'

A smile flickered. 'So you did. I do not believe you are the man to abandon those children to an orphanage. Not if you went to the effort to write to their relations and seek out my niece.'

'Two orphanages,' he said, avoiding the challenge. 'The difference in their ages meant they would not remain together.'

Her eyes narrowed. 'Tell me, Mr Guthrie, are you married? And no, it is absolutely none of my business.'

Montague made a sort of choking sound.

'No, it's not,' Hugo said steadily. 'I am a widower. No children.'

'Miss Price, really. All this is most unnecessary. I feel—'

She waved Montague to silence. 'Very well, Mr Guthrie. You have declined to discuss Althea's private business with me—very right, too, on reflection—but since you acted for my great-nephew, Frederick, may I assume you are aware that he cast his sister off?'

He nodded slowly. 'I am aware.'

'Have you read the letter he sent her, and chose to circulate within our family?'

'I have.' He couldn't keep his voice quite uninflected.

'One of his accusations was that she had squandered her inheritance.'

'All the more reason—' Again Montague quailed in the face of his client's gorgon stare.

Hugo wondered where this was leading, and in truth he had no idea what had happened to Althea's fortune. 'I cannot discuss Lady Hartleigh's finances with you, Miss Price. Not in any particular.'

She let out a frustrated sound. 'No. Of course not. Do you consider her a frivolous individual? Incapable of teaching those girls to manage their own affairs?'

He had to admire her tactics. 'No, Miss Price. I do not. While Lady Hartleigh certainly has a frivolous side, she is more than capable of teaching those girls to manage. I think perhaps it will not be improper to assure you that she has given this careful thought. She has made arrangements to ensure their ongoing safety and well-being should something happen to her. And it will *not* involve orphanages or going into service.'

Miss Price pursed her lips. 'Has she now? Thank you, Mr Guthrie. I'll take up no more of your time.' She rose and held out her hand. 'Good day to you, sir. Thank you. I know how to act now.'

Hugo shook her hand. 'Good day, Miss Price. Thank you for your understanding.'

Amusement flickered in her eyes, not unlike her great-niece. 'I believe I have understood a great deal, Mr Guthrie. And *you* may believe that I consider Wilfrid Price-Babbington's actions reprehensible. Far beyond anything I could possibly condone.' She let out a breath. 'Come, Montague. I have affairs to put in place. We will return to your offices immediately.'

With a final nod she stalked from the office. Montague, with an annoyed look at Hugo, hurried after her.

Hugo sat back in his desk chair as the door shut behind them. He closed his eyes and swore fluently. Then checked himself. No. That wasn't fair. This was precisely why his father had always advised against any personal involvement with a client.

'Under no circumstances whatsoever, my boy. I've

seen it happen. Leads to nothing but confusion and a devilish mess to sort out.'

He was pained to have to admit his father's percipience, but if his suspicion was correct it would put paid to any courtship of Althea, even if she wished it.

Elinor Price had discovered that Wilfrid Price-Babbington had refused to act as guardian to Kate and Sarah. He had inherited their father's estate and thrown them out as paupers. Hugo suspected that, unless Montague managed to talk her out of it, the old lady was about to change her will. Which would make the girls heiresses.

He drummed his fingers on the desk.

He couldn't possibly tell Althea any of this. It was no more than speculation, and although Miss Price was not a client, he was still bound by confidentiality. And without Althea knowing, as the girls' guardian, that they might stand to inherit something from Miss Price, he could not under any circumstances court her.

If she accepted an offer of marriage it would, at the very least, make him the girls' co-guardian. It would create the devil of a mess, and might even cause Althea to wonder about his motives for offering marriage. For an intelligent and beautiful woman, she seemed absolutely blind as to *why* a man might want to marry her rather than have an affair with her.

He was damned if he was going to hurt her, any

more than the world had already done so, by putting further self-doubt in her mind and heart.

And if Miss Price did leave the girls substantial sums of money, their marriage prospects went from possibly respectable to limitless. Especially with the Earl and Countess of Rutherford behind them.

Hugo swallowed. There was nothing he could do but remain Althea's friend and adviser, and wait.

Unsurprisingly Jacob strolled in a few minutes later. 'What the devil brings Montague here with a client?'

Hugo explained.

His gaze firmly on the top of the window, Jacob said, 'I believe you do not need me to spell out your only course of conduct in this situation.'

There was absolutely no hint of question there. It might not have been what Hugo had been envisaging when he assured himself that, in a clash of personal feeling and professional conduct, the latter must take precedence.

Still... 'I think, Jacob, that I may continue to supervise the girls' well-being and maintain a polite, professional connection with Lady Hartleigh. I believe we can be friends, without it tipping over into anything...improper.'

Jacob nodded slowly. 'Friends, yes. Very *platonic* friends. If you can do that, there is no problem. Like you, I cannot approve of the situation those girls were left in, and if Miss Price does alter her will it changes their lives materially. Keeping an eye on things is perfectly appropriate, and naturally two children will feel far more secure in their own home rather than these offices. But—*platonic.*'

Hugo nodded. 'I need to leave for the afternoon, Jacob. I have a couple of things to see to.'

Jacob eyed him narrowly. 'Things that involve Lady Hartleigh?'

'Yes.' He wanted to tell Jacob—his partner and one of his oldest friends—to go to hell.

Jacob frowned. 'Obviously you cannot tell her any of this. It would be highly improper. So—'

'It's a private matter, Jacob.' Hugo gritted his teeth. 'I can say no more than that.'

Jacob cursed fluently. 'Don't tell me you've already offered the woman marriage?'

'No.' Not quite. Hugo began tidying his desk. What the hell was he going to say to Althea?

Three nights ago I intimated that I was interested in asking you to marry me. Spoke too soon? I'm not interested after all? Something came up?

'Thank God for that. Very well. I'll see you in the morning.'

He was still wondering what he could say as he rang the doorbell of Althea's house. He could offer no explanation. Unless Miss Price chose to tell Althea that she was changing her will, he could not give so much as—

'Why, Mr Guthrie, sir.' The maid opened the door. 'I'll let the mistress know you're here. The young ladies have this minute gone for their walk with John. Let me take your hat and gloves, sir.'

'Thank you.' He handed them over and waited.

The maid set the hat and gloves down on a hall table, and opened the parlour door.

''Tis Mr Guthrie, ma'am.'

He'd noticed that Althea's staff never seemed to call her *my lady*. What did that say about her marriage, that she did not even care to use her title?

The maid turned, smiling. 'She'll see you, sir. Go right in.'

Althea was seated at her desk, a large notebook closed in front of her.

'Hugo.' She rose. 'How nice to—' She broke off, searching his face. 'Is something wrong?'

He swallowed. 'Not wrong exactly. Althea, when I spoke with you on Friday night, about…about—'

'Courting me?' She sat down again, her face composed.

'Yes. That. I—' *Should not have spoken?*

'You've changed your mind.' A light, calm voice, as though she commented on the weather.

'What? No. That is, I… I can't court you, but—' He floundered. 'It's not that I've changed my mind. It's a…a professional thing.'

She nodded slowly. 'I see. I did tell you that you needed to consider my reputation. Since you are here in the middle of a workday, I suppose your partner has concerns.'

'No. I mean, he does, but it's not about *you*. Exactly. It's a professional situation.'

'And will that professional situation change?'

'It…yes. But I have no idea when that might be, no control over it. And…' He forced the words out. 'I cannot ask you to wait under the circumstances. There can be no understanding between us. You…you must consider yourself a free agent.'

Her green eyes were carefully blank, her face betrayed nothing. 'Understood, sir. I never consider myself anything else.'

That clipped, cool voice said everything.

His heart cracked. 'Althea—I'm sorry. I can offer no explanation, no excuse.'

She rose. 'None is required, sir. After some considerable thought in the last couple of days, I am convinced that I would very much prefer to remain single anyway. Good day to you. I assume you will not wish me to apprise you of the date for Mrs Barclay's supper party?'

He hesitated. It might be better, safer, not to see her, but—

'Did we not agree to remain friends?'

'We did.'

'Then, if you wish to send me a note about the date, I would be happy to attend.'

'Very well, sir. Good day.'

* * *

Althea remained utterly still until she heard the front door close behind him. Then she leaned back in her chair and closed her eyes. It would be nice if closing your eyes closed off memories. The memory of his kiss, of his face as he corrected her assumption that he wanted an affair.

Althea, you idiot, I want to court you, not seduce you!

She couldn't blame his partner for having concerns. She'd raised them herself. But she wished—oh, how she wished—that Hugo had said nothing last Friday. She swallowed as the heat behind her eyes spilled over.

For two days she had been thinking, wondering if she dared try again. Perhaps it was better that Hugo had come to his senses. She had been perfectly content living by herself, managing for herself, in the past few years.

And yet these stupid tears slid down her cheeks. She didn't *need* marriage.

A few more tears spilled.

She might not need marriage, but apparently she had wanted it, with Hugo, more than she had cared to admit.

I am convinced that I would very much prefer to remain single anyway.

At least she could still tell a believable lie.

Chapter Nine

Hugo was more than slightly surprised to receive a note from Althea about the Barclays' supper party. He had fully expected her not to send one.

At supper, he took advantage of a brief private moment to say as much, under cover of applause for Miss Barclay's playing.

'Whyever would I not, sir?'

He tried not to let that polite *sir* sting. 'I thought you would prefer not to see me.'

Her eyes remained steady on his. 'It's not about me, though, is it? The girls wish to see you.'

'But you do not.' She was pale, and the circles under her eyes were still there. He wanted to ask what had caused them, but he had no right to ask her anything that encroached on the personal.

She bit her lip. 'As you see, remaining friends is a great deal more difficult in practice than it looks on paper.'

He reached for her hand. The quickest, lightest clasp. 'Perhaps we need to try harder.'

She sighed. 'Perhaps we do. I'll let you know about the next supper party, sir.' She gave him a ghost of her old smile.

'And perhaps you and the girls might come for a walk with me on Sunday after church, if the weather permits.'

She nodded slowly. 'They would enjoy that. Oh, look! Miss Barclay is getting Kate up to play.' Delight and pride beamed in her smile.

Sunday walks and informal supper parties. Slowly they reset their friendship, as Hugo accepted that Althea had retreated to a more distant friendliness. She did not always join the Sunday walks. Sometimes he just took the girls and Puck.

Even so, Hugo enjoyed the parties, especially the company of Will Barclay and Lord Martin Lacy. Lord Martin was about his own age and they struck up an unexpected friendship.

Lord Martin was startlingly down to earth. Especially for the youngest son of a duke. From everything Hugo had ever heard about the younger sons of the aristocracy, they were usually wild to a fault and had no idea of the value of money.

Lord Martin admitted as much.

'Comes of being raised in a luxury that we can't maintain once we leave home.'

Apparently he and Miss Selbourne had found a way of life that suited them both, which rarely involved society gatherings. Lord Martin, he knew, had a government job, but he spoke of that very rarely.

Spring leafed out and flowered, and London heated as May slid into June. Hugo's office baked in the growing warmth. Another month and he'd be taking his summer holiday at Petersham in the house his father had retired to.

His mother's sister, Sylvia—his Aunt Sue—lived there now. He wished, deeply, that he was looking forward to his summer holiday as much as he usually did. Long walks out along the river, watching for birds, noting them in the latest volume of the journal his father had started. Rambles in Richmond Park and quiet evenings reading aloud to Aunt Sue while she sewed or knitted, or—increasingly as she aged—dozed in her chair.

This year he kept thinking of Althea and the girls remaining in London as the city sweltered its way towards July. And those dark circles deepening under Althea's eyes.

Hugo took the note his clerk handed him, and his very humdrum day—drafting a will, writing a letter to another client and advising on a trust—brightened considerably. Sarah's handwriting. Now, what was so urgent that it couldn't await the planned supper in Soho Square this Friday night?

He broke the seal, smiling…

Dear Mr Guthrie,
Aunt Althea has asked me to let you know that
we cannot have our supper on Friday night this
week. Kate has chicken pox.

Aunt Althea says she—Kate—is not terribly
unwell, but very headachy, itchy because of the
spots and grumpy with it. I have tried sitting with
her because I had it years ago, but she won't
mind me at all—Kate, that is—so Aunt Althea is
sitting with her much of the time to see that she
does not scratch at her blisters. Aunt Althea says
this might make them scar or go nasty.

Aunt Althea asks me to say how very sorry she
is, and that she hopes you will understand.
Your Affectionate Friend,
Sarah Price

Hugo let out a breath. At least Sarah had already
had chicken pox, so was unlikely to catch it again.
Most children did catch it at some point. Sometimes
it was serious. He remembered his own mother and
Aunt Sue, nursing *him* in turns. How old had he been?
Nine? Ten? They had told him he was lucky to have
it then and not when he was older. In adults, they'd
said, it was often very nasty indeed. He hadn't cared.
He'd felt quite sick enough, thanks very much, and
there had been blisters in some very sensitive places,
too. He squirmed remembering his mother dabbing

calamine lotion on them. He suspected that he'd been a perfect little pest.

At times he'd been so desperate to scratch that only his mother's or aunt's presence had stopped him. And Althea was doing that alone. Even if Kate's illness were not serious, it was still exhausting.

He stared into space, drumming his fingers on the desk. Independence, of course, was a good thing. He valued his own independence, respected it in others. Then there was friendship...

Before he could overthink the situation, he pulled a fresh piece of paper towards him and dipped his pen...

My very dear Sarah...

The doorbell penetrated Althea's intermittent dozing with its insistent clang—why had she ever thought this was a comfortable chair?—but she ignored it. Kate was asleep, her fever somewhat reduced, but Althea had no doubt that if she left the room the child would be awake and scratching in minutes. Seconds, probably. Whoever was at the door, she didn't care.

She sank back into her doze, sore shoulders, aching neck and all, and hoped she could have a good night's sleep again soon.

Hearing the squeak of the doorknob she spoke softly without opening her eyes. 'She's asleep, Sarah. Her fever is down and she's not quite so itchy. I think the calamine is helping. Tell whoever it is to go away.'

'I'm very glad to hear it. But I'm not going away.'

Her eyes snapped open at that deep voice, and she shot out of the chair. Good God! Her oldest gown and she hadn't even bothered with stays this morning.

'Hugo.' She kept her voice as soft as his. 'What... what are you doing here?' What day was it? It couldn't be Friday already. Could it? Besides... Her mind cleared a little. 'Did you not receive Sarah's note?'

'I did of course. It occurred to me that you could use some assistance.'

'Assistance?'

'Yes. It's what friends do for each other.' He eyed her. 'Why don't you go and have a proper sleep, in an actual bed?'

'Kate—she might wake up, and—'

'I promise she will mind me just as well as she does you. I won't let her scratch her spots.'

'But what if you catch it?'

'I've had it. Off you go.' He made a shooing motion as he came towards her. 'Begone!'

She thought about narrowing her eyes at him. She ought to resent being shooed, and *begone*—as if she were some demon to be banished. But she was too grateful, and the kindness in his eyes disarmed her in the gentlest way. Besides, she didn't have enough energy left to narrow her eyes properly.

'Would you...would you like coffee?'

He brushed a strand of hair back from her brow, tucked it away. The light touch left her breathless.

'Sarah is bringing some up. Go and sleep. You need it.'

Did she look that bad?

'Yes, you do. Off you go.'

But his fingers remained lightly circling her temple. She wanted nothing more than to stay right where she was for ever, absorbing that soothing touch. How nice to lean on someone for a change.

And not simply anyone. *Him*.

For a moment.

As if he had read her heart, his arms came slowly around her. Offering, inviting only. There was no compulsion, just the invitation. And she accepted, stepping closer, allowing her head to rest against that steady shoulder, feeling his arms close in comfort, support. Friendship.

A moment. A moment's rest and kindness. That was all it could be. After that initial misstep, they had established a friendship, one she valued deeply. Friends did not demand of each other. Nor did they risk spoiling a friendship by asking for more. Not when someone had clearly stated that there could be no more.

He released her as she gathered herself to step back.

'Go and sleep, Althea.'

She didn't bother removing her gown and fell asleep almost before her head touched the pillow. Waking slightly puzzled to find herself in any bed at all, let alone her own, she had to think for a moment…

'Oh, Lord!'

She rolled over to look at the clock on the chimney piece, sat bold upright as the relationship of hands and numbers coalesced into meaning, and scrambled out of bed still blinking sleep from her eyes.

Over two hours, closer to three, she had left Hugo nursing a sick child. A quick glance told her that her gown was rumpled past shaking out. She got out of it, draped it over a chair and found a fresh one, along with a set of stays she could do up at the front without assistance. Her hair was a disaster and probably needed washing, but she brushed it out vigorously, twisting it up into a knot anchored with an army of pins.

Her mirror informed her in no uncertain terms that she looked far from her best. Then she rolled her eyes at her reflection, and hurried out of the room. Of all men, she did not have to worry what Hugo thought of her.

He was her friend who had come to help. He didn't care what she looked like. Still, a woman had her pride.

She opened the door to the girls' room, hoping Hugo had been given something to read, and that if Kate had woken up—

The room was dark and empty. She had told Kate that *if* she was a good girl and slept, and her fever did not return, she might come downstairs for a while that evening…

Her lamp illuminated a note on the pillow.

Fever not returned. Downstairs having supper.
H

Her heart light, Althea hurried out of the room.

The parlour door opened to admit Althea and Hugo looked up sharply. She smiled at him. He noted the colour in her cheeks as Puck got up from his basket and trotted across to greet her. She bent to pat the dog. She'd looked so tired and worn down, her eyes heavy and shadowed.

She didn't look so very much better now, but at least she didn't look as though a puff of wind might bowl her over.

He nudged Kate, nestled beside him on the sofa, half-asleep. 'Look who's woken up, sweetheart.'

'Aunt Althea!' Only a little croaky, the child sat up. 'Mr Guthrie said you were awfully tired and he sent you to bed. I slept and I'm not feverish still, so he carried me down and we had supper.' She wrinkled her nose. 'I had broth. Again. And Sarah put the lotion on my spots first. There are less of them now, I think.'

'Fewer.' Althea came across to them and leaned down to kiss Kate on the brow. 'If you can count them, it's fewer. But that's very good.'

Sarah stood up. 'Come and sit down, Aunt. I'll fetch

you a bowl of soup. It's being kept warm for you in the kitchen.' She hurried out, stopping to hug Althea.

Hugo watched as Althea sat down and the dog sat himself on her feet with a contented sigh.

She smiled at him again, and his heart shook a little, remembering that moment she had leaned on him, the feel of her in his arms.

'Thank you, sir.'

Comfort. She had needed comfort. And professional ethics still made anything beyond friendship out of the question. 'You look much better.'

She grimaced. 'Then judging by what I saw in the mirror just now I must have looked an absolute fright!'

'You did rather.' He shut his eyes briefly. 'My apologies. That didn't quite come out as I meant. Here.' He poured a glass of wine that he had brought. 'Have this while I get my foot out of my mouth.'

She accepted the glass with narrowed eyes. 'Hag-ridden, was I?'

He grinned. The most beautiful woman he had ever seen was referring to herself as *hag-ridden*? 'Completely.'

Kate giggled. 'I think he's teasing, Aunt Althea. You could *never* look hag-ridden!'

Her fairy smile dawned, and his heart stuttered as Althea reached out to touch Kate's cheek lightly.

'Ah. Is that it? Thank you, Kate.' She shot him a

gimlet stare. 'We shan't have to wash his blood out of the rug after all.'

Laughing outright, he raised his glass to her.

Chapter Ten

Four days later Kate, although still tiring easily and retaining a fair number of fading blisters, was on the path to recovery. Children could be amazingly resilient, thought Hugo, as he strolled through Soho with Althea in the early evening. But the child was still wan and crotchety.

Summer now beat down on London in full force. He knew most of the aristocracy, including Althea's friends the Rutherfords, had left the city for their country estates. Parliament had risen and would not sit again until the autumn session.

The day had been relentlessly hot and stuffy. Kate had not wished to go out and Sarah had shaken her head listlessly when asked if she wished to accompany them.

'No, thank you. I'll stay with Kate.'

He couldn't wonder at it. The city was stuffy and exhausting. They needed to be out of London, too.

As did Althea. She was heavy-eyed and pale still, as though she were not sleeping.

'Have you thought of taking the girls out of London?'

Althea sighed. 'Yes. Meg Rutherford wrote, suggesting I bring them both down to stay when Kate is strong enough to travel, and I would, but...'

'But?'

'She will have a houseful of guests, several of whom will *not* take kindly to my presence. For the girls I would deal with that, but the distance is considerable.'

'How far is it?'

'Three days' travel. That's the other problem.' She smiled. 'I'm beforehand enough with the world to go on the mail, but the thought! Kate in the coach for three days! And back again.'

'What about Petersham?'

'Petersham?' She stared up at him. 'You mean the village?'

'Yes. My father retired there.'

'To breed books?'

He laughed. 'You remember that? Exactly. My mother's sister lives there now. I always go out to spend a few weeks with her in the summer and at Christmas. Why not come with me? Or—' he thought about it '—go ahead? I can't go down for another three weeks, and I can promise you that Aunt Sue will be delighted to have company in the meantime.'

She didn't answer immediately, and he forbore to

press, content strolling with her in the fading light of the summer's day, imagining walking with her beside the Thames in the evening light, watching the last of the sun burn the far reaches of the river. If he took her there with the girls, would she see how it could be? Life with a family?

He caught himself up mentally. Althea and the girls had created their own family. He, for all his success, was the one who needed them.

He frowned a little. It shouldn't be about *need*, should it? *Need* was one of those slippery words. He might want Althea and the girls in his life, but it shouldn't tip over into *neediness*. That put a weight of obligation on the object of need.

Besides, there was still the matter of Miss Price's will. He hadn't thought of a way around that hurdle. If the old lady had told Althea what she intended, then it wouldn't matter. But, as Althea's solicitor, and since she hadn't discussed it with him, he had to assume that Miss Price was one of those people who preferred to keep the contents of their last will and testament a deep secret. Having seen some of the rows that could explode over the anticipated contents of a will, he couldn't blame her.

He could not imagine anything nastier in one's declining years than being pestered, or worse fawned over, by a set of relatives pretending to care about you when all they wanted was a slice of the fiscal pie. Or for that matter the best pie dish.

'Would we not be very much in your aunt's way? In your way?'

Her question brought him out of his ponderings. He smiled. 'I should say not. Aunt Sue enjoys company, but she is a little frail now at eighty. She doesn't like to go out much. But she will still fleece you at a game of picquet!'

'And what about Puck?'

He nodded. 'More than welcome. Aunt Sue had a very elderly pug that died a couple of years ago. She loves dogs but says she won't have another because she doesn't want to put the responsibility on me if the dog outlived her. She still has a cat. Spudge can take care of himself, believe me.'

'*Spudge*? Why Spudge?'

He'd often wondered himself. 'I have no idea. So, now that you know the family's darkest secret—a cat called Spudge—will you come?'

She laughed. 'If that's your darkest secret I don't think much of it. Yes. Yes, please. The girls need this far too much for me to stand on pride.'

They had turned and were walking back towards Soho Square. Glancing at Althea, Hugo thought she needed to get out of London at least as much as the girls. Was it his imagination, or had her steps slowed? Was she leaning more heavily on his arm? He doubted it was a good time to inform her that she looked nearly as washed out as little Kate.

She rubbed at one temple.

'A headache?'

'Not really.' She lowered her hand. 'Well, a little one. I slept badly. It's the stuffy weather. I'm sure a pot of tea will help.'

Two days later

Hugo looked at the note his clerk handed him with a stab of foreboding. Sarah's handwriting again. He broke the seal, opened it and swore as he read it.

'Is the servant who delivered this still here?'

'Yes, sir. Said he'd been asked to wait for a reply.'

'Tell him it's coming.'

He wrote swiftly. He had appointments this afternoon... 'What's on my slate for tomorrow, Timms?'

'Ah...' The clerk frowned. 'Mr Ellison at two o'clock. There's a deal of paperwork for you, too, sir.'

'Get that together for me, if you would. I'll take it with me to work on. I'll be in for Ellison's appointment but not before. Reschedule any other appointments for the following two days.'

Althea couldn't remember ever being this ill. Too hot, too cold, too damn *everything*, and especially too itchy. Someone had put mittens on her hands. Althea surfaced to the sound of voices. Sarah's shaking, frightened tones, and Hugo's deeper, reassuring tones.

'Did she tell you that she'd never had it, Sarah?'

'No. She wouldn't let the servants help nurse Kate, though, because none of them had.'

'Very well. Bring up more barley water for your aunt, coffee for me, and don't worry. She'll be perfectly all right once this fever breaks. I'll look after her for now. You go and sleep. You can spell me in the morning.'

The voices anchored her. She was in her own room after all, not some strange dreamworld where nothing made sense. She drifted back into the tossing sea of bizarre dreams, insensibly reassured that she would eventually come back to shore.

For three days Hugo sat with Althea, at first wondering if he had lied to Sarah and Kate about her being perfectly all right. Even the doctor, who had called twice, looked grave.

'A very nasty case.' He shook his head. 'Often worse in adults, but this is the worst I've ever seen. Are you a relative of Lady Hartleigh's, sir?'

Hugo shook his head. 'Family friend and lawyer. Her elder niece called on me for help.'

Doctor Harvey frowned. 'I can arrange for a nurse if you wish. Not quite the thing, is it? I mean, a man nursing a lady.'

'Doctor, I think we're beyond impropriety. Lady Hartleigh is perfectly safe with me and her elder niece is managing anything too personal.' Such as dabbing calamine lotion in sensitive spots, or persuading Althea to do it herself. He removed himself from the room at those moments.

He doubted Sarah had physically grown in the past few days, but it seemed as if she had suddenly leapt from childhood to womanhood. She looked exhausted, but she was bearing up under the strain, and stepping in to make household decisions that Althea would normally have made. And Kate was minding what Sarah said without argument—doing her lessons, even going to her music lessons again. Sarah had encouraged that wholeheartedly.

'Best to keep her busy.'

He could only agree with Sarah on that.

When the doctor left the second time, Hugo sank back into his chair. He'd barely left it in the past few days, except when Sarah sat with Althea to let him get some sleep on the very small sofa.

Althea woke properly to a dim light. Everything ached, but not in that hideous burning way. More like the memory of aches really. Turning her head on the pillow she saw Hugo, in his shirt sleeves, head tilted back, eyes closed, in the same chair she'd used when nursing Kate. Someone had hauled it back from the girls' room. Faint snores told her that he was sound asleep. Had he read to her? She thought he had. *Pride and Prejudice.* Even if she did occasionally want to kick Mr Darcy, she liked that one. Maybe because she had wanted to kick Darcy. In the end he gave himself a solid boot and that did the trick.

She assessed herself. Headache completely gone, although she felt washed out and as limp as wilted spinach. Itching almost gone. She wondered what would happen if she attempted to get up and use the commode. There were vague memories of Sarah or Mrs Cable helping her onto it. Not Hugo. That was something. Unless she'd forgotten?

Thinking hard, she brought up memories of him helping her to sit up, holding cups of barley water to her lips, spooning broth into her and, yes, reading to her… But no memory of him helping her to the commode. She wasn't going to ask. If she couldn't remember it, then it hadn't happened.

The light from the lamp was too dim to read the time on the clock, but the quality of silence, inside and out, suggested that it was the middle of the night. She *really* needed that commode. It was only a few steps away…

She pushed back the bedclothes and Hugo's eyes snapped open.

'You're awake.' He rose, stretching. 'How are you feeling?'

Desperate was the word that came to mind. 'Better.'

He touched her brow lightly and his smile dawned. 'The fever's broken. Good. Would you like something to drink?'

She shook her head. 'Er, no. Not until—' How was

she supposed to say this politely? 'Ah, if you could leave the room for a moment?' To prove that she *could*, she sat up. Wondered if she was going to collapse straight back down again. Regardless… 'I need to—you *know*.'

'Leave the—oh.'

'Yes, oh.'

'Compromise?' He came to the bedside. 'I'll help you over there, *then* leave the room. You call me when you're ready to get back to bed.'

That was a compromise? Althea thought about it, but her body was telling her very loudly that she didn't have much time for an argument. Nor did she have the strength. 'Oh, very well. If you insist.'

She ignored his grin, and the nasty little voice in her head that suggested she was being rather ungracious. She swung her legs over the edge of the bed and the world made an alarming swerve. Hugo's hand was there immediately, steadying her.

Drat it! She could stand up without—her feet touched the floor and her knees wobbled. Maybe she did need help.

Swallowing humiliation at her weakness, she muttered, 'Thank you,' and concentrated on making it safely to the commode with his arm around her waist.

She braced, gripping the back of the commode tightly as he stepped back. 'I'll…be all right now.' She hoped.

He nodded. 'I'll be outside the door. Call if you

need me.' His head tipped to one side, his mouth a little wry. 'I mean that, Althea. Call me.'

She stared. 'I—yes. Thank you, Hugo. For…for everything.'

He leaned forward and his lips touched her brow. 'You're very welcome.'

It took another three days before Hugo would permit her to walk downstairs without assistance. And even then he hovered. When she wanted to snap, she reminded herself that the first time he had permitted her downstairs he'd carried her. She also had to remind herself that she'd fallen asleep on the sofa, her broth barely swallowed.

The doctor had pronounced himself satisfied with her recovery. 'As nasty a case as I've ever seen, Lady Hartleigh. You're very lucky to have had such a skilled and devoted nurse.' He shook his head. 'Otherwise. Well.'

She reminded herself of that, too, when she wanted to snap. And instead asked for help back upstairs and took a nap.

Hugo had returned to work, but he still called every day late in the afternoon, remaining for supper. Mrs Cable had discovered all his favourite dishes and added them to her repertoire. Kate had been cajoled and outright teased into trying green beans and discovered that they wouldn't kill her after all.

Althea was touched that the friendships she had

made over those Friday night suppers had blossomed. Kit Selbourne and Psyché Barclay had each called several times since she had left her sickroom—Kit with an armload of books.

'I hear from Kate that you are off to Petersham to visit Mr Guthrie's aunt when you are feeling more the thing.' Kit set the books on the desk. 'I thought you might enjoy some of these to take with you.' Smiling, she added, 'When you come back from your holiday, we'll have you all to supper again.' A faint twinkle came into her eye. 'Mr Guthrie, too.'

Althea felt a slow burn on her cheeks. 'It's not like that.'

'Isn't it?' The twinkle remained.

'We're friends. Just friends.'

'Oh. That stage. I liked that stage. The next stage is even better, though.'

She knew better, but— 'The next stage?'

Kit grinned. 'The part where you seduce him.'

Althea nearly swallowed her tea the wrong way. 'Where I seduce *him*?'

Kit wrinkled her nose. 'If you wait for him to seduce you, you'll wait a very long time if I'm any judge. He's like Martin—too beastly honourable.'

Extrapolating, Althea said, '*You* seduced Lord Martin?'

'Only into bed,' said Kit with a cheerful lack of shame. 'I'll admit that he seduced me into marriage.

Marriage was very low on my list of priorities at the time.'

'It's nowhere on my list at all,' said Althea. Or it shouldn't be. Nor was having an affair supposed to be on her list. It hadn't been for years, even before the girls arrived to complicate things. Men were a complication in and of themselves, and she had enjoyed being free of expectations or demands. But here she was, still wishing she could have an affair with Hugo.

Kit smiled. 'Ah. Enjoy your time at Petersham. We'll look forward to seeing you rested and back to health when you return.'

Chapter Eleven

They arrived late on a golden afternoon, to the quiet house down from the Petersham Road. It sat on a rutted lane leading down to the river. The carriage Hugo had insisted on hiring for them drew up to the front door with a clatter of hooves and wheels on the gravel drive. Sarah and Kate scrambled down immediately, followed by Puck, his tail wagging madly.

'It's not far to the river from the house. The girls will love it. Richmond Park is close as well.'

Althea descended much more slowly from the carriage, steadying herself on the doorframe. Then Sarah was there, offering a hand. She took it, forcing a smile. 'Thank you, Sarah.'

Sarah's smile bloomed. 'Mr Guthrie said we had to be sure to look after you.'

Althea reminded herself that she had been very ill. The girls, according to Hugo, had been terrified that she might die. She had to remember that. But she hated it, simply *hated* it, that she still felt so utterly feeble at times. Especially if she didn't have a nap in the afternoon. Not that she had exactly missed her nap today. She had no recollection of anything between the Knightsbridge tollgate and Kate bouncing on the carriage seat as she announced their arrival.

Kate and Puck had reached the front door, which opened to reveal a plump, motherly looking female. 'Now, I daresay you'll be Miss Kate?'

Kate nodded. 'Yes. Are you Mr Guthrie's aunt?'

The woman laughed. 'No, my dear. I'm Mrs Farley the housekeeper.' She bent down to hold out a hand to Puck. 'And who might this fine fellow be?'

'This is Puck.' Kate gestured to Althea. 'And this is my Aunt Althea and my sister.'

Althea reached the porch. 'Good day. I am Lady Hartleigh. Mrs Farley, I think you said?'

The woman dropped a small curtsy. 'Yes, my lady. Come in. I've sent for one of the men to bring your bags in. Miss Browne is in the drawing room. She said to send in tea as soon as you've arrived.'

Miss Browne, Hugo's Aunt Sue, proved to be a kindly, if acid-tongued lady. She took an immediate liking to Puck, who viewed the enormous cat on the back of her chair with awed fascination as they drank tea.

'You'll try it once, my boy,' Miss Browne told the dog. She smiled at the girls. 'Once Spudge has demonstrated that he's in charge they'll be fine.'

Kate swallowed a mouthful of cake. 'Why is he called Spudge?'

Miss Browne reached back to scratch the cat's chin. 'Originally I called him Smudge, because of his blotchy markings. But he was quite a pudgy kitten. Possibly because he developed a talent for sneaking into the pantry, and he's also a very good mouser. So I found myself calling him Pudge rather more often than not, and then one day I muddled them up. I meant to say, *You're such a pudge, Smudge.* But what came out was: You're such a spudge!'

Althea laughed. 'So that's his name. Girls, if you've eaten enough, you should say thank you to Miss Browne and we should see to our unpacking.'

Miss Browne waved that aside. 'Oh, pish. Nice to see two gels who can eat a decent meal. Now, after being cooped up in that carriage for a couple of hours, I'm thinking, Lady Hartleigh, that they might like to walk down to the river with the dog. One of the maids will be happy enough to go with them if you are not feeling up to it.'

Althea hesitated. She *wasn't* feeling up to it. But—

'You're tired, Aunt Althea,' said Kate. 'And Mr Guthrie did say we should look after you. We'll tell you all about it when we come back, and then you can come with us tomorrow.'

'Sensible girl.' Miss Browne nodded approval. 'Your aunt may give me her arm for a turn about the

garden. Off you go and change your shoes. Ask Mrs
Farley for some scraps for the swans.'

'And don't let Puck chase the swans,' Althea warned
them. 'The King would be most annoyed if Puck hurt
one of his swans!'

As the door closed behind the girls and Puck,
Miss Browne snorted. 'If that good-for-nothing on
the throne takes the least interest in the well-being of
any creature besides himself it's news to me!'

That began a halcyon week of sunny days and balmy
evenings. Shuttlecock racquets and birdies were found
for the girls, and no one cared in the least how much
noise they made. Rambles by the river each morning, and sometimes in the late afternoon, left Althea
tired, but feeling that it was a good sort of tired. Not
the dragging weariness she had felt in the immediate
aftermath of her illness, but a feeling of tired limbs
that had taken a decent amount of exercise.

And, very unexpectedly, she found a good friend
in Miss Browne.

'Call me Aunt Sue, dear,' said the old lady as they
sat in the shade after a slow turn about the lawn. 'It's
Sylvia really, but Hugo couldn't say that as a small
boy, and after a while everyone called me Aunt Sue.
It will be nice to see him tomorrow. He would have
come sooner but he had work to do.'

Althea grimaced. 'That might be my fault. He spent

a great deal of time with us when Kate was ill, and then even more when I caught it.'

Sue smiled at her. 'I can't tell you how pleased I was when he asked if you and the girls might visit. As if he needed to ask! It's his house, after all.'

Althea laughed. 'Pleased to be invaded by two young girls and a dog?'

Sue patted her hand. 'It's been a very long time since Hugo took the slightest interest in any woman. Not since Louisa died.'

'His wife?' She had known Hugo was a widower. And she had suspected that his wife's death had shattered him.

Sue nodded, her eyes sad. 'Yes. Childbirth. And the baby, too. Poor little mite barely lived a day. After that he moved back into his parents' house, then lodgings, and buried himself in his work. When he mentioned the girls in his letters…' She patted Althea's hand. 'He grieved for that little baby girl as deeply as for poor Louisa, I believe.'

Althea could easily believe that. In the early days of her marriage, when she had fully expected and wanted to become a mother, every month that her courses arrived had been a grief in itself. And when finally the truth had become obvious, not only to her but to society, that it would never happen and that the fault lay in herself…

She pushed those thoughts away. She had ceased to mourn the loss of that potential long ago, even learned to be grateful that an innocent child hadn't been dragged into the disaster of her marriage. Hugo had not had even that miniscule comfort.

'Well. That's all ten years ago.' Sue gave a sigh. 'I think it's been good for him, that he was able to help your girls find a home with you.'

By Wednesday afternoon Hugo had his papers and files almost in order. He had a list of the few things he had left to do the following day and on Friday morning, before he drove out to Petersham. Usually he hired a horse and rode. There was already a horse and small closed carriage out there. But this time, with guests, he thought having a gig might be useful.

Timms knocked on the door jamb. 'Mr Montague to see you, sir.'

Hugo glanced at the clock. He had an appointment in half an hour. Time enough.

'Show him straight in, Timms.'

Hugo rose as Montague stalked in. 'Good afternoon, sir. Please be seated. Timms, the door. Thank you.' The door closed as Hugo settled himself behind the desk. 'How may I assist you, sir?'

Montague assumed a smug, not to say sneering, expression. 'I have some news that you may find pertinent, Guthrie. I have no idea how you or possibly your *client*, if we are to consider her as such, worked on a poor, frail old woman, but I think you should know that wiser counsel prevailed, and Miss Price has not altered her will.'

His father's voice sounded in his head.

'Never reply spontaneously in legal matters, boy. Always, even if you know the answer, give the impression of thinking about it first. Especially if your temper is involved.'

Excellent advice—his temper was boiling at the implication that Althea was something other than his client, something illicit and nefarious. For good measure he steepled his fingers and nodded thoughtfully, while he lowered the temperature to a simmer.

'How interesting, sir. Useful information indeed, although I'm surprised you're telling me. After all, I might think to *prevail* upon Miss Price again.'

Montague smirked. 'Given the state of her health, it is no longer possible for her to do so. And even if it were, how you might get past those dedicated to her interests I cannot imagine.'

'How you imagine I did so in the first place, when that meeting in this very office is the only time I have met her, I am not sure. Nor how my client may be supposed to have done so, when Miss Price's visit to Lady Hartleigh's home was the first and only time they had met in several years.'

Montague stiffened in his seat. 'Are you denying that you made such an attempt?'

'Categorically.' No hesitation this time. Montague had crossed a line here. 'You are accusing me of highly unethical behaviour, sir, with no evidence whatsoever. If you have discussed the matter further with Miss Price, I cannot imagine what brings you here to tell me so. It should be a matter of confidence between the lady and yourself.'

'Why you impudent pup!' Montague was half out of his chair. 'Are you telling me how to conduct my business?'

'I'm telling you that Miss Price's final will and testament is no business of mine, yet you have chosen to make it so. She came to me for information, which I provided, as far as I could without breaching my own client's confidentiality. How Miss Price acted on that information was completely up to her.'

Montague made a rude sound. 'Don't play games, Guthrie. No doubt your client was counting on that money and—'

'Why? Did you tell her?'

'*I?* Tell that woman—'

'Because I didn't.' Temper spilling over now, Hugo spoke straight across the older man. 'It would have been mere speculation, and subject to change if Miss Price changed her mind. As, apparently, she did. Moreover, the contents of an individual's will are for them to divulge if they so choose.'

Montague's mouth set hard. 'I believe it is of the first importance to the ongoing security of the Price family for that money to remain safely in the family.'

'And I will remind you that those two girls are

members of the Price family and, in justice, should have been entitled to some of that money. Their father failed to provide for them, Price-Babbington threw them out. If Miss Price was prepared to do something to redress that injustice, then she came to that decision without any advice from me, beyond what information you heard me give her. It seems, Montague, that the only person to influence her was yourself. Do you by any chance also act for Wilfrid Price-Babbington?'

A shot in the dark, but the man's darkly flushed face, and unwitting shift in his seat, told Hugo he'd hit the bullseye.

'How dare you, sir!'

Hugo shrugged. 'Your ethics are your own concern, sir. In truth, you've solved a dilemma for me in coming here. Your purpose, as far as I can tell, was to boast and put me in my place. Instead you've done me a favour.'

Montague stared. 'A favour? Done you a favour?'

Hugo grinned now. 'Not at all your intention, I'm sure, but I'll thank you anyway. Good day, sir. I have another appointment in a few minutes for which I must prepare.'

Hugo rose, strode to the door and opened it, to find Jacob, hand raised, about to knock. He strolled in. 'Ah. Montague. I thought I recognised your voice. To what do we owe the honour of another visit?'

Montague glared. 'I came to inform Guthrie here that my client Miss Price saw the value of my advice and decided against altering her will at the urging of, shall we say, *importunate* family members!'

Jacob nodded. 'I see.' He frowned. 'No, actually. I don't. I cannot conceive what business it is of mine or Guthrie's what dispositions—Miss Price, did you say?—chose to make in her will. But you may trust to our, er, discretion—I do like that word—that we shall keep this little lapse of yours *entre nous*.'

Montague, with no other choice, left with his nose in the air.

Hugo shut the door behind him and leaned on it. Anger still simmered. What Montague had done, dissuading Miss Price from leaving some money in trust for Kate and Sarah, was unconscionable. No doubt he'd make quite sure Price-Babbington knew who'd buttered that piece of bread for him, and pocket a very nice reward for his trouble.

Jacob let out a relieved breath. 'What the devil was the idiot thinking to come here boasting about that to you? Was he challenging you to attempt to change Miss Price's mind again?'

'No chance of that. It sounds as though she's dying.' And even if she weren't, attempting to influence her to change her will against her own lawyer's advice was out of the question.

'Pity.' Jacob scowled, a ludicrous expression on his normally cheery face. 'If ever a man deserved to be taken down several pegs, it's Montague. Damned idiot.'

Hugo went back to tidying his papers. 'It doesn't matter now, Jacob. It's done. And, as I told him, he's really done me a favour.'

Jacob sat down. 'I take it your friendship with Lady Hartleigh is about to become un-platonic?'

Hugo nodded. 'If she will have me.' He was not at all sure that she would consider him a fair exchange for her independence.

'I am convinced that I would very much prefer to remain single anyway.'

Since there was no longer the prospect of the girls inheriting any part of Miss Price's considerable fortune, then he was free to court Althea. She might or might not accept him. That was up to her. He might end up with a pair of ass's ears, but it was worth the risk.

Chapter Twelve

Hugo arrived at the Petersham house in the afternoon, the sort of golden summer's afternoon that made him think he spent entirely too much time indoors. Occasionally he thought about retiring and moving out here permanently, but he enjoyed his work. Even enjoyed the bustle of London most of the time. Perhaps if he kept a horse, or even a gig, which he could easily afford, he could come out more frequently.

Since he had the horse and gig this time, if he needed to go into his office there was no delay. Plus, the cob seemed very quiet—he might give the girls some driving lessons. His mind had been considering all manner of activities for days.

Would Aunt Sue mind if he visited more frequently? She would tell him not to be ridiculous. That it was his house, and he might be there whenever he pleased. Which was true enough, but he was very conscious that it was *her* home. Still, she was older now, and she could not live for ever, although she would not appreciate a reminder. He should spend more time with her while he had the chance.

Life was far from fair to most people, he thought, as he steadied the cob for the turn into the shady lane running down to the river. You could double that when it came to women. Sue had never married, but she had cared for her ageing parents until they died. In return, Hugo's grandfather had left her a pittance on which to survive. The old man had assumed that she would live with her married sister or some other family member as a poor relation. All the money had been left to his son and grandsons.

His own father had ensured Sue's welfare by leaving her a little more money, and asking Hugo to allow her to live in the house for the rest of her life. She was safe, but the more he thought about it, the less fair he considered it. Forbidden to earn a living, unless they became governesses or paid companions, women of his class were forced to rely on the generosity and kindness of their male relations.

This had been brought home to him by the plight of the girls when their father failed to provide for them. He had been on the verge of writing to Sue about them, when he had looked again at the appalling letter his father had been forced to deliver to Althea all those years ago.

Sometimes he thought about asking her *why* Frederick Price had turned on her like that. And then he told himself it was none of his business.

Turning into the drive, he put all thought of Price out of his head. He was on holiday, and for once he had something like a family with whom to enjoy it.

A few moments later, having handed the cob and gig to the gardener cum outdoor man, Hugo strolled through the house to the rear parlour that looked out over the garden. Sue, Mrs Farley had informed him, was taking a nap.

'Not as young as she was, Mr Hugo. Not but what the young ladies have brightened things up. Teaching them chess in the evenings, she is.'

He stepped out through the open French doors, onto the terrace, and viewed a scene of surprisingly silent action. Bare legged, shoes discarded and their skirts hiked up with their sashes, Kate and Sarah were playing at battledore and shuttlecock. Punctuated only by panting and the occasional gasp and stifled giggle, they were utterly focused on keeping the shuttlecock aloft. They didn't even see him as it flew back and forth between them. He could see Sarah's fierce concentration as she batted it back to her sister, and noted that Kate, despite her smaller size, was holding her own.

Eventually Sarah missed a shot and the shuttlecock hit the ground. A groan burst from her, but Kate was jumping up and down, practically crowing, albeit quietly.

'Were you counting, Sarah? *Fifty*! It was fifty shots

that time!' Dancing in a circle, she saw him. 'Mr Guthrie!' Her voice lifted as she ran to him.

He swung her up laughing.

'Did you see, Mr Guthrie?' Her voice had lowered again. 'Aunt Sue found the racquets and birdies for us and we've been practising. She's having her rest.'

He set her down with a smile. 'Is that why you were being so quiet?'

Sarah came up, holding her own racquet and the shuttlecock. 'Not entirely. Aunt Sue says she can sleep through anything and to make as much noise as we like, but...' She gestured with the racquet.

On the far side of the lawn, in the shade of an elm, a cane chaise longue was angled away from them.

'Aunt Althea brought her work out, but she's fallen asleep over it.'

Worry smote him. She'd been so ill... 'Is she still tiring easily?'

Sarah shook her head. 'Not so much. But we had a long walk by the river this morning.'

'Mrs Farley said she'd make us lemonade.' Kate tugged at his hand. 'Aunt Sue's lemon bush has lots of lemons. You can have some, too.'

After a glass of lemonade with the girls, and a re-assurance that there had been plenty of lemons for marmalade as well, Hugo left the pair of them inside playing chess. Bearing a tray laden with a jug and two glasses, he crossed the lawn to the elm tree.

Her bonnet discarded beside her, Althea still slept

with a shawl tucked around her. On the grass a note-book lay tumbled with a pencil. Smiling, he bent to retrieve it, and words caught his attention...

> *'I cannot imagine what folly has led you to be-lieve, sir, that I would be persuaded to accept an invitation to dance with you, let alone an offer of marriage!'*

For one horrified moment he thought he was read-ing Althea's private correspondence... Then—

> *'My dear Miss Parker! Permit me to inform you that such an intemperate response to an offer of marriage is most unbecoming in a young lady!'*
> *'No.'*
> *'No?' Sir Edwin sounded as though he thought his ears might be deceiving him. 'What do you mean, no?'*
> *'No, I decline to permit you to tell me ~~anything of the sort~~ such thing.' Lydia paused for thought. Best to be clear about such things. 'And, no, I do not desire to marry you, sir. Ever. Thank you.'*

It...it was a *story*. Althea was writing a *story*. A novel, in fact. His conscience woke up at this point and, burning with embarrassment at his transgres-sion, Hugo closed the notebook, setting it and the pencil on the wrought iron table, along with the tray of lemonade.

It took some doing. He dearly wanted to know more about Miss Lydia Parker and her antipathy towards the hapless Sir Edwin. He wanted to know what had led up to the fellow's clearly unwelcome offer, and exactly why Lydia disliked him. For he had not a doubt that she disliked him intensely…

He couldn't even ask Althea to let him read it, because that would tell her immediately that he *had* been reading it. Without her permission. Was this something she did as a hobby? Some ladies painted in watercolours…others wrote poetry…

'Aunt Althea brought her work out, but she's fallen asleep over it.'

Work? He'd assumed Sarah had meant embroidery or some such thing. *Needle* work of some sort. Had Sarah meant work quite literally? And Kate had once said something about Althea's work… As in something one did to earn a living? Or was it merely a creative outlet for an intelligent woman?

Music drifted through her dreams. Music and warmth. She didn't want to wake up. Althea let herself float a little on the melody. Allowed herself to dream a little more. No one minded if you dreamed here, even if you dreamed of the forbidden, the warmth of strong arms and a tender embrace, a kiss that meant love rather than conquest—

A damp nose shoved into her hand brought her back to the waking world—a reminder that someone at least expected another walk. Scratching Puck's ears, Althea opened her eyes, and wondered if she were still dreaming.

Music still drifted through the French doors. Kate at the piano again. And beside her, reading, sat Hugo. That treacherous warmth and longing twined through her. Safer not to dream of him. But there he sat, bareheaded, even his coat discarded in the heat of the afternoon. Companionable. Reading while she slept. Not in the least romantic or passionate, but so comforting and easy. Perhaps, later in the book, there might be a moment like this for Lydia and—Good God!

She sat up, stomach knotted as she understood precisely where her unruly mind was leading her.

'Althea. Are you all right?' His hand, gentle and steadying on her shoulder.

'I...yes. I was dreaming. My notebook—' She'd been writing, and she'd dozed off. Where was it?

'Here. On the table.'

And there it was. Closed. The pencil beside it. 'Oh.' Had she put it there? What the devil did she say? 'My...er...diary.'

Blast it. Now she'd lied to him.

'Your diary.' The merest hint of a hesitation. 'Of course. Ah, should you like a glass of lemonade?'

She forced a smile, grateful for the change of subject, even as she wondered at that odd hesitation. 'Yes, please.' Oh, Lord. What did she say now? Had he seen? Realised that it wasn't a diary at all? 'Have you been here long?'

He poured her a glass and consulted his watch. 'Perhaps half an hour.'

'How rude of me to sleep through your arrival.' *Keep it light.*

'I was enjoying the music.' He topped up his own glass. 'Have you thought about buying a piano yourself? For Kate?'

'Yes.' Another change of subject. Her glance slid to the notebook. She didn't recall putting it on the table, but she pushed that aside and thought about pianos.

With the bulk of the money she made from her books she had added to her capital. It was safer that way. With the sale of this book, however, she could afford to set money aside to buy a pianoforte.

'Do you play?' Hugo asked.

She laughed, sipped her lemonade. 'Yes.' *All* young ladies learned to play and she had been no exception. Not that she had ever had Kate's talent, but she had enjoyed it, found it relaxing—when she wasn't expected to play as a sort of advertisement for how accomplished and ladylike she was. It was only after she was married that she had fully understood that. No one expected her to play after dinner any longer— that was the province of unmarried girls. Instead she had played privately, for herself, but music had been one of the luxuries she had given up when she first moved to Soho.

Then every penny had been counted twice and polished thrice before it was spent. The importance of balancing the household budget had outweighed her love of music. Back then she had asked herself *Is it necessary?* every time she had to make a purchase. She had known the fear of having bailiffs at the door, and every month she balanced her books to a penny. Even now she hesitated to spend money on anything but essentials.

But listening to Kate fumble a passage, go back and correct it, play it over and over until she was satisfied, as Miss Barclay had taught her—Althea tossed all that to the winds. She was not going to end up in the Fleet Prison for debt if she bought a pianoforte.

Hugo rose. 'I should go in and see if my aunt is up from her rest. I'll leave you in peace, Althea.'

Over supper Althea's suspicion that something was bothering Hugo deepened. He seemed awkward, unwilling to meet her eye.

She waited for a chance to speak privately with him, but Kate and Sarah were eager to tell him all about their adventures. And he was more than happy to be told—she would have known if he were faking it.

What would he have done had she refused to take the girls in? Watching them over the supper table, she knew the answer. He would have adopted them himself. Hugo would never have abandoned them. He hadn't been able to do it when they arrived in London, but had housed them and protected them. Therefore he would never have done it after he had come to know them, and, she thought, love them.

As she did.

After supper Althea listened as Kate's description of a bird she had seen that morning sent Hugo to the top of the bookcase. He brought back a pair of books on birds.

'Let's see…' He paged through the first volume. 'Ah. Here we are. Red-tailed kite. What do you think?'

Kate leaned over the book. 'I think…maybe. Can we look tomorrow? Would you mind?'

He smiled. 'I wouldn't mind at all. My father used to know all the birds you'd see around here. These are his books. We often used to walk along the river, seeing how many different birds we could spot. His journals are here, too. You might enjoy looking through those, too.'

Seeing the small dark head bent over the book with Hugo, Althea knew envy. Her own father had never spent time with her. Always it had been Frederick, the son, the *heir*, who was the focus of Papa's interest. She had been her mother's business. But Mama had died when she was ten, and she had been left to the servants and her governess. Papa had mostly ignored her.

Until she was fifteen and there had been her godfather's death, and her sudden change in status from respectably dowered daughter to heiress.

Then Papa had finally noticed her.

He had been furious. She swallowed. Better not to think of all that. At the time she had scarcely dared say a word lest Papa turn on her.

'Oh, so the fine lady, the heiress, has something to say, does she? Pah! Giving yourself airs won't catch you a husband, girl.'

Had he ever called her anything but 'girl' after that? She didn't think so. He had never sat helping her to identify the birds she had seen on her morning walk. And, if he thought she had seen a red-tailed kite, he would have gone looking for it with a gun.

Soon enough Kate's ill-disguised yawns raised the spectre of bedtime. To Althea's amusement there was no protest this evening. Hugo had promised to help her spot birds the following morning… 'But you need a good night's sleep so your mind and eyes are sharp.'

Kate got up. 'Yes, sir.'

She came over to Althea. 'Goodnight, Aunt Allie.'

Althea held out her arms for the hug. 'Goodnight, sweetheart. Sleep tight.'

Kate hugged her hard, whispered, 'Do you think Mr Guthrie would mind if I called him Uncle Hugo?'

Althea kissed her temple. 'Why don't you ask?'

Kate's eyes widened. 'But—'

'He won't mind you asking.' She knew that as surely as she knew her own name.

Kate took a deep breath. 'Mr Guthrie? Sir?'

He smiled. 'Yes? Whatever it is, ask away.'

'Would you mind… Would it be all right if I called you Uncle Hugo?'

For a moment he stared, and Althea wondered if she had been wrong, if she should have sounded him out first.

But then, his voice oddly constricted, he said, 'I should be honoured, Kate.'

Althea caught Sarah's gaze, nodded slightly.

Her voice a little gruff, Sarah said, 'Would you… would you like a game of chess? Uncle Hugo?'

She saw, clear in the dancing glow of the fire and lamplight, the naked pain in his eyes, mingled with… acceptance? Resignation?

An odd smile twisted his mouth. 'I…yes. Very much.'

A faint snore came from the corner.

Kate nudged Althea. 'Aunt Sue is asleep. Shall you take her up?'

But Hugo was already on his feet. 'I'll take her up. Set up the board, Sarah, and we'll play when I come back down.'

Chapter Thirteen

'Shall we walk towards the sunset or the moon?'

They had reached the end of the lane. The river murmured ahead of them, and soft light danced on its hurrying surface. To the west the embers of sunset still flamed. In the east the moon rose over London. Further upstream at Teddington the tide had turned and was hurrying back toward the sea.

'We can have both.' Althea bent to release Puck. 'If we walk west now the moon will still be there to light us home.'

She shut her eyes and cursed silently as she straightened.

'Very wise.' He offered his arm, and against all her better judgement she placed her hand on it. Walked with him along the darkening, singing river toward Richmond. A faint splash near the bank told her something had gone into the water. Or perhaps it was a trout.

Home. Why had she called it that? *Back to the house*

would be accurate. But in the past week she had felt so at ease, so comfortable, that it was easy to think of River Lane House as home. Easy, and dangerous.

Her hand on his arm felt at home, too. That was even more dangerous. Waking up to find him beside her this afternoon—why had her heart skipped a beat? More than one beat if she were honest. Safer, much safer, if she lied to herself about that. But lying was the problem.

She had lied to him. Lied directly this afternoon, but she had been lying by omission since they met. Once it had not mattered, or she had told herself that it did not. But somehow, against all the odds, they had become friends.

He had come when she needed help, and had very possibly saved her life. At all events he had nursed her through a horrible illness, opened his home to her, and she had repaid him with a lie. You didn't lie to friends. You might keep your private business to yourself, but you didn't lie. Not to friends.

If he disapproved of how she had rescued herself from debt, then so be it. She knew what some in society murmured—that she had dug herself out of debt by taking lovers. If she didn't care about that, why should she mind if Hugo disapproved of her writing?

She didn't care to look too closely at the answer. It cut too close to something she had determined upon years ago—never to allow herself to care what a man thought of her ever again.

'I have to apologise.'

'I need to apologise.'

They both stopped, stared at each other. Then, by mutual consent, they walked on. And somehow Hugo's free hand covered hers on his arm—a dangerous, comforting weight.

'Ladies first seems a little self-serving,' he said.

Despite the thumping of her heart and the knots squirming in her belly, she choked out a laugh. Then, before she could change her mind—'I lied to you.'

'Ah.' His hand tightened a little.

'About the diary.' How to explain? Where to start?

'You do know it was none of my business, Althea?'

'Yes, but—'

'First, will you tell me *what* Sir Edwin did to earn such a set down from Lydia? She's clearly furious with him.'

Althea tried to collect her thoughts. Lydia had dealt Sir Edwin three set-downs so far. She'd been writing his first proposal of marriage, though, and—

He'd read it.

A chill shook her, despite the warmth of the evening.

'Are you cold? Shall we turn back?'

His immediate concern banished the chill.

'No.' It was far too late for that. She could tell him it was a hobby, something to pass the time. And it had been that. Once.

Ahead of them a pale shadow drifted silently from

the trees. Her breath caught. A barn owl on the hunt. 'We'd better not mention that to Kate. She'll slip out to see for herself.'

She felt a quiet laugh shake through him. And in their shared amusement, their mutual awe at the silent ghostly flight, the last chance of prevarication died.

'He offered marriage to her younger sister first.'

Hugo let out a crack of laughter. 'What a tactless clodpoll! What on earth possessed him to do that?'

Althea blinked. He'd spoken of Edwin Jamison exactly as he might on hearing of the folly of an acquaintance, someone *real*.

'It's a little complicated,' she said carefully. 'That's only his first proposal. He'll get it right in the end.'

'What? Lydia is going to forgive him for that stunning lapse of good sense and marry him?' He spoke of Lydia as a real person, too.

'Eventually. Once he learns his lesson.' She smiled a little. 'And once she learns that people, and the world, are not quite as cut and dried as she would like them to be.'

He chuckled. 'She's not perfect then?'

'Of course not. Who is?'

'No one. I don't suppose you'd let me read the rest?'

From her silence, the tightening of her fingers on his arm, he decided he'd gone too far.

'You…you could read it, as it is. Or… I could give you one of the first copies.'

'First copies?'

'Yes. When it is published.'

He took a deep breath. 'You're hoping to publish it?' Oh, lord. Publication was a risky business, especially for a woman. She would likely be expected to take all the financial risk, and—

He took another breath. Best someone explained it to her...

Did she ask for your advice? Do you know her to be intelligent? Competent?

'How do you go about it?' he asked instead.

They walked on in the velvet dusk, wrapped in the murmur of the moonlit river, a blackbird singing nearby. He always liked hearing a blackbird sing in the moonlight. And Althea remained silent.

Yet he did not believe she was ignoring the question or annoyed. Just...thinking.

Eventually she said, 'It's hard to know where to start.'

He understood that. Where did anything truly begin? When had he fallen in love with Althea? From the very first? When she had asked him to draw up her will? Five minutes ago? Or perhaps he was going to keep falling in love with her for the rest of his life.

'When Hartleigh died he left the devil's own mess. Mortgaged estates, half the family jewels turned out to be paste when his cousin and heir tried to sell some of them. He also left a pile of gaming debts. His friend and executor considered paying those far more important than working tradesmen.' Disgust sounded clear in her voice.

'What about providing for the widow?'

'Me? Provide for a barren widow?'

Barren? He set that aside. None of his business.

'I was probably below the tradesmen.' Now a little amusement slid through her voice. 'Anyway, once the dust settled, there was very little left for me.'

He knew from his father that she had inherited a fortune from her godfather, but very possibly that had gone to Hartleigh. It wouldn't be unusual, unless her family had seen to it that her money was very carefully tied up in trust.

She went on. 'My world had turned upside down. During my year of mourning I simply clung to the wreckage. The one thing I did own was the London house where we lived. It had been my godfather's, and it was mine absolutely. A separate trust. Even I couldn't sell it without consent.'

'So you stayed there.'

'I thought I had no other choice,' she said quietly. 'I was, although I didn't quite realise it at the time, in desperate straits. I had very little income, a house I couldn't afford to run or maintain, and no one to advise me. Reluctantly, I came up with the plan of marrying again.'

'Plan?' *Reluctantly?*

A bitter laugh. 'Oh, yes. It was definitely a plan. It

wasn't what I wanted, but I saw no other way out of the trap I was in. I fully intended to marry Rutherford.'

'For money.' He had no right to judge, but he hated that she had been forced to that.

She shrugged. 'For money, status. For safety. We were involved in an affair, and he was kind enough in a distant sort of way. We both thought we would suit.'

Now a hint of laughter, genuine affectionate laughter, came into her voice. 'Fortunately for Rutherford he met Meg, and she thawed him out beautifully.'

'But not so fortunate for you.' Despite his liking for the man, he couldn't keep the anger from his voice. 'Did you enter into the relationship believing he meant marriage?' And how often did that happen? Wealthy nobleman embarks on an affair, holding out the lure of marriage, then meets a beautiful, younger woman, and drops his lover faster than—

'No, no!' She was still laughing. 'It wasn't like that at all. Don't blame Rutherford. Marriage was mentioned *after* we became involved.'

'And then he discovered how little you had?'

She patted his hand. 'Stand down, Hugo. If money had mattered he would not have married Meg. She had even less than I did. Stop looking for a villain and let me tell this story!' She was silent for a while as they walked. 'Sorry. I'm editing a little. There are things I cannot tell you, that are not mine to tell.' Another pause. 'Let us say, through sheer luck, I was able to help Meg out of a horrible situation.'

'I daresay Rutherford was grateful.'

She grimaced. 'Embarrassingly so. I did very little, and it wasn't at all heroic. The thing was that Meg decided she didn't care that I had once been her husband's mistress, and—well, we became friends. She insisted on it.'

'Rutherford did not object?'

'No. *I* objected, but Meg wouldn't listen.'

He could believe it. The countess's quiet loveliness cloaked a spine of pure steel.

'Where does this fit with your writing?'

'I'm getting to that. I sold the house in Mayfair.' Another silence. 'I found out a little about the trust my godfather had set up and I… I persuaded the trustees that I couldn't afford it. I couldn't afford to go about in society either, so I sold the house and moved to Soho, which provided me with a little capital. A smaller, cheaper house, far less expensive to run, and away from all the gossip. Frederick had written that letter, which somehow was seen by the entire world, so I was very much persona non grata with society anyway.'

'What about Rutherford and his countess?' Couldn't they have helped her face down the gossip?

She shook her head. 'I wanted their friendship, not their protection. And I was tired of society. When Meg tried to invite me to anything but a very private dinner, I declined.'

'So you wrote a novel?'

'Not exactly. Should we turn back now?'

'When you've finished your story.'

'Very well. Where was I? Oh, yes. I'd always written, you see. Poetry, too, when I was a girl. But Hartleigh never knew. No one did except my father. He tore up most of a story once, saying writing by a female was a waste of time. After that I hid it from everyone.'

He wanted to drag her father out of the grave and then pummel him back into it.

'It was my…escape, I suppose,' she continued. 'Private and freeing. Especially after I married. By the time I accepted the reality of my situation and moved to Soho, I had six novels more or less completed.'

He blinked. *Six?* 'And you had never tried to publish one?'

She shook her head. 'You're a lawyer. You know better than that. How should I have gone about it? During my marriage it was impossible. Hartleigh would not have helped. He would have been mortified that his *wife* was doing such a thing, and as a married woman I couldn't have signed a contract without his permission. Even if he had permitted it, the money I earned would have gone to him. But after his death it was different. Before that, publishing my stories never occurred to me. They were just for me.'

'Your escape,' he recalled.

'Yes. But now I needed money. I knew Meg enjoyed novels. She'd loved a book called *Pride and Prejudice*, which I had also read and enjoyed. So I asked her to read one of mine. Swore her to secrecy, and made her promise to tell me the truth.'

'Would she have?'

'If she hadn't, Rutherford would have.' Althea chuckled. 'She showed it to him, without telling him where it had come from, and asked his opinion.'

He caught his breath. '*They* helped you get it published?'

'Yes. Rutherford approached the publisher, negotiated, and it earned me one hundred and fifty pounds.'

Even now he felt the little bounce of delight in her step.

'I'd never been so proud of anything in my life.'

For a moment he couldn't speak. Pride in her achievement swelled in him. Finding herself in a mess, she had somehow dug herself out of a hole. Ahead of them a shadow whisked across the path away from the river and under a hedge. A fox. He registered that, hoping the chickens were safely secured for the night.

'And the other books?'

'Rutherford negotiated the second sale. That earned quite a bit more, because the first book sold out, and made a profit. Then he advised me as I negotiated the next sale. I wanted to be able to do it myself, and he agreed that it was better that way.'

'And since?'

'This is my second novel since publishing the first six. I did have to look at the early ones again. Revise them. Bring them up to date.'

'Up to date? You mean, the fashions?'

She laughed. 'There's that. But more the writing style. My earliest started life as an epistolary novel. Very old-fashioned. I had to rewrite that one completely.'

He stopped, turned to face her and held her hands lightly in his. 'You turned everything around for yourself.'

'I was lucky. And I didn't do it alone.' She tried to tug her hands away, but he held fast. 'I had—'

'Althea, you wrote the books. They sold.' He gave her a little shake. 'Taking advice on the business side of it was the sensible thing to do. Like you took my legal advice on setting up trusts for the girls.' He shook his head. 'That doesn't make you less independent. And you said you learned to negotiate for yourself.'

'You don't disapprove?'

He stared. 'What? No. Of course not.'

'Many would, you know.' She shrugged. 'Women, *ladies*, are not supposed to pursue anything intellectual, and many still think novels are rubbishing things that corrupt girls' minds.'

He laughed. 'Yes, I know. I don't happen to agree, but possibly my mind has been hopelessly corrupted already.'

She sighed. 'I thought my life was complete earlier this year. Oh, I'm nowhere near as rich as I once was, but I'm secure. I thought I had everything I could possibly want. Peace. Contentment. That financial security to assure my independence. Even some good friends.'

'All very fine things.'

'Yes.' Her laughter sounded odd. 'But then you arrived on my doorstep with the one thing I was missing, and didn't even know I wanted, let alone needed—a family. Thank you for that.'

He spent most of his life sitting in his office listening to clients, drafting wills, occasionally setting up trusts. Sometimes he wondered if he did any good at all. When he came to the end of his life, would one single person mourn him?

Except for Aunt Sue, for the past ten years he had not had the joy of family. In that, he and Althea were much the same. She had been dispossessed and reviled by her family. His had died.

And when he had met those girls off the stagecoach he had known he could never abandon them to orphanages. He had given Althea the family he had wanted. And now... Words hovered in his heart, longing to be spoken.

But they had to stay there. At least for now. She had confided in him as a friend—the suitor, the lover, must wait.

'What was the title of your first novel?' A much safer subject.

'Barnabas Flowers; or, the Recalcitrant Suitor.'

He stopped dead in his tracks. '*That* chucklehead?'

She gave him a sideways glance. 'You read it?'

'I wanted to kick his—' He broke off, did a quick mental edit. 'I wanted to kick his backside. Telling the woman to whom he was betrothed that love was for silly, immature girls?'

'You didn't like it then.'

He caught the flat, even tone. Grinned. 'I didn't say that. I said I thought Flowers needed a good, swift kick. And he got it, too, when Susanna cried off, saying she loved him too much to inflict him with a silly, immature bride.' He laughed out loud. 'And then she tried to match him up with her friend, who thought exactly the same way? Which he found cold and calculating.' He shook his head. 'You wrote that? I really didn't think he deserved her until nearly the end. You're sneaky like that. Showing the poor devil at his absolute worst, and then putting him through hell to mend it all.'

'Oh.' A moment's silence. 'You bought my book.'

He kept a straight face. 'Well, no. Sue gave it to me for Christmas.'

'Of course.'

He relented. 'But I did buy the next one. And the others.' He shook his head in disbelief. 'I thought you were selling your jewellery bit by bit to build up your capital.'

She laughed. 'I did that right at the start when I sold the Mayfair house. I had some pieces that had been my mother's, which Hartleigh hadn't been able to get his hands on. Rutherford helped with that, too, at Meg's suggestion. Jewellers are very good at offering extremely low prices in those circumstances.'

They had reached the bottom of the lane that led up to the house and on to the Petersham Road. On one side of the lane the woods clustered darkly, blocking the light of the rising moon.

He held her back a moment as they stepped into the shadows. 'Let your eyes adjust.'

They stood, enveloped in the balmy, velvet darkness. Neither had bothered with a hat or gloves. Who was going to see or care? The night breathed around them, faint rustlings in the woods attesting to the presence of some small creature.

'Hugo?'

Yes, love? He managed not to say that. 'Yes?'

'Thank you. For everything.'

He swallowed. 'That's a great deal.'

He felt her turn to him, saw the pale shadow of her face look up. 'It's true. The girls, and…everything. Your advice—'

'You paid for that,' he reminded her. She'd insisted on paying for his legal advice. Except the letters to her relatives. He'd held the line on that.

'You don't judge,' she said quietly. 'Ever. You know all the discreditable things about me, and you don't judge.'

'It's not—'

'Your business?' She shook her head and the faint

light shimmered on her hair. 'It's more than that. You have given me your friendship, you came when I needed help. Thank you.'

'That's what friends are for.' He wanted more, so much more that he shouldn't ask for yet. He wanted to take her in his arms and… They needed time. She needed time. To see him as more than her friend, time to see what could grow between them, and time to trust that he would never use it to control and confine her.

Her hands slid into his and she rose on her toes. 'Thank you,' she whispered again, and touched her lips lightly to his.

Everything rose up in him, but somehow he found the strength only to return what she offered, to brush his lips over hers, and not take her into his arms. Slowly she stepped back and, the spell broken, they walked back up the lane through the velvet shadows to the house.

He could wait a little longer. He must wait.

Chapter Fourteen

Althea had enjoyed the first week at Petersham with the girls and Aunt Sue. She had enjoyed feeling her strength return, no longer being exhausted and requiring a short stop when they reached the end of the lane. She enjoyed the simple routine of country life again. Of walking along the river each day, with Kate becoming more and more enamoured of the bird life around them.

The second week with Hugo there was something more.

At his suggestion she had finally told the girls her secret—that she was an author and that was how she established an income.

They love you. Even Kate won't blurt it out when she knows it has to remain private between the three of you.

And it was a relief to tell them. To no longer have to hide her work away when one of them entered the room was a relief in itself, and no longer having to work quite so late into the evening was a blessing. Kate had accepted it, and that it was something quite private that only they must know.

Sarah found the whole idea of writing a story fascinating.

'You had to change a character's name because we came to live with you?'

She had giggled over that, at the idea of a real Sarah being a complete distraction from the fictional Sarah.

More though, her interest went beyond the writing itself to how Althea managed the money. She was startled by the idea that, instead of using the money paid by the publisher as income, Althea invested it. And Althea used that curiosity to teach her a little about managing money, about knowing how much you had and how far it would go. The child—and she was nearing fourteen, no longer a little girl—had even asked if she might learn how the household accounts worked.

'Because I'll have to do accounts like that one day, won't I?'

Sarah was growing up, and it was joy itself to witness that blossoming.

Would she have told them without Hugo's prompting? She thought not. And she would have been wrong. Perhaps it was easier to know when to tell children things when you had brought them up from babyhood, been witness to all those changes in them.

And Hugo himself became part of the rhythm of their holiday life. He walked with them in the mornings, took one girl or squeezed both into the gig with him for a drive in the afternoons. Sarah, he said, was becoming quite adept at handling the placid horse he'd hired.

So much that she alone had not been able to give the girls. Already Kate was asking if they might come again next summer. If they were invited, of course. Even if they weren't, and Althea was shocked to realise how much she hoped they were, she would have to set money aside to take the girls into the country for a week or two next summer. She could afford to stay with them at an inn for a few days or even rent a small house.

She was thinking about this as she relaxed in the shade a week after Hugo had arrived. He had taken both girls out in the gig. A squeeze, but they managed somehow.

She smiled, thinking of Hugo's comment as he helped Kate in. 'We'll need a bigger gig if you keep growing like this.'

Her intention had been to work, but the drowsy warmth of the summer afternoon was seductive. The notebook and pencil were on the table beside her, untouched. Aunt Sue had gone upstairs for her rest, and the golden afternoon, the soft breeze and the green embrace of the elm were a lullaby.

She dreamed.

She knew it was a dream, but it seemed so real. The house and garden were as they were. But she was not alone. Her eyes were closed, but she knew Hugo sat beside her reading. She knew that he loved her. There was no need for words. She simply knew. In the same way that she knew that this was how it was supposed to be. Them. Together. But would he still be there if she opened her eyes...?

Hugo was there, sitting beside her reading, as she opened her eyes. It felt right. As if he and she were both exactly where they were meant to be. Together. He looked up, as if her gaze had touched him, and smiled.

Her breath caught at the unguarded expression in his eyes. As if he were looking at everything he wanted in the world.

Her world lurched dangerously. 'Hugo? You're back?'

He leaned forward and murmured. 'Yes. I'm here.'

As if he meant not just here now, but always. As he had been in the dream. Was that it? Was that what he wanted?

Her?

And could she give him that and retain herself?

'Mrs Farley made lemonade while we were out!' Kate's bright voice shattered the spell. 'She made enough for all of us.'

Aunt Sue seemed to think they should come back sooner than next summer. 'You should come for Christmas as well as next summer,' she said that evening, her knitting needles flying. 'It will be lovely to have young voices in the house, not only dear Hugo and myself. Kate might join the carol singers. She has a pretty voice to go with her talent on the piano.'

'I'm going to buy one for her,' Althea admitted. Kate had already gone up to bed, and Hugo and Sarah were having their nightly game of chess. 'I haven't mentioned it to her yet. I thought a surprise when we get home. But I have already written to Mr Gifford at the music shop, and to her teacher for advice.'

Hugo looked up from the chess and smiled. He said nothing, but his smile turned her heart inside out and upside down, as it had done this afternoon. She wished there was someone she could ask for advice on what to do about Hugo. His smile deepened and her foolish heart danced a slow waltz against her ribs.

'Check!' Sarah managed to control the glee in her voice a little, but not by much.

'The deuce you are.' Hugo looked back at the board. 'Let me see.'

The two heads bent over the board again, and Althea looked away to find Aunt Sue smiling a small, wise smile over her knitting needles.

The evening walk had become *their* time. Each evening after supper, after a game of chess with Sarah, after Kate's piano playing, when the girls were in bed, and he took Aunt Sue upstairs with the old cat winding about their ankles. After he came back down.

Althea waited for him in the front hall, Puck bouncing around her in excitement at the prospect of this night-time adventure. Tonight should have been no different.

But this afternoon there had been that moment when his control had cracked for a second and she had seen. Seen what he tried to hide. And he had seen the returned yearning. And again this evening before Sarah, taking advantage of his distraction, had mopped the chessboard with him.

They walked largely in silence as they often did. He carried a lantern tonight, since the half-moon had not yet made its appearance. The dog, released from his leash, ranged ahead of them, occasionally dashing back to reassure himself that his humans were safe and still coming along behind him.

'So, a piano for Kate?' He broke the companionable silence as they turned for home.

'Yes. She enjoys the piano here so much. She practises at least once a day, and I enjoy listening in the evenings. I might play again myself.' She smiled a little. 'It's not just for Kate. But I need to think of something Sarah would enjoy as much. Not that she's jealous. It seems fair.'

He liked that she thought that way. Not of alleviating jealousy, but of fairness. 'I've noticed Spudge doesn't make you sneeze.'

'No. Cats don't. What made you say that?'

'She wants a kitten.'

'Sarah? How do you know that?'

'She slips Spudge bits from her plate all the time. You don't sit next to her at supper.'

A choked laugh. 'Well. That's easy. And since Puck is now used to Spudge, I suppose he would adjust to a kitten. Thank you.'

'My pleasure.'

They walked on until they reached the lane, the dark tunnel of trees and the shadows of the wood. It was as though the lantern cradled them in a little world of light, holding back the shadows. Even at night the air was cooler under the trees—a gentle benediction.

Puck, caring nothing for benedictions gentle or otherwise, stiffened at a rustle and squeak in the woods and dashed off to investigate.

Hugo felt Althea turn to call him back, but he placed his fingers against her lips. 'Give him a moment. He never goes far and we're not in a hurry.' He could speak to her now, tell her what he felt, and ask her to think, to consider…

He took a deep breath. 'Althea, would you—?

Somehow she was much closer than he had realised, and her mouth was even closer. Then there was no distance at all. The lightest, merest brush of a kiss. A feather could not have touched him with more care, nor a burning brand have set him alight more completely. All the things he had been going to say before he touched her dissolved in the dusky shadows—his arms closed slowly about her.

He didn't rush, didn't grab her and haul her to him. She could have stepped back. Her choice. She did not. Instead, with the softest of sighs, she stepped into him and together they deepened the kiss. In the velvet shadows and lantern light there was nothing but the silken mating of mouths, the match of their bodies, and the mingling of sighs and breath.

He'd stepped back a week ago, wondering if he had misinterpreted. And if he had, *what* he had misinterpreted. Had he been wrong in thinking that kiss had signalled desire? Or was he insane to have stepped back, rejecting her?

Now she'd kissed him again. He knew her well enough to know that if she didn't want something he'd be the first to know.

So he gave himself without reservation to the kiss and to her. Soon he would want more than the kiss, would want to touch, to explore, but for now this was enough, and not enough. More was there, a fragile waiting and beckoning, but it was not now. *Now* was this tender, dreaming kiss in a world of shadows and banked longing. Then he could speak. Not rush her, give her time to think about his offer, his feelings.

'*Six nights.*'

It took a moment for the words, breathed against his lips, to penetrate his hazed mind, another moment for their meaning to register, and for him to understand what she was saying, offering, there in the perfumed night.

She returned to London in a week, and she was offering to be his lover for these last six nights. Six nights when he wanted a lifetime. And that was the one reason he couldn't give her. If she was offering six nights, the offer of a lifetime might send her running.

Weeks ago he had spoken. Spoken and been forced to back away from what he wanted. He could explain that to her now… Ask her to marry him as he had wanted to do.

There were other reasons they shouldn't do this. One in particular. One he thought she would accept as rational, even when everything in him screamed that this once he should toss rationality into the river.

'Althea, the risk. If I were to get you with child, then—'

In his arms she stiffened. 'I'm barren.'

He remembered she'd said that once, referring to herself bitterly as *a barren widow*. There had been pain then, too.

He held her closer. 'You say that, sweetheart, but—'

'In eight years of marriage I never quickened.' Calm, resigned. 'And in that time Hartleigh sired two illegitimate children that I know of.'

His heart broke for her. What could he say to that? To the quiet pain in her voice that spoke of tears long since shed. Seeing the way she had responded to Sarah and Kate, he did not doubt that she would have loved any children she had been granted.

'I'm sorry.' He pressed a kiss to her temple.

She let out a shuddering breath. 'Any regret is over long ago. But you need not worry about an un-wanted—'

'A child, any child, would *not* be unwanted.' He heard the sharpness, his own deeply buried pain, in his voice.

'Hugo?'

He swallowed. 'You knew that I was married, that Louisa—my wife—died.' Ten years later, even as he was falling in love again, that pain seared, still rough-ened his voice.

'Yes.'

'She died in childbirth. Our daughter survived her by a day.'

They walked on for a moment, hand in hand, by mutual tacit consent. Althea had no words. There were some things, some hurts, for which words were a mockery, worse than useless. She had known this, too. But hearing him speak of it, she knew the grief, the pain, the loss that would never quite go away.

She stopped, turned into him and put her arms around him. Held him as his arms came around her. What could she say? There could be no comfort for such a loss. Her heartbreak each month had been for a child she had hoped for. Hugo had held the fulfil-ment of hope in his arms and lost it. She could only hold him and thereby tell him that he was not alone.

I wish I could give you what you want.

And she did wish it. But she couldn't say it. An empty wish at best. One she was safe from ever having to make good on.

After a while they walked on again, still hand in hand.

They were nearly at the gates before he spoke.

'Let me put it this way.' His words were precise, careful. 'Hypothetically. *If* you were not barren, *if* you conceived, would you accept an offer of marriage?'

What choice would she have? The difficulties and disadvantages, social and legal, faced by an illegitimate child were enormous. She could not inflict that on an innocent any more than he could. And the damage to her own already shaky reputation would harm Sarah and Kate.

She let out a breath. 'Yes.'

'You said once that you never wished to be married again. Would you hate it?'

Would she? Once she could have answered categorically *yes*. But she was no longer the same person, and she honestly did not know any more. And marriage to Hugo? That was another question altogether.

'I would not wish to give up my writing. Nor would I wish to stop publishing.' And God only knew how they'd squirm around the legal issues.

'Of course not.'

Another shaky breath. A man who didn't mind that his hypothetical wife might have a life and pursuits that were completely her own and not melded to *his*

life, *his* pursuits? 'Then marriage to you would be...'
Wonderful, glorious, joyful... 'Acceptable.' Hurriedly
she added, 'Hypothetically speaking.'

'Well.' They turned in at the gate. 'Don't drown me
in enthusiasm.'

'I... I didn't mean...' Oh, damn! Why did this have
to be so difficult?

Because this time it matters.

Afterwards would matter. They had to remain
friends, not just because of the girls, but because she
couldn't bear to lose him as a friend. He mattered too
much to risk that.

'You are having second thoughts,' he said.

Third and fourth thoughts, for that matter.

With him of all men, she must be honest. 'Can we
do this and remain friends? And what about that professional situation?'

He halted her short of the front door. 'Answer me
this. Why have you made this offer here, when you
rightly stepped back from it in London? This wanting, on both our parts—it's not a new thing.'

Her breath caught. 'Because here we may be private. In London we cannot have that privacy. No matter how careful, how discreet. And I will not harm the
girls with a scandal.'

He bent to her, pressed a kiss to her temple. 'Then
you have answered your own question. We both understand the limitations of what can and cannot be.
So yes, we can remain friends.'

She nodded slowly. He was right. They understood each other.

'There is one other caveat I must make.' They had reached the door as he spoke. 'You already mentioned harm to the girls. That, for me, comes under the same heading as an unexpected pregnancy—harm to an innocent.'

He opened the door as she digested that. 'You would offer marriage if there were to be a scandal.'

'Yes. Under those circumstances no professional situation would stop me. And I would expect you to accept it.' He closed the door behind them, locked and bolted it. 'Those are my terms. Half an hour.'

'Half an hour?' She swung off her cloak and he took it from her to hang by the door.

'Yes. For you to think. If you cannot accept those terms, lock your door and I will understand that to be your answer.'

She lifted her chin. 'Half an hour for us *both* to think. You may decide the risk is too great.'

A soft laugh broke from him. 'My risk? Finding myself obliged to marry a beautiful, fascinating woman? Dangerous indeed.'

She scowled at him. 'What about your professional reputation?'

He grinned, quite insufferably. 'My profession? I'm a lawyer, not a monk, love.'

She swallowed, desperate to focus on the important issue. Not the casual endearment that should *not* have speared her to the heart. 'And what do you imagine your partner, your other clients, might think about your marriage to a female bearing my reputation?'

He nodded slowly. 'I think it would not bother my partner. As for my clients? It's none of their business.'

'And if they made it their business?'

He shrugged. 'I am fairly comfortable. I own this house. I have a sufficient sum invested that I could retire quite happily. I enjoy my work and I prefer to be busy, but I would not starve should my clients desert me *en masse*.' He kissed her lightly. 'As you say, that's my risk. Think about your own. My risk is for me to assess.'

Chapter Fifteen

Hugo walked Althea to her door. 'Half an hour.'

He went to his own room at the far end of the upper corridor, considering his options for what the well-dressed lawyer might wear to an assignation in his own home. Certainly not his dinner attire. If anyone saw him still in his evening clothes in the middle of the night, especially dishevelled, there would be absolutely no doubt about where he'd been. He could change ready for tomorrow morning, but the same thing applied. It would raise questions.

Best if he changed into his nightshirt and a dressing gown. It was his house. Even with guests it was not unduly outrageous for him to wander about the upper corridor like that. Besides, he didn't dare stay the entire night with Althea. Much as he wanted marriage, it must be her choice. He couldn't trap her that way. If anyone saw him, he could say he'd heard a noise, wondered about an intruder...

Every night for six nights?

He'd worry about that when he had to.

He glanced at his watch. Twenty minutes. God help him, he was hard already. He already knew he was going to her room despite the risk. And the risk she had raised for him was not the one that terrified him.

There were times when risks were necessary. He knew that. His reputation?

He tossed his waistcoat and cravat over a chair. A moment later his shirt followed them. He didn't mind the risk to his reputation.

He risked his heart. Again. If he wanted her, then he had to accept that risk. He had already had his heart broken into a thousand pieces. Somehow, over the years since Louisa's death, it had reassembled itself. It wasn't quite the same heart it had been. Some of the pieces were different. Others seemed to be in different places. Perhaps it wasn't supposed to be the same. The problem was that it could be broken again.

The risk to Althea was the destruction of the life she had built for herself, the loss of her independence. He had told her not to weigh his risks in her decision, but he couldn't help weighing hers. She had built that world for much the same reason he had buried himself in his work—to protect herself. Her heart had not been broken as his had been, but she had been hurt, damaged somehow, by her marriage.

In an odd way he thought she had not been damaged by the affair with Rutherford. Somehow they had remained on friendly terms without any whiff of either holding a torch for the other. Rutherford's countess clearly loved Althea, and would have done far more than Althea would permit to help her.

He stepped out of his trousers, folded them neatly and put them away. She had weighed the risk to herself and her carefully constructed life. If she deemed that risk unacceptable then her door would be locked, and he would be in for a highly unpleasant night of frustrated desire.

He might also have to accept that winning Althea was beyond him. He wasn't sure which would be worse. Having her and then losing her, or never having her at all. It would be far more logical to remain in his own room and leave things as they were. Unconsummated.

Safe.

His gaze went to the little portrait of his father hanging by the door. One always thought of one's parents as staid arbiters of good sense and propriety. And yet he had heard a few stories about his father from his youth. Old friends who chuckled over their port and memories. And something his father had once said to him...

'The things I regret for the most part are the things I didn't do.'

Carrying a candle, he padded barefoot down the corridor to the big corner room he had insisted that Althea should have. It had been his parents' room and the one he usually used. He had told Aunt Sue not to mention that. Sneaky of him. One way or another he had wanted Althea in *his* bed. Even if he didn't share it with her. It was the principal of the thing.

He hesitated before reaching for the doorknob. All the what ifs in the world hung on this. Screwing himself to the sticking point he gripped the knob, and...

It turned. The door opened, and, the what ifs answered, all risks accepted, he stepped inside.

She was already in bed, a lamp burning on the bedside table. Seeing that he blew out his candle and set it on the little table beside the door, which held a bowl of Aunt Sue's potpourri. Rose and lavender scented the room, but he thought he could already smell the soap she used, the sweet fragrance of her hair.

Everything in him yearned towards her.

She smiled in the lamplit shadows. 'We did not change our minds.'

'No.' How could he have pretended even for a moment that this was anything as logical as a decision? Something he could choose, or not choose.

It simply *was*.

And he had absolutely no idea how to conduct himself. It wasn't *his* bed, even if he owned it and frequently slept in it. Tonight it was her bed. Did he climb in with her? Or should he wait for an invitation?

His breath caught and his blood hammered as Althea pushed back the bedclothes and slipped out of bed. She stood, slim and straight in those lamplit shadows, her simple nightgown falling to her ankles, her glorious honey-gold hair in a loose braid over one shoulder.

For how long had he wanted to see it loose? He wanted to unravel the braid, unravel *her*, and bury his hands and face in the silken gleam of her hair. He reached for control as she came to him, bare feet silent on the wooden floor. Desire was a slow burn in his veins, but he held back, hesitant.

It had been so long—if he reached for her he might explode, and he wanted to savour, explore, to *love* her, not just have her. There might be a time for that, but it wasn't this time.

And now she stood before him and he dared not move, in case—

'Hugo?' Her voice stroked his senses, he felt it deep inside. '*Are* you changing your mind? Is this not what you want after all?'

Her uncertainty undid him. 'I'm terrified,' he confessed.

Her lips parted, he thought in shock. 'Of *me*?'

She stepped back, but he caught her hands, drew her to him. 'Of dragging you to the floor and ravishing you there.'

'Oh.' That wicked faerie smile beckoned him straight to perdition. 'That sounds promising.'

He choked out a laugh. 'Promising?'

'Mmm…' She came a little closer. 'We should try that sometime.' *They should?* 'But for now…' She rose on her toes, still holding his hands, until her mouth was a whisper from his. 'Kiss me,' she breathed.

His heart pounding, he brushed his mouth across hers, then rested his forehead against hers. 'What if we end up on the floor, not sometime but this time?'

The soft, sultry laugh matched the wickedness of her smile. 'It's your floor, Hugo. I'll go on top.'

Her mouth returned to his and they took mutual pleasure, mutual delight in the deepening intimacy. Mouths mated, at once urgent and tender. Tongues touching, sliding in a dance of discovery, her taste a heady elixir, her arms an eagerness about him.

He learned her body through the veil of her night-gown, and thanked God for his own nightshirt as well as hers, because her touch, even muted by the linen, threatened to destroy him. And she was all grace-ful curves, warm secret hollows that promised every earthly delight. His hungry mouth found the beat of her heart there in the curve below her jaw. He joyed in the speeding dance under soft, fragrant skin, the trembling catch of her breath.

The ribbon securing her braid gave at a single tug, and at long last he slid his fingers into the twining silk, loving the cool fire of it slipping between them. It tumbled over her shoulders, sweetly alive, curling around his fingers, tempting and luring.

He buried his fingers in her hair, kissing, just kiss-ing, as her careful fingers undid the button closing the neck of his nightshirt, and loosened the laces. He shuddered at the first touch of her lips to his bared throat, unwinding the tight coil of his control.

'Althea?' Something had happened to his voice, roughening and deepening it.

She had happened to his voice, his life, his heart.

'Yes. Please.'

He hadn't even been able to think what he needed to ask, but she understood, placing his fingers on the first of the ribbons that held her nightgown closed. A gentle tug and the bow was undone, along with more of his control.

More unlacing, and more of the dainty bows fell victim to desire, until he nudged the nightgown to bare one shoulder. He kissed his way along the grace of her collarbone to the curve of her throat. Warm skin, trembling breath, his name a soft gasp.

'Hugo, please.'

Beyond words, he swept her up into his arms.

Shock slammed through Althea as her feet left the ground and she found herself being carried naked to the bed. She felt small, dainty and utterly vulnerable in every way. What had she been thinking to allow this, to suggest it?

'Are you…are you ravishing me?'

He lowered her to the bed and discarded his nightshirt in one swift move. Her breath burned in her lungs as he leaned over her, braced on his hands either side of her, so that their noses touched.

'What do you think?' His voice, rough and gravelly, brushed over her nerves. He reached out and turned down the lamp.

She gave him the truth, there in the enveloping dark. 'I'm not.'

'Good,' he murmured. 'Thinking…' A nibbling kiss along her jaw stole her breath, had her tilting her head back in a wordless plea for more. He gave it and she moaned. 'Where were we? Yes. Thinking. Very useful for work…' He nipped her ear and her body shot fire straight to her centre. He licked where he'd nipped and she melted. 'But right now…'

He joined her on the bed, gathered her into his arms, and there was another searing shock as warm skin met warm skin.

'Right now?' she murmured against his throat. She had wondered if she would even remember what she was supposed to do in bed.

A rumble of laughter. 'I thought you'd have stopped my mouth by now.'

She found it with her own and did exactly that. She didn't need to remember anything. With Hugo it was at once new and deeply familiar.

He was everything she wanted, and everything she feared. The one man who could make her want something more than the quiet, contented life she had carved for herself out of the ruins of the old.

And then it was too late. Too late for anything but this fierceness of mouths and bodies burning. His weight, hard and male, pressing her deeply into the mattress, the salt taste of his throat. Fires lit everywhere under her skin, dancing along her nerves where he touched her, and everywhere she wanted him to touch her.

He seemed to know, finding all those places, learning them, learning her. Discovering what she liked, even as she remembered. And yet it was not as she remembered at all. There was pleasure, yes. She remembered that. But had it ever been like this? Wanting to return pleasure as much as she wanted it for herself. Not in fair exchange, but because hearing his soft groan as she stroked his flank was a delight in itself. She slid lower and found him hard and ready for her. More than ready, she knew, as he cursed softly. She stroked, curious, loved that she could make him shudder. Knowing it made her ache, there where she wanted him most of all.

'Witch.' He murmured it against her lips, and gently, carefully moved her hand. 'If you keep doing that it will all be over.'

Shock rippled through her as he captured her other hand, trapped them over her head in a gentle grasp. She stared up at him, wriggled, tested that grip. It held.

'Hugo?'

He kissed her deeply. 'You just say *no*.'

You just— She didn't want to say *no*.

She wanted, needed, it to be now. Five minutes ago. Every breath, every tender touch, raked fire through her. But he held her safely, held her back from what she wanted.

His free hand, his lips, quested over her mouth and breasts, drifting lower over her quivering belly. And then those careful, shaking fingers were finally at her core. Tender, curious, learning her inside and out, slick in her sudden wild need.

Now, surely now...oh, please!

'Soon, love.'

And she knew she had spoken, begged. But yet he held back, pinning her to the bed with a powerful thigh flung over hers, holding her open to his touch, stroking shock after shock through her so that all the fiery tension built and built. And at last, at last he rose over her, came to where she needed him to be.

Soft, wet, Hugo's world stilled, contracted to this place they occupied in space and time, his body pressing into hers, her body both giver and receiver. She gave a startled cry at his entrance. His heart threatened to burst as he forced himself to stop, barely inside her.

'Sweetheart?' It was all he could manage, fighting the demand of his body, as he saw her closed eyes and trembling lips. It had been a long time for her, if he was hurting her—

Her eyes opened, dazed, her breath coming in gasps. *'Yes.'*

She shifted under him, and all control shattered.

He plunged deep, taking her next cry with his mouth, and she moved with him, as frantic, as wild as he. He knew, he could feel when her body leapt to peak, broke with him into a shattering beyond oblivion.

He thought he could happily lie right there for several eternities, cradled on her soft body slicked with his and her own sweat.

'I think you just ravished me.'

He raised his head, with some effort, at the slightly slurred murmur. 'I think we ravished each other.'

Her silent laughter shook through him. 'I think you're right.'

He was probably squashing her and made to get off, but her arms tightened.

'You're not at all—' a yawn '—too heavy.'

He smiled in the darkness. 'I will be if I fall asleep on you.' He eased to one side, disengaging from her lax body, to settle half over her, their legs entwined. Utterly sated and relaxed, he drifted, felt himself sinking, and vaguely hoped he didn't snore…

That jolted him back to reality. He didn't dare fall asleep in her bed.

'I can't stay.' He felt Althea stiffen, realising too late how it sounded, and he wanted to swear. 'Althea, love, if I'm caught in your bed—'

'I know.' She sighed. 'We're trapped.'

That couldn't stand.

He levered up on his elbow to look down at her. At

his lover, warm and rumpled from their loving, her lips soft and damp from their kisses. 'It's not a trap for me, sweetheart. And there's nothing I'd like more than to spend tonight with you.'

And all the tonights for the rest of my life.

He couldn't say that. Not yet. Instead, he stroked a damp curl back from her brow. 'I want to wake with you in the dawn and love you again, but by then the servants will be awake.'

A gentle finger traced the line of his jaw. 'I know, but you can stay a little longer.'

He could stay a little longer. Settling back down with her, he drew her close. She snuggled against him with a contented little sigh.

After a while she murmured drowsily, 'This is nice. Lying here, holding each other. I had no idea.'

He rubbed his cheek against her hair. That her marriage had not been happy, he knew. But that she had never known this simple joy, of lying in a lover's arms after making love, told him exactly how lacking that marriage had been in affection. Not untypical of aristocratic marriages, though, with husbands visiting their wives' rooms only to bed them, and then leaving.

He wanted to give her all the intimacy and affection she had been starved of, that she hadn't even realised she was missing. And he was so close to falling asleep with her in his arms that he needed to leave immediately.

A soft sigh and the heaviness of her limbs against him told him she was close to sleep herself.

'Althea?'

There was no answer. He pressed a kiss to her temple. She'd had that at least. Now she knew the pleasure of falling asleep in a lover's arms. Very carefully he set about disentangling himself from her sleep-weighted arms. A sleepy protesting murmur, but she didn't wake fully.

Tenderly he pulled the covers up around her shoulders. She gave a contented little huff and snuggled in. Relying on the faint moonlight, he located his nightshirt and dressing gown and donned them.

Safely clad, he bent over his sleeping lover and brushed a kiss to her brow. 'Sleep well, my darling.'

He opened the door a mere crack and peered out, letting his eyes adjust to the darkness of the corridor. Absolute silence. He opened the door further and slipped out, shutting it quietly behind him.

Five more nights. And five days. All the time he had left of her holiday to convince her that, together, they could have everything. Everything he'd thought lost to him for ever, and everything she'd never known she could have.

Waking to the chorus of birdsong in the soft darkness before dawn, Althea reached for him. And sighed, remembering. They had agreed they could not have this joy. And it would have been joy. Below, she could hear the faint sounds of the servants, the bang of the kitchen door, quiet voices.

Hugo had been a great deal more careful and responsible than she had. She didn't remember him leaving. The last thing she remembered was lying in his arms, her head on his shoulder, their legs entangled. Just lying together, sated and sleepy. She closed her eyes to bring back the intimacy, the tenderness.

I had no idea.

Her eyes shot open. Had she actually said that to Hugo? She thought she had.

Restless, she sat up. She supposed her bed was no emptier than it usually was, but somehow it *felt* empty, lacking.

Taking a lover will do that.

She shoved the nasty, cynical little thought away, along with the bedclothes. She had not *taken a lover*. She and Hugo had taken each other. For six nights. And she was terrified that after these nights her bed would feel empty for the rest of her life.

Chapter Sixteen

Hugo knew what happiness was. He knew what joy was. There had been happiness and joy in his life before. In fact, Hugo admitted to himself, he had learned to be perfectly content, and even happy again in his life, before he met Althea.

Summer holidays, and the Christmas holiday, had always been special times out of his deliberately busy life. Times when he could come out here to the Petersham house, sometimes for several weeks at a time to be lazy, to read, walk by the river, watch birds, spend time with Aunt Sue, and generally do whatever he liked, when he liked. He could sleep in if he liked, drink his morning coffee in the garden, and just be. It was as close as he could get to the carefree summers of his boyhood.

This year had been different. If he'd wanted to sleep in, there would have been no opportunity. Not with leaving Althea's bed before dawn to avoid the servants, and tossing and turning in his own bed for an hour or so in order to make sure it looked slept in. Then the girls rose early and there was always something to be doing.

Kate was working her way through Aunt Sue's music and his father's bird journals. The child had started a list—two lists. Birds she had already seen, and birds she wanted to see. Sarah was spending a good deal of time poring over the chess board. She was determined to excel. Apart from that she had taken to spending time in the kitchen, learning Mrs Farley's recipes.

If I learn how to manage the house, I can do it for Aunt Althea—that would save her time. Then she can write more if she wants to.

And then there was Althea herself. She wrote openly now, not bothering to hide what she was doing from them, although she didn't allow anyone to read it.

'It's not ready. I'm still scribbling. You can read more when I've tidied it up.'

He wasn't sure how he could go back to his London life as it had been without Althea. And yet he had not found the way to tell her what he wanted. She seemed perfectly content with things as they were.

Each night he went to her, and they made love. For that was what it was. He wasn't merely a man bedding a willing and beautiful woman. It wasn't mere bedsport. It was Althea and Hugo making love to each other. And each night she fell asleep in his arms, and he left her with increasing reluctance.

He wanted to sleep with her. Literally. He wanted to fall asleep with her. And not only that, he wanted to wake up in the dawn to make love with her again. Without caring if the servants or anyone else knew he was in her bed. Or that she was in his bed.

He'd thought of a way around it. Not completely around it, but enough. Maybe. It meant he had to buy a new, very expensive, watch.

All his life, unnecessary expense had been something to avoid. It was cold? Don an extra layer. Put a rug over your knees before heaping extra coals on the fire, even if you could afford the coals. Waste not, want not. He already had a perfectly good, functional watch. One, moreover, that he was very fond of. It had been his grandfather's watch and had been passed down to him through his father. He had one day hoped that he would give it to a son.

That last was irrelevant. The point was that he had a watch that kept time perfectly. He ought not to be thinking of buying another watch. Except he was. Because there was something his watch did not do that he needed it to do.

Two more nights. He had two more nights with Althea before she and the girls returned to London.

He announced his intended trip into Richmond over breakfast. 'I have something I need to do. Is there anything I may collect for you, Aunt Sue? Althea?'

Aunt Sue pursed her lips. 'You might buy some nice

cakes for tea, dear boy. And strawberries. I think the foxes have been eating ours.'

He grinned. 'Cakes and strawberries. Anything else?'

'May I come with you, Uncle Hugo?'

He looked at Kate in consternation. Half of him— curse it, *all* of him—was more than happy to take her, but—

'We were going to walk back towards London as far as Ham House, Kate.' Sarah looked puzzled. The previous evening they had discussed very seriously the thrill of seeing Ham House again. Althea had admitted to a slight acquaintance with the owners, and that made it even more of an excitement. Even viewing it from the river gate.

Kate stuck her nose in the air. 'I should like to go to Richmond with Uncle Hugo if it won't bother him.'

Althea looked at him. 'What does Uncle Hugo say?'

He sipped his tea. 'That I would enjoy the company.'

Richmond was an easy drive along the main road. Leaving the horse and gig at the inn, Hugo strolled through the centre of the town, Kate chattering brightly and holding his hand.

'Where are we going, Uncle Hugo?'

He steered her into a narrow lane that led through to Richmond Green. The shop he wanted was a few doors down. 'Right here.' He opened the door for her. 'In you go.'

She looked around. 'It's a jeweller's shop. Oh!' Her eyes widened. 'Are you going to buy Aunt Althea a ring?'

'What?' *Oh, Lord.* 'Ah...no. Not right now, Kate. I need a new watch.'

'Oh.' She frowned. 'Is something wrong with the old one? I'm sure they could mend it. Aunt Althea's clock stopped, and a man came to the house and made it work again.'

'No. It's working perfectly. I, er, need a spare watch.' He nodded to the woman who came out of the back room.

'Good morning, sir.' Then she smiled. 'Why, it's you, Mr Guthrie! How nice to see you again. And how is Miss Browne? I was hearing she had visitors apart from yourself.' She looked at Kate. 'Would this be one?'

'It would. Miss Kate Price, Mrs Henderson. And Miss Browne is very well. No need to ask how you go on.' He smiled. 'You look famously.'

Mrs Henderson fussed with her cuffs and blushed. 'Thank you, Mr Guthrie. How may we help you today?'

Hugo explained what he needed.

She nodded. 'Of course, sir. This way.'

Half an hour later he walked out with Kate, the dazed owner of a very expensive striking watch, guaranteed to sound on the hour, when you activated the mechanism. Just the hours. He had gently but firmly rejected the notion of a watch that would also strike the quarters. Life, he had noticed, seemed to move a great deal faster than it had when he was a boy longing for the end of the school term. He didn't need to be reminded of every passing quarter hour.

Fortunately, Kate had lost interest very quickly and made friends with the black and white shop cat, who was more than happy to be petted. Her distraction was complete when Mrs Henderson found a small, carved wooden brooch in the form of a bird, which she gave to Kate. This had Hugo, not wishing Sarah to be left out, selecting a small silver rose brooch. Mrs Henderson wrapped it with the watch. Kate already had the wooden bird pinned to her bodice.

Walking back towards the inn, Kate gave a little jig, swinging their hands. 'We mustn't forget the cake and strawberries. I'm glad you bought Sarah the rose, but should we find something for Aunt Althea and Aunt Sue?'

He laughed. 'Good point. Since you and Sarah have your brooches, I'd better find something for our aunts.'

Remembering that Althea had enjoyed her ginger ice cream at Gunter's, he chose a jar of crystallised ginger for her. For Aunt Sue he bought pretty handkerchiefs and a new cap with bright pink ribbons.

When Kate looked a little puzzled over the handkerchiefs he chuckled. 'Aunt Sue would be the first to tell you she has more than enough *stuff*, as she calls it. But she does like pretty handkerchiefs, and she loves pink.'

Kate nodded slowly. 'Is it like when I told Mrs Henderson I liked watching the birds and she found the brooch for me? And she told me she had enough things to give something away.'

'Exactly like that. And your aunt likes ginger, and the jar is pretty afterwards. She can keep something else in it.'

'Because she's not as old as Aunt Sue, so she doesn't have as much stuff.' Kate nodded.

Hugo hid a smile. 'Something like that. Come along, and we'll find the cake and strawberries.'

Althea saw the little wooden brooch on Kate's bodice, and her heart tumbled helplessly. 'That's very pretty, Kate.'

Kate jigged. 'When Mrs Henderson, the shop lady, asked what I liked, I said birds, and she found this. And Sarah has—'

'Perhaps, Kate, love, you could let me present Sarah's gift first?' Hugo said mildly. He reached into his pocket and brought out a small parcel, which he handed to Sarah.

She stared. 'You bought me a present. Thank you.'

'A very little one.'

And Althea's heart misbehaved again as she watched Sarah unwrap a little box and take out the silver rose.

'Kate liked the bird and we thought, because you pick roses for the breakfast table, that you might like this.'

The girl looked up, eyes shining. 'It's beautiful. Thank you, Uncle Hugo.' She pinned it on at once, went to him and hugged him hard. 'I love it.'

Kate jigged up and down. 'Are you going to…'

This time she shut up with a mere look.

Looking slightly shame-faced, Hugo offered Aunt Sue a small parcel. 'I promise it's not *stuff,* Aunt Sue.'

She laughed. 'It feels like *stuff,* but never mind. If an old lady can't accept a gift from a handsome young man, even her nephew, then who? Thank you, my dear.'

Opening it, she smiled. 'Not *stuff* after all. Thank you very much, Hugo. My favourite colour, too. And what pretty handkerchiefs!'

Then he turned to Althea, and her heart stuttered. 'What? You didn't.'

He raised his eyebrows. 'And exactly what do you think Aunt Sue would say if I'd brought home gifts for her and the girls and forgotten you?'

'It would have been nasty, and quite pointed, I assure you.' Aunt Sue carefully unpinned the cap she had put on that morning. 'My sister and I brought him up better than that. And even dear Hugh, this one's papa, always brought me a little something when he bought Cecily a gift. Which was often.' She pinned on the new cap. 'How does that look, girls?'

Hugo smiled at Althea, and leaned close as he gave her the parcel. 'I remembered your preference in ice cream.'

Small, yet heavy. She resisted the urge to shake it. He couldn't possibly have brought home ice cream from Richmond. As a child she had always ripped the wrappings off presents, now her fingers trembled a little as she carefully undid the ribbon and removed the paper.

'Oh.' All these months and he'd remembered she had chosen ginger ice cream. For that matter she often had ginger biscuits. Mrs Cable knew she liked them. And he'd remembered. The little ginger jar turned misty. For goodness' sake! She was not going to turn into a watering pot over a jar of ginger!

'Thank you.' She had to push the words past a lump in her throat. She didn't remember a present that had ever moved her more.

'There's cake, too,' Kate announced. 'It's ginger cake.'

After supper they all settled in the parlour with the doors open to a glorious evening. Birds still sang as the shadows lengthened.

Kate sat down at the piano and, instead of riffling through the music as she usually did, opened the piece on top of the pile. 'Aunt Sue asked me to learn this one for her this afternoon. She said she used to play it.'

Hugo looked at his aunt curiously.

She smiled. 'I think you'll remember it.'

Kate struck up a waltz. And he did remember it. Aunt Sue playing it, on this very instrument, on a summer evening a few years ago. And his father, well into his seventies at the time, laughing and asking Mama to dance. They had danced here in the parlour as if they were in their twenties again. He'd been more than a little surprised that either of them had known the steps.

They had both been gone before the next summer, yet it was as if they were still here somehow, dancing and loving.

He rose, went to Althea. 'May I have this dance, ma'am?'

Words proved impossible. Althea placed her hand in his, felt his fingers tighten briefly on hers—it felt as if he held her heart. Careful, gentle and utterly dependable. What had she done?

She rose and he took her into the dance. She had danced in some of the grandest ballrooms in London once. Danced with dukes and earls, been sought after as a supper partner for her cursed beauty. As if she were some sort of prize. Hartleigh had married her for it—that and her money. Yet none of those grand rooms or wealthy aristocratic partners had meant as much as this waltz in a parlour, the tune from an elderly, battered piano, played by a small girl, winding its way around her heart.

The room wasn't huge, but there was space enough if they danced in small circles and he held her close. And he did. So close that her body, attuned to his over the last few nights, hummed with delight.

What have you done?

She smiled up into his eyes, deep grey eyes that smiled back, and couldn't bring herself to care. Only two more nights, but she'd had this. If it hurt for the rest of her life, she'd had two glorious weeks with him, and this last week when he'd come to her each night had been the loveliest week of her life.

Two more nights.

They would make them nights to remember for a lifetime.

Hugo slipped down the hall to Althea's room shortly after midnight. He should have come earlier, but he had hesitated, even after the house had fallen silent and the servants were abed. That dance had shaken him to the depths of his being. How could they continue this for even one more night without him speaking what cried out in his heart?

They needed to talk. And he needed to know what to say. Or perhaps not what to say, but how to say it. So now it was after midnight and he reached for the door handle, half expecting her to be in bed and sound asleep...

A single candle stood on the chimneypiece. Althea, standing by the open window, turned as he came in and shut the door. Consciously, he turned the key. He hated that. Hated the secrecy that felt as though he were somehow ashamed of this, what they did, but it was the only way he could protect Althea from being forced into choosing a path he was still not sure she wanted.

They needed to talk.

'I'm sorry. I've kept you waiting.'

She shook her head. 'It's all right. I was thinking.'

'Thinking?' About the same things he was thinking of?

'We have only tonight and tomorrow.'

His breath caught. 'Althea, we need to talk. We—'

'Yes. Later though?'

Her hand went to the sash of her robe. One tug and it was undone. And he was undone with it. Her gaze held his, not challenging but steady, a half-smile dancing in her eyes. A shrug of her shoulders and the robe slid to the floor.

Leaving her naked.

His blood hammered and the rest of the world blurred. His breath came in hard—like something else—and stayed there.

'Shocked, sir?'

He couldn't think enough for shocked. That velvet voice, all teasing seduction, stroked every nerve.

'You are...utterly—'

Now her gaze did turn challenging. 'Not beautiful, I hope.'

No. She *was* beautiful. That spoke for itself, not requiring words.

'Wicked.' He shook his head. 'Beautifully, wonderfully wicked.'

Her laughter danced. 'I think I like that, being wicked. For you.' She came to him, a pale sylph in the candlelight and shifting shadows.

Just for me?

She smiled. 'I intend to be more wicked yet.'

Hugo reached for her, drew her close, one hand on the sweet curve of her bottom. 'And if I wish to be wicked as well?' He nibbled along the line of her jaw, felt the jolt of her breath, her pulse speeding under his lips.

Althea stood on tiptoe, her arms lifting to wind about his neck. 'We can be wicked together.'

Together.

He wanted that more than his next breath. To spend the rest of his life with this woman—loving her, being driven to distraction by her independence, loving her all the more for it.

But her mouth was right there, warm and inviting. He accepted the invitation, tasted her deeply and was lost. He was never sure quite how they found the bed, but somehow they did, minus his nightshirt, and rolled together until she sat up, somehow straddling him.

The single candle on the chimneypiece danced light and shadows over her face. She smiled down at him. 'Wicked enough?'

'I'm not sure,' he murmured. 'Keep going.' She rose up, reaching between them to guide him to her entrance. He wanted to pull her down, possess her utterly. So soft, so wet... He held back, fighting for the control to allow her to set the pace. Slowly, slowly she took him into that wet heat, an endless possessive slide until she had all of him. Or he had all of her. Did it matter? They had each other and it was glorious.

She rocked a little and he reached up to cup one pale, lovely breast, stroked the tip, and felt her breath catch. Her hair tumbled forward around her face, framing it. *'Yes.'*

'More?' He lightened his touch, felt her quiver.

'More,' she breathed, moving on him. 'Much more.'

He gave her more, rocked under her, matching her slow rhythm, his hand on her hip only to anchor himself. Pressure built, his grip hardened as she finally, finally moved faster, until, with a smothered cry, she broke. Her head fell back as the storm caught her, and he watched in wonder as it swept across her, through her.

She collapsed onto him, trembling with the force of her release, and he caught her, held her trembling body close, as his own consummation stormed through him.

They lay, a tangle of limbs and pounding hearts, and he wondered if the world would ever—could ever right itself. He should speak now, tell her how he felt, what he wanted. For himself, for them.

'Althea, love.' The odd little sound she made told

him that she was right on the cusp of sleep. Very gently he lifted her so that she lay warm and relaxed against his side. Wasn't it men who were supposed to fall asleep immediately?

'Althea?' A contented little sigh breathed out of her, and he smiled into the darkness. In the morning then. He would speak in the morning. Perhaps it was better to speak then, when they weren't dazed with lovemaking and half-asleep. He smiled again—fully asleep, in Althea's case.

Meanwhile, he would enjoy the sweet intimacy of actually sleeping with her. Carefully he reached out and set the striking mechanism on his expensive new watch. Praying it would do its job, Hugo settled Althea in his arms and closed his eyes.

Chapter Seventeen

Althea jolted awake, wondering what had disturbed her, and realised that the pillow tickling her nose was Hugo's chest. What time was it? Something had made a noise. The servants? Why was he still here? She tried to sit up, but was held in place as his arm tightened.

'Hugo, wake up!' she whispered. 'We both fell asleep and—'

'My watch did its job and woke us.' He still sounded sleepy, but there was no mistaking the smugness in his voice.

'Your watch?'

'I bought one that strikes on the hour.'

She digested that. Watches were expensive at the best of times, and one that chimed on the hour… They weren't just *expensive*. 'That was what you bought at the jeweller? So that you could stay without risking—'

'So that I could sleep with you, yes.' He sat up and stretched. 'I wanted that more than I can say. We need to talk this morning, sweetheart. Not now. I can't risk falling asleep again. The servants will be up in another hour.'

He pushed back the bedclothes and got out of bed. She could hear him moving about in the dark, hear the small movements as he found his nightshirt and dressing gown. Then he was back at the bedside, tucking the bedding around her as he always did. Making her feel cherished and cared for.

One more night.

She could feel the heat pricking at her eyes and thanked God for the friendly darkness that had cradled their loving and now hid her tears. He bent, a darker shadow, to kiss her as he always did. Sometimes she wasn't quite awake when he left, but she always knew when he kissed her. Those kisses were going to have to last her for the rest of her life.

'I liked waking up with you, too,' he murmured. 'I'm looking forward to doing it again.'

One more time. He'd bought a disgracefully expensive watch so he could sleep and wake up with her. Twice.

Her lips clung to his, drawing out the kiss, drowning in the sweetness. Somehow she had to navigate her way back to their friendship, without him ever realising how much he'd come to mean to her.

He broke the kiss gently. 'Go back to sleep, sweetheart. I'll see you at breakfast.' Another swift kiss. 'We'll talk during our walk.' Then he was gone, a shadow moving quietly to the door, which opened and closed with the faintest of clicks.

Althea stared into the darkness and let the tears come. She wasn't sure what he wanted to talk about. Perhaps that they should continue their affair in London. And that she couldn't allow.

She didn't mind the risk to herself, but she couldn't allow the risk to the girls, or the risk to him, if a scandal ensued.

Like a fool she'd fallen in love. It wasn't the sleeping with him that had tipped her over that fatal edge. It was the living with him. He was easy to live with. He had his own habits and routines, but was more than happy to accommodate others. She found it endearing that he preferred tea first thing in the morning, but coffee later in the day, and a return to tea in the late afternoon.

He had brought some legal work down with him, and sequestered himself for a couple of hours each day after their morning walk. Now that she had told Kate and Sarah about her writing, she used those same two hours for her own work. The girls either read, kept Aunt Sue company playing cards, or visited Mrs Farley in the kitchen. Kate had learned how to make lemonade. Sarah had learned how to bake Althea's favourite ginger biscuits.

He had remembered her choice of ginger ice cream and brought her a jar of candied ginger.

How could she have *not* fallen in love?

She had told herself that it was attraction, desire, that had made her want to start this affair. The truth was, she had already been in love. The affair itself had opened her eyes to that truth. That and his insistence on protecting her. She had been protecting herself for a long time. Both during and after her marriage. She was good at it. But oh, it was such relief to have someone who also thought her worth protecting, not because she might sully *his* good name, but because she was intrinsically important to him.

And simply because he was a good man. The antithesis of her husband, her brother and her cousin Wilfrid. None of whom had protected the women and children in their lives.

Hugo did. It was that simple. And he did it without making you feel useless or obligated or inferior. He made her feel that she mattered.

She rolled over, breathed the faint scent of Hugo on the sheets, on his pillow, and closed her eyes, hoping that she might dream of sleeping in his arms and waking the same way, of making love in the dawn.

Hugo had thought carefully about how he should raise the topic of marriage with Althea. He was still thinking about it over his eggs at breakfast. Aunt Sue generally breakfasted in her room, and the girls and Althea had yet to make an appearance, so his musings were uninterrupted.

Tell her you love her first. Then explain about Miss Price's will.

He topped up his teacup, considering. It was a very long time since he had told a woman he loved her. Hopefully things hadn't changed, but he was no longer a young man of twenty-five, who had fallen in love with a colleague's daughter.

Telling her you love her is still the best way to start.

First he had to get her alone. It wasn't the sort of thing a man wanted to blurt out in front of two young girls, especially when one of them already thought he should be giving her aunt a ring.

On their walk. The girls always ran ahead with the dog. Oh, one or the other of them came racing back from time to time, but mostly they could be assured of a reasonably private conversation. He glanced out the window. Sunshine poured from blue skies.

Perfect.

'Good morning, sir.' Sarah came in with a bunch of roses. She placed them in a waiting vase on the breakfast table. Something inside him bloomed at the thought of becoming used to that. To Sarah arranging a few flowers on the table each morning for years to come.

'Kate and Aunt Althea are just coming. They are still in the garden with Puck.' She helped herself to eggs and a piece of bread. 'Have you been to Paris, Uncle Hugo?'

'No. Why?'

'Aunt Althea has, and she says they have delicious pastries for breakfast each morning.' Sarah buttered her bread thoughtfully.

'The Scots like black pudding,' he offered. He did, too, for that matter.

Sarah screwed up her face. 'Ew! I'd rather try the pastries.'

'Practise your French,' he advised. 'Then you can tell them which ones you want.'

Sarah grinned and bit into the bread, as Kate trotted in, followed by Althea and the dog.

'Good morning.' Kate poured milk for herself and took it to her place. 'It's such a nice morning, we can walk for ages. Maybe all the way to Richmond and back through the park?'

Althea smiled as she sat down and poured tea. 'We'll see.'

He considered that possibility. If they did that, if Althea said yes, then he could stop at Henderson's again... They could choose a ring together.

A clatter of hooves on the drive distracted him from a vision of walking home across Richmond Park newly betrothed with Althea.

He returned his thoughts to the immediate issue. 'Can you really walk that far, Kate?' he asked.

She hunched a little. 'If we have a rest in Richmond I can. And maybe a rest on the way home?'

'I think we can—Mrs Farley.'

The housekeeper stood at the door, a letter in her

hand. 'Messenger from London for you, Mr Hugo. He's waiting for an answer.'

Something minor, please.

Something he could scrawl an answer on the bottom and send back... He took the missive, broke the seal—Jacob's signet ring, not the firm's office seal. His heart sank. Not simple then, if Jacob had used his personal signet...

Opening it out, he scanned it. His stomach executed an ungainly roll. He read it again, slowly.

How in Hades had that happened?

He folded the letter carefully, placed it in his pocket. The last two weeks—the last week especially, and this morning in particular—all turned to ash in his heart.

What have you done?

'Hugo?' Althea's worried voice broke into the wasteland of his thoughts. 'Is it very bad news? Can I help?'

'What? No. I mean, it's not good news. I must return to London. Immediately.'

Dear God, the mess this would cause!

The outcry from the girls should have been heartening. Instead it tore at him. 'I'm sorry, girls. This is something...' He blew out a breath. 'Something I've made a mess of and now I have to mend.'

If it can be mended.

He rose, looked straight at Althea. 'I'm sorry. For... for everything.' He couldn't even explain now.

He saw her stiffen and cursed himself. Cursed all

the things he couldn't say, both because the girls were there and because of his blasted ethics.

'Must you go immediately, sir?'

'I'm afraid so.' Beyond caring, he went to her, caught her hand. 'I'll see you as soon as I can. But this is bad. And…it changes things.'

Her face went utterly blank. 'Of course, sir. I quite understand.'

No, she didn't. And, since he couldn't explain yet, he needed to shut up. Now. He was making everything worse.

The sun was as bright, the birdsong as lovely and the river as beautiful as it was every morning. And yet to Althea it might as well have been pouring with rain and smothered in a suitably gloomy fog.

How had she become so attuned to his presence that she missed it like a limb? After he'd slipped from her room that morning, she'd lain awake, wondering what it would be like to awaken in the dawn to find him still in her bed, and to make love in the blooming light. As she'd drifted between dreams and the waking world, it had seemed that it might be possible.

'We'll talk after breakfast. On our walk.'

She had allowed herself to believe that one day she would open her eyes and know what it was like to have him there, smiling at her in the light, or perhaps have him kiss her awake.

But now something had changed for him.

You aren't going to find out. You had this brief in-terlude to enjoy yourself. With no obligations, no expectations. Don't spoil what you had by wishing for what you can't have. You set the rules yourself.

She hadn't understood that she'd be breaking her own heart.

They turned back a little way before Richmond on their walk. Somehow no one wanted to stop for cakes without Hugo. Sarah had been very quiet, lost in her own thoughts, and Kate was dancing ahead as they approached the lane up to the house, hoping, Althea knew, to spot a squirrel in the woods there if she were very quiet. Sarah had stayed back to walk with Al-thea, and they had leashed Puck. Otherwise the odds of Kate seeing a squirrel were little to none. Puck's attitude towards squirrels was that they had been cre-ated especially for him to chase and, if out of reach, which they always were, to bark at.

Kate safely ahead, Sarah finally spoke. 'Do you think *I* could write a book one day?'

Althea smiled. So that was what she'd been mull-ing over.

'I have no idea. Nor will you until you try.'

'Is that what you did? Sat down to write a book?'

Althea laughed. 'When I was your age, I used to wish desperately that I had a sister.' She had been so lonely when Frederick went off to school. He had come back changed, far less willing to have a younger sister tag along behind him. And then there had been her inheritance, and his bitterness that he, the boy, the fêted heir, had been passed over for a mere female. It should have been *his* inheritance. Even the Pater—he had taken to referring to Papa as *'the Pater'* in that lordly way—said so.

She swallowed, pushing away the hurt. 'So I imagined a sister for myself, but because she lived somewhere else we had to write letters to each other. So of course, I had to make up a reason for her to live somewhere else.'

'Was she married?'

'Oh, goodness, no! That would have been far too ordinary. I imagined that she was travelling with her godmother so she could write to me about all her exciting—who is that?'

At the foot of their lane a small black carriage stood, a nondescript pair of bays facing up the hill towards the main road. One man stood beside it, another on the box. Kate was very close, and the man stepped forward to speak to her.

Instinct had Althea lengthening her stride. No doubt he was only asking directions, but—the man gripped Kate's arm.

'No!' Althea leapt into a run as the man dragged Kate towards the open carriage door.

Kate's screams ripped through her. She'd never make it. Her skirts wrapped around her legs—she hitched them up, not bothering to yell. There was no breath for it and no one else to hear.

The man nearly had Kate to the carriage, her childish struggles useless as he clapped a hand over her mouth to stop her screaming.

He let out a yell, lost his grip and Kate was free, bolting back down the path towards Althea, even as Puck charged past, barking furiously.

The man on the box yelled. 'Come on! You've lost her!'

Puck reached the would-be abductor, snarling, snapping at his ankles. The man kicked out, missed, then ran for the carriage, harried by the dog. He leapt for the open door and swung up into the carriage.

The driver whipped up the horses and the coach rattled off up the lane.

Reaching her, Kate flung herself, panting, into Althea's arms.

'He wanted me to get in the carriage! He asked where the nearest house was. I started to tell him, but he said I had to show him, and he grabbed me!'

Her own breath shuddering in and out, Althea held her close.

Sarah came up breathless as Puck returned, his tail wagging, hackles still bristled. She dropped to her knees. 'Good dog!'

Althea turned. 'You let him off.'

Sarah nodded. 'He was tugging on the leash, and I knew *we'd* never be fast enough.'

'I *bit* that man!' said Kate with relish. 'And he *yelled*. Then Puck came. He was going to bite him, too.'

Sarah nodded. 'Good idea, but you should probably clean your teeth.'

Hysterical laughter threatened to erupt from Althea. 'Are…are you all right, Kate?'

The child nodded, but she pressed close. 'Why did he want me to go with him?'

Althea could only think of one reason—the same one that had ensured Hugo met the stagecoach when the girls came to London. It wasn't a reason she was going to tell them.

Sarah frowned. 'Maybe he thinks we're rich? Sometimes rich people are abducted, and their families have to pay to get them back.'

Kate looked unconvinced. 'We're not rich though.'

'No.' Sarah straightened up from petting Puck. 'But he might have thought we were. Don't you think, Aunt Althea?'

'It's possible. That does happen.' Surely any kidnapper worth his hire would make sure the victim's family had enough money to make it worthwhile? If only Hugo hadn't returned to London. Today of all days.

She wanted to hurry the girls back to the house, tell him what had happened and know that he'd sort it—she drew a deep breath and set her jaw.

For whatever reason, Hugo had gone back to London. She could sort this out for herself. She'd been sorting things out for herself for the last six years. With varying success, admittedly, but in this instance she knew exactly what to do, and she didn't require a man to do it for her.

Gathering Kate close, she spoke with a confidence she was far from feeling. 'Back to the house now. We'll send a message to the local magistrate with one of the servants.' If someone was prowling the area, looking for girls to sell into brothels, the sooner the authorities knew the better.

The illogic of it niggled at her, though. Luring unprotected girls off a stagecoach was one thing. Evil, yes, but not particularly dangerous for the perpetrators. It happened. People wrung their hands and said how dreadful, but nothing much was done about it. Abducting obviously cared for young ladies, even if they weren't wealthy, was something else entirely. The sort of thing that would have people looking out for these men with blood in their eye. It was stupid.

The magistrate himself called in the early afternoon. He was inclined to dismiss the brothel theory.

Kate, clutching Sarah's hand, had described her would-be abductor, then been sent off for milk and cake while the magistrate conferred with Althea.

'Mistaken identity, Lady Hartleigh.' Sir William Banner steepled his fingers as he frowned over their story. 'As you say, you are not really wealthy enough to attract a serious ransom demand. However, there are families hereabouts who *are*. Some with young girls. We're a little far out of London for the brothels to be looking for prey, I believe. And, as you so rightly say, it's a very risky business for them. I think your niece was mistaken for someone else.'

Althea nodded slowly. 'That does make more sense. You will warn those families, then, Sir William?'

He smiled. 'You may be very sure of it, ma'am.' The magistrate rose. 'In fact, I will call on a couple of the nearer houses on my way home. Thank you for alerting us to this, Lady Hartleigh. Ah, you may be sure I will keep your name and your nieces' names out of this.'

She hadn't even thought of that. The last thing she needed was gossip. 'Thank you, sir. I appreciate it.'

'You are a friend of Miss Browne? I believe she has her nephew staying? I've met Guthrie a time or two. Excellent fellow.'

'Yes. Unfortunately he was obliged to return to London this morning. His partner sent a message requesting his presence. Otherwise he would have been walking with us.' That niggled at her. What were the odds—the very morning Hugo was not with them, someone would attempt to abduct Kate?

'Most unfortunate. I doubt those fellows would have dared try for the child in his presence. I suggest you keep your nieces close, Lady Hartleigh. Perhaps take a male servant when you walk out until Guthrie returns. Good day to you.'

Chapter Eighteen

Hugo stared at Jacob Randall. 'I don't understand. You're saying that Althea Hartleigh's nieces *have* inherited money from old Miss Price? But Montague informed me that, in his words, *wiser council prevailed,* and Miss Price had not asked him to draw up a new will.' He paced around his office. 'You were there, damn it! You heard him.'

Jacob sipped his tea. 'I did. And that's perfectly true as far as it goes. Montague *didn't* draw up a new will for Miss Price. Robert Kentham, of Kentham & Hardbrace, drew it up.'

Hugo didn't know whether to laugh or swear. 'Have you spoken to Kentham?' He knew the man, a few years older than himself. Kentham was likeable and utterly trustworthy. He couldn't quite see the man poaching clients.

'He came in yesterday looking for you. That's why I sent for you. Apparently the lady named you as executor as well as trustee to the girls.'

'Montague must be apoplectic.' He could spare a moment for a little pleasure at that thought.

'He's not happy, no. He showed up yesterday, fortunately after Kentham left, breathing fire and brimstone and demanding your head on a pike, as it were.' Jacob didn't seem unduly perturbed by that. Then again, it wasn't *his* head being demanded. 'According to Kentham, Miss Price asked her neighbour to recommend a reputable lawyer—who turned out to be himself—wrote to him and requested that he call on her without announcing his profession. She sent him a visiting card with her signature scrawled on it. Then, after the will was drawn up, signed and witnessed, she made the neighbour promise to alert Kentham the moment she, er, shuffled off her mortal coil.'

Understanding flashed. 'She didn't trust Montague to draw up the will properly.'

Jacob nodded. 'She said as much to Kentham, although she also thought, even if Montague did draw it up, he might destroy it and pretend it never existed. As you divined, he also acts for the principal beneficiary of the previous will, Wilfrid Price-Babbington. Which—' he pursed his lips in mild disapproval '—does strike one as slightly poor form.'

'So Elinor Price found another lawyer to conduct her business, and let Montague think he'd won.' He had to admire the lady's tactics, even as he mentally cursed the mess this had left him in.

'That's it in a nutshell.' Jacob set his teacup down.

'Those two little girls you were supposed to consign to orphanages are now heiresses. And there's more.'

Suspicion bloomed. 'What more are we talking about now?'

Hugo listened to the *more* and thought that, if Montague ever realised the mess this left him in personally, the idiot might consider the loss of a slice of Price-Babbington's fortune worth it.

He groaned and buried his face in his hands.

Jacob frowned. 'Should have thought you'd be delighted at this outcome.' He rose from his chair. 'Come now, Hugo. There's no real question that you did anything at all dubious. Montague caused this mess by forcing his own client to go around him and use Kentham.' He snorted. 'If the way he bleated to me yesterday, about the folly of allowing women to manage their own money, is any indication of his manner with Miss Price, it's a wonder she left Price-Babbington so much as a groat. *I'd* have disinherited him entirely for the pleasure of knowing how much it would annoy Montague!'

Hugo straightened. 'You don't know the half of it. I've made a complete mull of this. I need to return to Petersham at once.'

Jacob shook his head. 'You can't. Montague and Kentham are both coming here tomorrow. I assured them you would be here.'

Now Hugo did swear.

Jacob raised his brows. 'Rather ripe for you, isn't it?'

Hugo didn't answer, considering the alternatives. He could send a messenger to Althea, but what good would that do? This was something he needed to explain in person. And she was returning to town tomorrow anyway. He'd have to call on her in Soho and tell her what had happened. All of it.

The sky wasn't going to collapse even more completely if he told her in London rather than Petersham.

Assuring Kate that she had been mistaken for someone else, someone wealthy, didn't convince the child that she wanted to go for a walk that afternoon.

Not without Uncle Hugo.

Even the suggestion of taking one of the male servants with them failed to get her through the front gate.

'You and Sarah go, Aunt Althea. I... I don't feel very well.'

Shock, Althea thought. The fierce bravado of biting the kidnapper and escaping had worn off, leaving the child scared and insecure. She even looked pale.

'Perhaps a sleep, Kate.' The child might feel better after a rest.

It spoke volumes for how shaken Kate was that she didn't argue against the prospect of an afternoon nap, and allowed herself to be tucked up and the curtains drawn.

She woke screaming from a nightmare.

Aunt Sue urged Althea to stay on with the girls. 'Hugo won't mind at all, dear.'

But Althea held firm. 'I'll take them back to London in the morning as we planned, Aunt Sue.'

Aunt Sue sighed. 'If you think it for the best, dear. I'll keep an ear out and write to you when those men have been caught. It won't take long. They sound most inefficient. And Kate gave Sir William a very good description of the man she bit.' She leaned over and patted Althea's hand. 'Then you can bring them back for another visit later in the year. Come for Christmas, as I suggested. Kate won't feel scared if Hugo is here, and when she knows that the fellow is in Newgate!'

Althea and the girls reached Soho by the middle of the next day. Kate was still pale and inclined to cling. The suggestion that they might send a note around to see if she could visit Miss Barclay for a piano lesson brightened her considerably.

'May I?' Then her face fell. 'But, what if that man—'

'He doesn't know where we live, Kate,' Sarah pointed out.

Still, Kate bit her lip as she unpacked her clothes.

'John and I will both walk around there with you,' Althea assured her. 'And we'll both come to fetch you.'

The note being duly sent, a reply came back that Miss Barclay would be delighted to see Kate for a lesson.

Althea walked back, missing the fresh air of the

countryside, and reminded herself that she did like London. That she liked the bustle, even the noise, although perhaps not so much the smells. She wrinkled her nose at the persistent odour of over-boiled cabbage, and all the refuse of a large city full of animals and humanity.

Reaching home, she discovered that Sarah had removed herself to the little garden behind the house and was doing a watercolour of a pot of flowers.

'For Uncle Hugo, to thank him for having us to stay,' Sarah explained when Althea walked out to check on her. 'And I thought to do another that he can take out to Aunt Sue when he visits again.'

With time to herself Althea settled down at her desk and started reading herself back into her neglected book. Two days away from the story and she had completely lost the flow. Frowning, she picked up a pencil to make notes on a sheet of paper. Half an hour later the clanging doorbell dragged her away from the belated discovery that Lydia hated seed cake because the seeds became stuck in her teeth. Puck's nose appeared hopefully from under the desk.

Althea's heart leapt. *Hugo?*

She squashed the thought instantly. If he called, he called. If he didn't, she was perfectly content to be as she was.

Blessedly single.

The door opened to admit John. 'Ah, there's—'

'Stand aside, man.' John was hustled aside by a

blue-coated man Althea recognised for a Bow Street Runner. Two more followed him.

She rose politely. 'Good afternoon, Officer. Is something amiss? Is this about that business at Petersham? Have they caught the men?'

'Lady Hartleigh?'

His tone chilled her. 'Yes.'

'Lady Hartleigh, you are under arrest for abduction.'

Her jaw dropped. She felt it. Thought, let alone speech, was an impossibility.

'Aunt Althea, what do you—oh. I'm sorry.' Sarah stood in the doorway, sketchbook in hand. 'I didn't realise you had someone with you.'

The Runner turned. 'Miss Sarah Price?'

'Yes.' She gave the Runner a tentative smile. 'How do you do, sir?'

'Very well, thanking you, miss. Where's your sister?'

Sarah looked at Althea. 'Aunt—'

'Officer Derby. Bow Street, miss. We're here to get you back where you belong.'

Althea found her voice. 'What the devil are you talking about? *I* reported the attempted abduction of my younger niece at Petersham yesterday! My nieces belong with me.'

Derby strode forward. 'Not according to the magistrate, they don't.'

'*What?* Which magistrate?'

'You'll have to come along with me.' He glanced

at his men. 'Marston, you stay with this young lady. Phipps, search the house for the other girl. The pair of you are to take them back to their guardian when you've found her.'

'Yes, sir.'

One man left the room and the other strode forward to set a hand on Sarah's shoulder.

'Aunt Althea isn't going anywhere with you!' Sarah shook off the officer's hand and ranged herself at Althea's side. 'She's our aunt! You should be looking for the men who tried to abduct my sister!'

'I don't know about that, miss, but I was warned you'd likely not understand.' Derby's voice was not unkind. 'The fact is you and your sister were abducted by your aunt. It's my job to get you back to your home.'

'Abducted by Aunt Althea? What are you talking about?' Sarah's voice rose.

Derby cleared his throat. 'Well, miss, *abducted* means—'

'My niece knows what it means.' Althea pressed a warning hand to Sarah's shoulder. 'She wants to know why you think they were abducted by me. There must be some confusion. I reported the attempted abduction of my younger niece to Sir William Banner in Petersham yesterday. And how dare you set your fellow to search my house?'

Derby's eyes narrowed. 'We've a warrant, ma'am. For your arrest and the recovery of the two girls. And it's not my place to explain your lies to the poor young lady. Her guardian will do all that. Now. You'll come along with me. Let's not have a fuss and make things worse for the lass.'

Guardian? Althea's mind started to move again. As far as she knew, there was only one other person who could legally claim to be the girls' guardian.

'Officer, if my cousin—'

Derby stepped forward, reaching for her, and Puck growled furiously, ranging himself in front of his mistress.

Derby stopped dead, his expression grim. 'Call him off, Lady Hartleigh. I like dogs, but I have to do my duty and the little chap deserves better.'

Althea's stomach churned. 'Puck. Sit. Enough.' She turned to Sarah. 'Hold his collar.'

'You aren't going with them?' Sarah clutched at Althea's hand, even as she bent to grip the dog's collar.

What choice did she have? She patted Sarah's hand. 'I'll have to.' She found a smile. 'Don't worry. I'll be back before you know it.'

'It must be a mistake! A…a silly joke someone is playing! No one else wanted us. Not even Cousin Wilfrid!'

The child's voice shook, ripping at Althea's assumed calm, but the mention of Wilfrid hardened her fear into resolve. 'And the easiest way to sort all this out will be for me to go with this officer and see what's what.' She turned to Derby. 'If you would permit me to walk out of the room without laying hands on me, that will ensure my niece keeps control of my dog. Or rather...' She turned to John. 'If you would be so kind as to carry that message...' She hesitated. The last thing she wanted to do was give away Kate's whereabouts. 'To Lady Martin. Take the dog with you, please.'

The flicker of John's eyelids suggested that he understood completely. 'Aye, ma'am. I'll do that.' He took Puck's leash from its hook and walked over to him, bending to attach it. He looked up. 'Should I take him to Mr Guthrie for safekeeping, ma'am?'

Her breath caught. 'Thank you. I can trust him to care for a dog.' Please God, let Hugo still be in London. 'Go now.'

Before the other officer came back without Kate.

Derby frowned. 'I don't know that's—'

'You have a warrant for me, sir. Not my servants. And certainly not for my dog.'

Derby backed down, scowling, and John left the room with a reluctant Puck. A moment later Althea heard the front door bang. She breathed a little more easily. Kate was safe. For now.

She turned to Sarah, bent close. 'Will you trust me?'

Sarah nodded. 'Kate?' she breathed.

'You have no idea where she is. Be brave.' She straightened up and spoke louder. 'I assume Cousin Wilfrid has thought the better of his decision not to act as guardian to you and Kate.' She caught the tell-tale flicker in Derby's expression. 'A shame he didn't think to write and tell me.'

Sarah's face turned even more mutinous. 'Then you could have written back that we don't want to live with *him*.'

Phipps strode back into the room. 'Sir, there's no sign of the other child. Housemaid and the cook said they had no idea where she might be.'

Althea caught her breath. Mrs Cable and Milly were lying. Deliberately lying for her. They knew exactly where Kate was.

Derby glared at Althea. 'Where is she?'

Althea lifted her chin, ignoring the fear twisting sick and cold in her belly. 'I'll discuss that with a magistrate. Shouldn't you get on with arresting me?'

Please God, she wasn't about to spend the night in Newgate. And please, please God, Hugo would be able to sort this out. Clearly Wilfrid had decided that he wanted the girls. Perhaps there had been gossip about his behaviour in throwing them out, but why go about it this way?

Derby's jaw hardened. 'Right. Phipps, Marston, you take the young lady we do have back to Mr Price-Babbington. I'll deliver our fine lady to Bow Street.'

Hugo strode into Bow Street Magistrates' Court late in the afternoon, his mind ice cold. He had a suspicion he knew exactly what was going on, and cursed himself for not seeing this possibility as soon as he'd known that Montague had been outfoxed by Elinor Price. If he'd sent a message out to Petersham explaining the situation, Althea would have remained there rather than returning to an ambush. He shoved that aside. What mattered now was getting her released.

Please God, he wasn't going to find her in a cell!

When he'd reached Soho Square to inform Althea that Elinor Price had died, he'd found the cook and housemaid in a state of panic.

'Just marched her off, sir,' Milly had sniffled. *'And they took Miss Sarah. Said she'd been abducted by the mistress!'*

'My lady foxed them, though. Good an' proper.' Mrs Cable had said it with pride leaking through the fear. *'Little Miss Kate was gone for her music lesson. My lady refused to say where she was, an' we played dumb. John was already gone to find you.'*

Hugo thought he knew what had happened. Price-Babbington, realising his mistake in throwing the girls out, had brought abduction charges against Althea to cover his own callousness. Hugo clenched his fists. He had to remind himself that the law was his best weapon, and he had to wield it with logic, not emotion.

At the magistrate's, at this hour, there was only a clerk still at his desk to raise his head as Hugo stalked in, Puck beside him. Upon reaching his chambers after leaving Soho, he'd found John and the dog waiting in his office. He had tried to leave Puck with his own office clerk, but Puck had howled piteously, scrabbling to follow him. In the end he'd given in and taken the dog with him.

Now the court clerk stared at the dog, then raised his eyes to Hugo's face. 'May I help you, sir?'

'I am looking for Lady Hartleigh. I hope—' he paused for effect '—I hope, as will her good friends, the Earl and Countess of Rutherford, and Lord and Lady Martin Lacy, that she is being looked after, and that she has not been subjected to any distress.' That was a large assumption, as the earl and countess were away in the country. Lady Martin, though—or perhaps it was Miss Selbourne, as she had been in the shop—had immediately sent a note to her husband when Hugo had gone to the bookshop to ask her where he might find Lacy.

To do the clerk credit, he looked as though titled gentlemen and their ladies were tossed about so regularly as to be inconsequential. In fact, he scowled. 'The lady is here, sir. I don't know that I have any authority to allow you to see her, though.'

Hugo kept his expression inscrutable. 'I will see her immediately, if you please. And Birnie, if he is here.' He had a nodding acquaintance with Sir Richard Birnie, the Chief Magistrate.

The scowl deepened. 'And who might you be, sir?'

'Guthrie, of Guthrie and Randall.' He gave the address in Lincoln's Inn. 'Lady Hartleigh is my client.'

The clerk nodded slowly. 'Right. Sir Richard's not here, sir. 'Twas on the authority of one of the other magistrates that we put the lady in his office with a Runner on the door. Being as how there was some concern that the cells might not be the best place.'

Inside him the knot of fear unclenched itself. *Thank God.* 'Very wise.'

'But I've no authority to allow the prisoner—'

'The *what*?' Hugo leaned forward, resting clenched fists on the desk. 'Let me be very clear, my good man. Arresting Lady Hartleigh was a mistake of some magnitude. I advise you not to compound it.'

The clerk swallowed. 'I'll fetch Mr Wilcox, the magistrate on duty. He'll know what should be done.'

Hugo nodded benignly. 'An excellent idea. But first you will conduct me to Lady Hartleigh.'

For a moment the air hummed with the clash of wills.

Hugo smiled. 'Come, my good man. Do you imagine that I am about to slip Lady Hartleigh out from under your nose? It can do no possible harm for me to see her, and may do those in charge of this institution a great deal of good with her friends.'

'Ah, yes, sir.' He rallied. 'Er, the dog—'

'Stays with me.'

Puck walked sedately at heel until they reached the door of Sir Richard Birnie's office. At which point, ignoring the Runner guarding the door, he lunged forward, snuffling and scrabbling at the door.

The Runner blinked at Puck, then looked at the clerk. 'Mr Sutherland?'

'Yes, yes.' Sutherland waved. 'Officer Derby, this is Lady Hartleigh's solicitor. I have said he may wait with the lady while I fetch Mr Wilcox.'

The Runner frowned. 'You're not armed, I hope, sir?'

Hugo snorted. 'Hardly. Nor is the dog. Don't worry. My intentions are to remain law abiding.'

As long as possible.

The Runner opened the door and Puck shot forward, barking, ripping his leash from Hugo's grasp.

Chapter Nineteen

Althea shifted position in the chair yet again. It was not at all a comfortable chair, but there was a limit to how many times one could circumnavigate a magistrate's office. There was also a limit to how long one could sit still with nothing to do. A lengthy inspection had convinced her that the many books on the shelves, while doubtless interesting to a magistrate, were not at all the sort of thing she could contemplate poring over.

She froze at the faint commotion outside the door. Male voices, and…scratching? For the past three hours she had slowly sunk into herself, wondering exactly when someone would decide that she was a great deal less trouble in a cell, with whatever other prisoners they happened to have on hand.

Or in Newgate itself. Perhaps she could put in a plea for the Fleet if they decided she was destined for an actual prison.

She had pinned all her hopes on dealing directly

with Sir Richard Birnie, with whom she had a very slight acquaintance, and persuading him to allow her to go home. Mr Wilcox, a very junior magistrate, had declined to acquiesce in this without Sir Richard's authority. Much against the advice of the office clerk and Timms, Wilcox had decided that she would remain in this office for the time being. No doubt that was a great deal better than a cell, but—

The door opened. Perhaps someone had made a decision—she stiffened her rapidly wilting spine and prepared to argue in favour of the less dangerous Fleet Prison.

Barking wildly, Puck hurled himself across the room and onto her lap, nearly oversetting the chair and herself with it. Dazed, Althea clutched the dog, submitting to having her face thoroughly licked, hearing the frantic whines. It was a moment before she managed to look past the dog and see who had followed him into the room.

Hugo.

Her throat closed on a choking lump, and she realised in horror that she was seeing him through a mist of tears. She would *not* cry. Not in front of Hugo, and not in front of the Runner who had arrested her, or the clerk who had wanted to lock her in a cell.

'You will accord us a few moments privacy, gentlemen.'

Had she ever heard Hugo speak with that air of cool command? As though he not only expected to be heeded, but the notion of not being obeyed wasn't to be considered.

It worked. Derby and the clerk frowned, but the door closed behind Hugo.

He stood there for a moment, and she struggled for words. A simple thank you. Anything.

'I—' Her throat closed, and a lump rose up. She dragged a breath past it to try again. But Hugo crossed the room, hauled her up out of the chair and had her in his arms in the space of that despicably shaky breath.

That was all it took. Her control broke and she wept. Great, racking sobs that horrified her even as the fear ebbed. Whatever happened now, even a prison cell, she wasn't alone. And he didn't tell her not to cry, but held her close, stroked her back and somehow lent her his own strength.

Slowly the sobs eased—she sniffled, and found a very large handkerchief pushed into her hand.

'It's perfectly clean,' he assured her.

She managed a watery laugh. Of course it was. She wiped her eyes and blew her nose. She became aware of Puck, standing on his hind legs, pawing at her gown, whining. 'It's all right, boy. Everything's all right now.'

Hugo cleared his throat. 'A slight exaggeration. John told me the charge was abduction. Of Kate and Sarah.'

She nodded. 'Yes. I don't understand. The only person who could have brought a charge of abduction is Cousin Wilfrid, but why would he bother? And the girls aren't heiresses, which is what the Runner said. Wilfrid of all people—'

'I'm afraid they are.'

'What? That's what the Runners said, but—'

The rest was smothered against his chest as he pulled her back into his arms. 'I'm sorry. This is my fault.'

'Your fault?' She looked up at him. 'Were you supposed to anticipate that Wilfrid would slip his moorings?'

He let out a frustrated breath. 'Yes. I suspected weeks—months ago that the girls were heiresses, but I said nothing to you. I couldn't. And then the day before I came out to Petersham I was told, point-blank, that they weren't, so—'

'What are you talking about? You're not making sense.'

He wasn't, either. Best to give her the pertinent information straight. 'Your great-aunt changed her will.'

'*Elinor*?'

He raked a hand through his hair. 'Yes. Your great-aunt, Miss Price—'

'Great-Aunt Elinor? She's died?'

'Yes. She called on me in the office. Not long after she called on you. Before she died. Asked a number of very nosy questions—'

'A talent of hers.'

He smiled briefly. 'Most of which I declined to answer, because they encompassed your private affairs. But I confirmed for her that the girls were with you because their father had left them penniless, and Price-Babbington had given instructions for them to be entered in orphanages.'

Althea frowned. 'There was no secret about that.'

'No. She'd gathered that from various other sources, but she wanted confirmation from me.'

'I don't see why that makes you think—'

'Althea, love, she had her own solicitor there.'

He told her the rest. Montague's subsequent visit, and the contents of the message that had brought him tearing back to London from Petersham. 'I'm sorry, Althea. I should have brought the three of you with me, or at the very least told you what was afoot, but I thought there must be some mistake.'

Althea's stomach turned over. 'Wilfrid must know.' She shut her eyes. Two penniless orphans were one thing. Two heiresses were quite something else. And he'd let them slip through his fingers.

Hugo spoke again. 'This is going to make them Wards of the Chancery Court. I'm sorry. I should have said something.'

She shook her head. 'Never mind that. This explains the abduction attempt.'

'*Abduction?*' He gripped her shoulders. 'What happened?'

She told him.

He swore. 'Price-Babbington has overreached himself with this. I know they removed Sarah, but John said Kate wasn't home, and Mrs Cable and Milly told me they lied—told the Runners they didn't know where she was.'

Althea bit her lip. 'I didn't tell them to say that, but she's only a baby. Surely—'

'Sweetheart, if we're to have the least chance of winning this, and of avoiding spending the night in a cell together—'

'They haven't arrested *you*, have they?'

'No, but if you think I'd let you spend the night in a cell by yourself, then you don't know me at all.' He gave her a gentle shake. 'Kate. We're going to have to produce her.'

She understood what he was saying, but—

'Abduction, Althea. It's serious. Especially when heiresses are involved, depending on how Birnie looks at it. I think if we promise to bring Kate tomorrow, then I can have you released into my custody. It shows good faith.'

Her stomach roiled. 'And you think Wilfrid will show good faith?'

He snorted. 'Not willingly. But I think we can force his hand. And if we can show that he hasn't acted in good faith? Show that he did not act in the girls' best interests? The magistrate won't like that. As for trying to snatch Kate at Petersham, if that's what it was about, he's sunk.'

'Will the magistrate care?'

'Yes, I think he will. I need to consult my law books

for the precise wording, but a guardian must act in the best interests of his ward. And there's something else. Sarah is nearly fourteen. She is old enough for the court to give consideration to what she says. She can request a change of guardian.'

'But Wilfrid wouldn't bring her with him.' Althea knew that. He considered women, let alone girls, flibberty creatures, not to be permitted within spitting distance of any serious *men's* business, let alone a court of law.

Hugo's smile was close to a smirk. 'If the court requests that he bring her and he doesn't, then he is not merely showing bad faith, he'll be disobeying a court order. His solicitor, even an idiot like Montague, will advise against that.'

Her stomach twisted. 'But how *can* the court make that request? Sir Richard isn't even here. He wouldn't know about—'

He smiled. 'You're friendly with an influential countess. Not to mention Lord Martin Lacy. You changed your own will and set up trusts for the girls. You've been seeing to their education. You've demonstrated yourself to be a responsible guardian. I think we can count on Birnie being fully informed as to those particulars before he reaches for his after-dinner port this evening. I've sent a message to Lacy about the importance of having both girls present. Lady Martin assured me that he would run Birnie to ground for us and see to it.'

It took another half-hour before the magistrate on duty agreed to release Althea into Hugo's custody. Finally it was done, and he could escort her out onto Bow Street, Althea's hand on his arm and Puck at their heels.

Althea took a deep, shaky breath. 'I know I was lucky—no, privileged, because most other females would have been tossed into a cell, but I thought—'

He pressed his hand to hers as she broke off. 'Don't. You're safe now. Come. We'll find a cab and get you home.'

If he thought about Althea in a prison cell, he'd go insane. He couldn't imagine what it had been like for her.

The clatter of traffic between Bow Street and Soho was hideous, but Althea was only vaguely aware of it. The din was somewhere *out there*, beyond the circle of safety within the hackney cab, the reassurance of Hugo's large hand clasping hers.

The conditions of her release into his custody were stringent. He must remain with her at all times. She must not so much as step outside her house without his escort. If she defaulted, or failed to present herself at Bow Street with Kate at ten o'clock the following morning, she would be arrested when found and placed in prison. As would Hugo.

Desperate to control her panic, she focused on the practical. They had to collect poor Kate. The child would be frantic by now. What would Psyché Barclay have told her? That her aunt had been arrested for abducting her? That her sister had been taken? She pushed all that down.

'Kate may share my chamber tonight,' she said carefully. 'That leaves the girls' room free for you to use.'

He nodded. 'Thank you. If you permit, I will send John to collect some items from my lodgings.'

'Of course.'

At the Barclay house a servant informed them that the mistress was visiting Miss Selbourne's bookshop. Althea swallowed hard. She wanted nothing more than to get off the street, be somewhere private that she could fall to pieces. She took a breath. She could walk back down Compton Street to Kit Selbourne's shop. The strength of Hugo's arm under her hand, the sheer calm of his presence, his quiet voice as he thanked the servant, were more comfort than she could have expressed. She smiled her own thanks at Psyché Barclay's servant and accompanied Hugo blindly back down the street.

Kate was safe. She had to concentrate on that, on Hugo's steady conviction that they could get Sarah back. If they failed, if she lost Kate as well—

She couldn't think like that. She had to remain strong, steady, the sort of woman who could care for two orphaned girls. Her stomach roiled. Wilfrid would use every means at his disposal to discredit her.

Her less than virtuous past, the fact that it looked as though she had lost her own fortune.

The shop was already shuttered for the evening, but Kit opened the door to let them in.

'She's here. Quite safe but very upset. I'll let her know you've arrived. We persuaded her to stay upstairs with my boys until you did.'

Althea gripped her hands. 'Thank you. I... Thank you.'

Kit squeezed Althea's hands. 'You're very welcome. Martin has gone to do what he can to ensure Birnie knows what's going on. He's also going to seek out someone from the Chancery Court, a school friend's father. Come. Sit down. You must be exhausted.' She beckoned to Psyché Barclay, who stood in the archway that led through to the circulating library. 'Psyché, sit Althea down and pour her a glass of wine.' She smiled at Hugo. 'And you. Thank you for bringing her back.'

She left them and her swift footsteps sounded on the stairs.

Psyché hugged Althea, guiding her through to the library. 'We brought her here because it seemed a little safer. And I'm afraid we sneaked her around through the back alleys. Your servants all knew where she was and, really, you couldn't have blamed them if they'd let it out when threatened with arrest. She told us some fellow tried to abduct her out at Petersham.'

Althea was nearly beyond words. 'Thank you. Yes.

We…we think my cousin, the one who kicked them out, was behind that.' She gripped Psyché's hand. 'Thank you. More than I can say.'

Psyché shook her head. 'It was nothing. We're having supper here, all of us, to help you work out how to present your case tomorrow. Although,' she nodded at Hugo, 'you already have Mr Guthrie on hand.'

Scrambling feet sounded on the stairs, and a moment later Kate shot through the archway and hurled herself at Althea.

'You escaped!'

Althea's arms closed tightly around her as the child wept. 'Escaped?'

Psyché winced. 'We told her the truth. Anything else seemed pointless. One of Kit's boys promised her that Mr Guthrie would break her out of prison if necessary and that his father would help.' She gave Hugo an apologetic look. 'He's only fifteen. They've been up there working out the details with Kate.'

Althea gave a choking laugh as she guided Kate to the settee. Slowly she became aware that Hugo was sitting at Kate's other side, gently stroking her back. Her eyes burned, but she forced the tears back. Hugo's kindness threatened to undo her completely.

'Not quite an escape, Kate, love. I did a great deal of talking, as solicitors are wont to do, and persuaded a magistrate that he could either release your aunt into my custody or listen to me talk all night.'

He glanced up at Psyché. 'Do you happen to know where Lady Hartleigh's manservant is, ma'am? I need to send him to my lodgings.'

'He's here, Mr Guthrie, but if you require a change of clothes or a nightshirt, my husband said you were very welcome to borrow what you needed.'

He blinked. 'How very kind. Unfortunately I also need to consult my copy of *Blackstone's Commentaries on the Laws of England*.'

'I have a copy upstairs.' Miss Selbourne came through the archway. 'I'll take you up and we can bring them down if you wish.'

'*You* have a copy?'

Psyché gave a snort of a laughter as she poured another glass of wine. 'If it has a leather binding and pages in between, the odds are high that Kit has a copy somewhere.'

Miss Selbourne picked up a candle. 'I only wish! Come up and fetch the volume you need, Mr Guthrie.'

Hugo followed Kit upstairs into what he supposed was a dining parlour overlooking the street, wholly lined with bookshelves. He wondered if he could somehow invite himself back some time to explore this paradise properly. And why hadn't he ever thought of lining a dining parlour with bookshelves?

Unerringly, she went to a shelf by the window.

'Here we are. Which volume? I would assume the first, since it deals with the rights of persons, but—'

He stared in bemusement. It was one thing to have the books on her shelves, but for a female to be familiar with the contents of *Blackstone's Commentaries* was unusual to say the least. 'You are absolutely correct, Miss—' He broke off, still unsure how to address her.

She laughed, taking out the volume. 'Miss Selbourne is appropriate. If I am out somewhere official with Lord Martin I become Lady Martin, but here at home, or in the shop, I am Miss Selbourne for the most part.'

He took the volume she passed him. 'Is that confusing?'

'To me, no. Nor to Lord Martin. We know who I am.' Her smile was challenge incarnate. 'The sort of woman who knows her way around Blackstone's.'

Downstairs in the library Althea watched from the sofa, Kate snuggled against her, as Hugo opened the volume on the table, checking the table of contents.

'Won't the magistrates already know all this?' she asked.

He glanced up, flipping through the book. 'They do of course.' Here it was. *Chapter the Seventeenth: of Guardian and Ward.* 'But possession is involved here—your unspeakable cousin has Sarah—and there is the inescapable fact of your brother's will. We need to make our case, and make it in law. I want to be quite sure I have it all at my fingertips.'

He took a careful breath. What had Kit Selbourne said?

'The sort of woman who knows her way around Blackstone's.'

Althea was the sort of woman who could learn to find her way around Blackstone's. A woman with a spine of tempered steel, and a mind that thought for itself.

'Come and look.' He returned his attention to the page, as Althea—and Kate, clinging to her hand—joined him.

'Why does Cousin Wilfrid have Sarah?' Kate demanded. 'He didn't want us. I heard him say so.'

Hugo looked up sharply. 'Did you, sweetheart?'

Althea looked down at her. 'You never said anything about that.'

Kate wriggled closer. 'I didn't want to think about him at all.'

'What exactly did he say, Kate?' Hugo pulled a paper towards him, picked up a pencil. The child had a musician's memory—he'd heard her recite a half-heard conversation before.

'That he wasn't going to be saddled with the cost of two blasted little pauper bitches, and he wouldn't have tainted goods in his house corrupting his sons.'

'He said that in front of you?' Althea's voice remained even, but Hugo heard the bite of fury underneath. It found an answer in the fury simmering under his own outward calm.

Kate hung her head. 'Not exactly. I was hungry, so I'd gone downstairs to the kitchen to ask Mrs Minchin for something to eat. He was saying it to Cousin Mary—you know…his wife—in the parlour when I was on my way back, but the door was open a little bit and I heard him. Then he said he'd write to *"Frederick's lawyer fellow"*—that was you I think, Mr Guthrie—and tell him we'd be on the stagecoach the next week. He was washing his hands of us because there was little enough money as it was until the old lady died.'

Hugo met Althea's gaze. 'And he did write to me, and I met you.'

'Yes. And we weren't so scared any more.' Even with her tear-blotched cheeks, Kate gave him a trusting smile.

They must have been terrified, but he doubted even Sarah had fully understood the dangers that had awaited two young girls stepping off that stagecoach. Even now he wondered what might have happened to them had Wilfrid's letter gone astray. The girls' youth would not have saved them. Quite the opposite.

He pushed the pencil and paper towards the child. 'Write it down, Kate.'

She stared at him. 'Write what down?'

'What you just told us. And anything else you can remember that Wilfrid Price-Babbington said, either to you or about you.' Even if he didn't use it in tomorrow's hearing, it gave Kate something to do. Also, it might bring up a bit more evidence he could present to the magistrate.

'Even the rude words?'

He inclined his head, suppressing a grin. 'Certainly the rude words. Never tamper with the text in a legal document, sweetheart.'

She looked up at him very seriously. 'Why not?'

'Because you might change the meaning of what was said. It's important that the magistrate tomorrow knows *exactly* what your cousin said.' And what he'd meant.

'It doesn't make him sound like a very nice person, though.'

Hugo let the smile come. 'No. It doesn't, does it?'

Pauper bitches. It was an admission that Wilfrid Price-Babbington hadn't given a damn about the girls until they inherited money.

As the child settled into a chair and began to write, frowning in concentration, Hugo turned his attention back to *Blackstone's*.

He read slowly down the page, fiercely aware of Althea at his side, scanning the text with him.

'There. Is this what you need?' She looked up, her finger paused on the line that read: *at fourteen is at years of legal discretion, and may choose a guardian.*

Close, so close to him, her light scent enveloping him as it had every night at Petersham for nearly a week. It was oddly soothing for a change—it meant she was here, safe with him, not in prison. 'That's part of it. When does Sarah turn fourteen precisely?'

Althea bit her lip. 'Next month. Will it make a difference that she isn't quite fourteen yet?'

'I doubt it.' He reached out, laid his hand over hers and felt the slight tremor. 'We lawyers are very good at holding things up and stringing things out.'

She raised those elegant brows, even as her hand turned under his and clung. 'To everything there is a season, and a time for every purpose?'

He smiled. 'Quite so.' Hearing the airy sarcasm back in her voice lifted his heart, just as her fingers, warm and delicate in his, made it beat the faster. He pushed his mind back to *Blackstone's*. 'And there's more in here that I can use. Price-Babbington has made a mull of this.'

Kit Selbourne spoke. 'You may take those volumes along with you tomorrow, if you wish, Mr Guthrie.'

He looked up. It would help—

'There's no need.' Althea smiled at Kit. 'Thank you, though. Sir Richard Birnie has a set in his office.'

Hugo blinked. 'I suppose he would, but—you're sure?'

She shrugged. 'There wasn't a great deal to do in that office *except* look at the bookshelves. None of it looked frightfully inviting, but I do remember the name Blackstone. That was our coachman's name when I was a child.'

Chapter Twenty

Hugo listened to the little house creak and settle into comfortable darkness around him. Sleep held off, out of reach in the shadows. The room, even in darkness, seemed full of the girls, brimming with their energy—a discarded ribbon on the dresser, along with several pretty crystal bottles. They didn't look new, but he knew they hadn't had them when they stayed with him, so Althea must have found them. Had they been hers? Something treasured that she had given the girls to help them feel at home? Loved? Secure?

He lay back with a sigh. Althea loved those girls. What if he couldn't persuade the courts that she was the right guardian for them? Her past and reputation wasn't going to help, and he had no doubt that Price-Babbington wouldn't hesitate to use it. And even if he had the time and means to dig up some scurrilous affair in the man's life, it was always different for men.

Men were expected to have affairs. Oh, there might be a little tut-tutting over it, but no one was going to declare a man an unfit guardian because he'd bedded a dozen women not his wife—even if he'd been married at the time. Whereas Althea, from all he understood, had indulged in a couple of reasonably discreet affairs once she'd been widowed.

He laced his fingers behind his head, reviewing his strategy for tomorrow's meeting at Bow Street. It was vital to show that Wilfrid was an unfit guardian because of the way he had treated the girls. Casting them out, not caring where they ended up, He had not acted in their best interests, and that was a basic tenet of guardianship. He had only taken an interest once they had become heiresses.

His mind caught on that. He didn't know the exact terms of Elinor Price's will. Robert Kentham had explained the gist, and given him a copy, of course, but he'd left it on his desk when he'd gone to call on Althea.

Who was the next heir if something happened to the girls? He could assume that if one of the girls died the other would inherit her sister's share. But what if something happened to both of them? The courts ensured that children left in ward were cared for by someone who could not inherit. Kentham would have seen to that, surely. If not, then the court would have no choice but to name another guardian.

Hugo let out a breath. He knew, as surely as he knew the colour of her eyes, the way her mouth curled into that delicious, wicked smile, what choice Althea would make if she could. She would refuse the bequest rather than lose the girls.

Staring into the darkness, Hugo called down every curse he could think of on the head of Frederick Price for leaving his daughters in such a mess.

Althea lay awake, unable to sleep with the lamp burning. But Kate, poor little Kate, even curled up in the same bed, with Puck snuggled against her, had begged for the light. Even with the lamp it had taken a long time and several stories for the child to doze off, her eyes red and swollen with tears.

She had heard Hugo come up to bed long after she had taken Kate upstairs. There had been a comfort hearing him move around the girls' room, hearing the bed creak under his weight. Before the girls came, she had learned to enjoy living alone, to savour her independence. Now she dreaded tomorrow, and the likelihood that Wilfrid would take Kate and Sarah from her.

Long ago she had decided that regrets were a waste of energy. You might come to the conclusion that something or other had been a colossal mistake. You acknowledged that and put it aside. If your mistake had hurt someone else, you tried to make amends. You did not waste time beating your breast over it. Or at least she didn't. Much. Sometimes, though, you couldn't help it.

This was one of those times.

Sitting up against her pillows in the lamplight, she

wished bitterly that she had not indulged in those affairs. Not because she thought that she'd been wrong to do so. Those affairs had harmed no one, and after the cold mockery of her marriage she had wanted *something*. She had been a widow, for God's sake. Neither gentlemen involved had been married at the time. No one would have cared a finger-snap, if her idiot brother had not wanted to cover up his own misdoings by painting *her* as a feckless, irresponsible slut.

By having those affairs she had handed him all the ammunition he could have wanted. Society always enjoyed a good scandal and she had provided one. Ironic that the one person who might have resented her, Meg Rutherford, had become a close friend.

And Meg would have used her influence to facilitate her return to the *ton*.

'*Don't, Meg. And for heaven's sake, don't allow Rutherford to do so. Even if I wanted it, I can't afford it. If I am careful I have enough to live simply.*'

'*You truly don't want to come back?*'

'*Truly.*'

'*What about the truth? Doesn't that matter?*'

She had smiled. Meg was still young and naïve enough to believe that truth would always out.

'*Even that is no longer important. You know the truth. Rutherford knows. And a few others. People I am fond of. Who are fond of me. Why should I care what the rest think?*'

And she no longer had the energy to fight back.

Meg had scowled. *'Because lies can always come back to bite you.'*

Althea sighed. Perhaps Meg had not been so naïve, and she should have fought back against Frederick's lies. Instead she had removed herself from society, and the lies he had told to protect himself, and made a new life. She had found peace, contentment and just lately joy. But now those lies had come back to sink their teeth into everything that mattered, and tear it to pieces.

Beside her Kate tossed, muttered, her voice rising in panic.

'*Shh*, dearest.' She stroked the soft hair. 'It's a dream. Only a dream. You're safe.' A lie, but what else could she say?

But the nightmare held Kate fast as she thrashed, crying out. On the child's other side Puck sat up, pawed at her shoulder, whining.

Kate came awake on a scream—*'Sarah!'*—as the door flew open.

For a moment Althea thought the child was not quite awake, her eyes dazed and confused as she struggled against the bedclothes. Then her arms closed around the dog, now in her lap, and she folded over him, weeping.

That Hugo was now on the bed, holding Kate as she wept, seemed the most natural thing in the world.

'There now, Katie, love. Was it your old dream? It's gone now. You're safe.'

His voice, low, tender, made Kate sob even harder. 'It's not gone. It's worse. Because I did lose Sarah. She's gone! I ran and ran, but it was dark and I couldn't find her.'

Althea's arms tightened on the sobbing child. 'Only for now, Kate. We'll get her back. I promise you.'

Oh, God! What had she said? That was a promise she shouldn't make, couldn't be sure of keeping.

But between them the child's shuddering sobs eased.

On Kate's other side Hugo spoke. 'Listen, sweetheart. How old is Sarah?'

'Th…thirteen.'

'There you are.' He bent, pressed a kiss to Kate's temple. 'Nearly fourteen. And at fourteen she can choose her own guardian. It says so right in the law books. Do you really think she would choose your cousin Wilfrid?'

'No. But I'm not even *nearly* nearly fourteen. He might take me!'

Hugo's grim eyes met Althea's over Kate's head. 'Not once I've finished with him, he won't.' Cold determination burned in his voice and eyes.

'Can you stay here with us? Like you used to?'

Like you used to?

Althea *felt* Hugo stiffen, knew exactly what he was thinking, heard the indrawn breath.

'Would you feel safer if he did, Kate?' She kept her voice casual.

'Yes. He used to tell me a story after.'

'That seems like a very proper thing to follow a bad dream.' Althea smiled at Hugo's slightly stunned, questioning gaze. 'Now, what story shall we hear from Mr Guthrie?'

By the time Hugo had wound his way through the tale of *Beauty and the Beast*, Kate was sound asleep between them. Althea had an arm around the sleeping child. Her head rested on his shoulder, her arm wedged against his side, and Kate herself was half on top of him. He suspected Althea was more than half-asleep, too.

So much for his skill as a storyteller. Damned if he knew how he was supposed to extricate himself, and he didn't mean from the bed. The dog at least had removed himself to the foot of the bed and lay on his back, snoring.

'She's had that dream before?' Althea murmured.

Not asleep then, although her head didn't move.

'Yes. I should have told you. She had it several times in the first week they stayed with me. After that—'

'She must have felt safe.' Althea sat up a little, but left her arm where it was. 'I don't think she's had it here before. What was it?'

Rage burned in his throat, but he kept his voice soft. 'She dreams that they get lost when they leave the stagecoach. It's very dark. At first they're together, but she becomes separated from Sarah in the darkness.'

'And when you heard her, you went in to them and comforted her.'

He squirmed. 'It's no more than anyone would do.'

A soft snort. 'Really? Can you see my cousin Wilfrid comforting a terrified child? Telling her a fairy tale to ease her back to sleep?'

He had no answer for that. 'Do you think we can shift her now? I... I ought not to be here.' No matter that it felt as though he were precisely where he ought to be, they had enough trouble without complicating it any further.

They tried. But when Hugo attempted to move the sleeping child, she stirred, muttering distressfully.

Althea let out a breath. 'I'll go and sleep in the other room. You stay here.'

She started to ease her arm free, and Kate cried out.

They stared at each other over the sleeping child.

'I think,' he said carefully, 'that we are sleeping together. Again.'

The movement of her throat as she swallowed did impossible things to his heart.

'Apparently so.' A moment's silence. 'Interesting pair of chaperons we've acquired.'

He smothered the escaping crack of laughter. 'Um, your head.'

Her eyes narrowed to glints of green. 'My head? Is something wrong with it?'

'What?' *Oh, Lord!* 'No. Not at all. It felt rather nice,

er, where it was.' And his tongue felt as though it had tied itself in a Gordian knot, along with his heart.

'Where it was.'

He held his breath, unsure if he were about to be annihilated. Then, miracle of miracles...

'Like this?'

Her head rested on his shoulder again and the entire world seemed right and good.

'Yes. Yes, exactly like that.' The slightly astringent fragrance of her hair surrounded him. Chamomile. His mother had planted a chamomile lawn when he was a small boy. He'd loved to lie on it reading on hot summer afternoons. Warily, he lowered his cheek to those silken tresses, relaxed when she shifted closer.

'This is nice,' she murmured. 'Even without your new watch.'

Walking into the Bow Street Magistrates' Court the following morning, Althea half wished she'd woken up with a crick in her neck so that she could at least have something to regret about the night before. Had she lost her mind permitting that simple, unspoken tenderness between them? What if one of her servants had come in?

Fortunately Kate, ever an early riser, had stirred before the servants came up. Althea had awoken, her head still on Hugo's shoulder, to a very serious conversation between Hugo and Kate about the merits of a boiled egg and toast soldiers versus a poached egg on a slice of toast.

Now, with Kate clutching her hand as they walked into Bow Street, she wondered how it was that a man should be as unspeakably appealing discussing eggs as he was telling fairytales. He walked beside Kate now, holding her other hand, a quiet, protective presence.

'Will Sarah really be here?'

Althea hesitated.

Hugo said calmly. 'Perhaps not yet. We are a little early. But we know your cousin Wilfrid received the message that he must bring her this morning.'

Kate nodded solemnly. 'Because Lord Martin said so.'

Lord Martin had called during the consumption of toast soldiers and boiled eggs to say that, in addition to finding Sir Richard Birnie, he had spoken to a friend's father the previous evening.

'Found him in the club after speaking to Birnie. Whittenstall is a decent chap, and he's appointed to the Chancery Court.'

According to Lord Martin, Whittenstall had been more than a little annoyed that Bow Street had become involved in a case of wardship, which was within the purview of the Chancery Court.

'Whittenstall has agreed to go along to Bow Street this morning to sort things out. He also agreed that both girls should be present, but particularly Sarah, and sent a note to Sir Richard about it.'

Althea plastered a calm smile to her face and lifted her chin. They had done everything that could possibly be done to prepare for this meeting. Please God, it would be enough.

Sir Richard was seated behind his desk and rose as they entered. He was not alone.

Sarah leapt to her feet from her place beside Wilfrid and hurled herself at them.

'Sarah!' Kate flung herself into her sister's arms, hugging her. 'You're safe!'

'Really! What an extraordinary thing for the child to say!' Wilfrid remained seated. 'I cannot imagine what you have been filling their ears with, Cousin Althea.'

Althea favoured him with a sweet smile. 'It was rather the other way around, Wilfrid. Until the girls turned up on my doorstep, I hadn't given you a thought in years. I believe you are acquainted with my solicitor, Mr Guthrie?'

Price-Babbington stared at Hugo, his eyes widening. 'I…er…yes. We have…ah…corresponded.' Turning to Sarah, he scowled. 'Kindly do not behave like a hoyden in here. Sit down, if you please, and conduct yourself as befits a young lady.'

Sir Richard spoke coolly. 'If this is for my benefit, Price-Babbington, I saw nothing untoward in Miss Price's behaviour. Only a very proper sisterly affection.'

Sarah bestowed a smile on the magistrate. 'May I sit with my sister, sir? I worried about her all night.'

Sir Richard eyed her closely. 'You may, but why would you have worried about her?'

'Because I knew she would be scared about what was happening, worrying about being taken away as I was. Especially after that horrid man tried to abduct her the other day.'

'I must protest, Sir Richard!' Wilfrid did rise now. 'Sarah was precisely where she ought to have been last night. Under my guardianship and protection. I have attempted to explain that to her, but I fear her mind has been poisoned against me!'

Sarah opened her mouth, caught the slight shake of Hugo's head, and shut it again.

Sir Richard frowned. 'We will come to all that. You will all please be seated. This should not take very long at all.'

Hugo frowned. That sounded as though the magistrate had already made up his mind.

'Your Honour, we should await Whittenstall from the Chancery Court, since we are dealing with a disputed guardianship.'

'So I have been given to understand, Mr... Guthrie, is it not?' Sir Richard inclined his head. 'I daresay that will prove useful on this occasion, but in future understand that I prefer to make my own arrangements in such matters.'

'Of course, Your Honour.' Hugo handed Althea to a

seat. 'I felt that with the meeting set for this morning, and to avoid further distress to the young ladies—'

'As to that,' Price-Babbington fairly galloped into his speech. 'I have suggested to Sir Richard that all this may be very easily cleared up. I am willing to accept that there has been a misunderstanding, and if Lady Hartleigh relinquishes in writing, here and now, all claim to my wards, then I am prepared to withdraw the charge of abduction.'

Hugo narrowed his eyes. *What the devil?*

Sir Richard leaned forward. 'You see that this simplifies matters. What does your client say, Guthrie? Less upset for the young ladies, and your client avoids the very nasty charge of abducting two heiresses.'

'*No.*'

Chapter Twenty-One

Althea had spoken before Hugo could even draw breath.

'It is a very generous offer, Cousin!' snapped Price-Babbington. 'And one that I shall not hold open for long!'

'I'm only surprised that you made it at all,' Althea began. Then she frowned. 'Or perhaps not. You didn't know Guthrie had become my solicitor, did you, Wilfrid? You seemed a little put out to see him.'

And Hugo understood that Althea had seen Hugo's miscalculation as quickly as he had himself. Price-Babbington had not considered that he might be here this morning. The idiot had assumed that Althea would be attempting to defend herself, or at best might have a solicitor who would know nothing about the background to the situation.

And yet he had been prepared to withdraw the charges… It dawned on Hugo that Price-Babbington had brought the charge as a ploy to frighten Althea into giving the girls up. The mud that would stick to her name when word got out would not have mattered to him in the slightest.

He spoke coldly. 'With respect, Sir Richard, Mr Price-Babbington has brought a very serious charge against my client. I believe Lady Hartleigh deserves the opportunity to clear her name. Then, assuming Whittenstall—'

He broke off as the door opened. A clerk ushered an elderly, black-clad gentleman into the room.

Sir Richard rose at once. 'Good morning, sir.'

The old man nodded to him. 'Birnie. Good morning.' He looked around, his gaze settling on Hugo. 'And I suppose you're old Hugh Guthrie's sprig. Good man, your father. I was sorry when I heard of his death. Now, what's all this fuss about an heiress?'

Whittenstall seated himself beside Sir Richard, pulled out a pair of eyeglasses and settled them on his nose. He peered over them at the girls. 'Which one of these is the heiress anyway?'

'Ah, both of them, sir.' Sir Richard shuffled through some papers. 'We haven't progressed quite that far. We're still on the abduction charge.'

'We *weren't* abducted!' Sarah burst out. 'Cousin Wilfrid refused to let us stay!'

'Eh?' Whittenstall frowned.

'Sarah.' Althea reached over Kate and patted Sarah's wrist. 'I think we need to allow Mr Guthrie to explain, and then answer any questions.'

'But—'

'Sarah.'

'Yes, Aunt Althea.' She bit her lip. 'I'm very sorry, Your Honour.'

Whittenstall nodded. 'Not at all, my dear. I'm sure all this is quite a shock.'

Sir Richard pulled out a paper. 'I have here, Guthrie, a copy of the last will and testament of Frederick Price, in which he very clearly names Wilfrid Price-Babbington as guardian to his daughters, Sarah and Catherine.'

'Yes, your honour. I am fully apprised of the terms. Although my late father drew up that will, it fell to me to enact it.'

'Then I fail to understand why, on receiving instructions to enter these girls in a good school, you should have taken them to Lady Hartleigh.'

Hugo caught Price-Babbington's eye and smiled at the man's panicked expression. No, the man had not expected him to be present.

'This is all a misunderstanding!' Price-Babbington blustered. 'My intention in writing that letter was to have both girls enrolled in some suitable school! An educational institution! I... I have offered to withdraw the charge of abduction already!'

'Perhaps this letter will enlighten you, Sir Richard.'

'That's my private correspondence!' Price-Babbington lunged at Hugo, snatching at the letter.

Puck growled, hackles up, but didn't move.

'Control that brute, Cousin!' Price-Babbington jerked back, his face white.

'He's sitting, Wilfrid. Perhaps you should follow his example?'

Hugo smothered a crack of laughter as he passed the letter to Sir Richard. 'And there's this. Miss Kate noted down a conversation between Price-Babbington and his wife.' He handed Kate's deposition to the magistrate.

Whittenstall rose slightly to lean over the desk and look at Puck. 'Nice little chap. Some sort of terrier, is he, ma'am?'

Althea raised her brows. 'It's possible, sir. A friend found him as a puppy, in the yard behind her shop, and gave him to me. I've never enquired very closely into his ancestry.'

Whittenstall nodded. 'Very wise. Breeding's not always the most important thing, eh, ma'am? These crossbreeds often have a deal of game about them. And an excellent nose for a rat, I daresay.'

Althea inclined her head gravely. 'So it would appear, sir.'

His jaw rigid, Hugo met Sir Richard's gaze. To the man's eternal credit there was only the slightest flicker at his jaw to show that he'd heard the exchange.

Turning to Whittenstall, Hugo said, 'I took the precaution of making a copy last night, sir, thinking it might speed things along this morning. I had no chance to have it notarised, but you may check it against the original I just gave Sir Richard.'

Whittenstall took the offered copy. 'Thank you, Guthrie. Much appreciated.' He adjusted his glasses and scanned the document, as Sir Richard did likewise with the original and Kate's evidence.

Sir Richard passed the latter across to Whittenstall without comment, but with an icy look in his eyes.

When Whittenstall had read that, the two men exchanged glances.

Whittenstall spoke first. 'Interesting. Birnie, might we have that clerk of yours back in? Helpful to hear an unbiased, chap-in-the-street sort of view on this.'

Duly summoned, the clerk looked enquiringly at Sir Richard.

Sir Richard held out the letter. 'Read this, if you please, Sutherland. And tell us what sort of institution you think is meant.'

'What?' Price-Babbington sputtered, half out of his seat. 'I have already told you that I meant—'

'Hold your tongue, sir!' Sir Richard Burnie picked up his gavel and banged it down—Puck barked. 'You will leave Sutherland to form his own conclusions.'

Price-Babbington subsided.

Sutherland read the letter carefully. He looked up, scowling. 'Exactly what did you want my opinion on, Sir Richard? Seems clear enough to me.'

Birnie gestured to Whittenstall. 'My learned colleague will explain.'

Whittenstall nodded. 'What type of institution do you think is meant, Sutherland?'

The clerk frowned. 'Says it right there. A charitable institution.'

'There are many charitable institutions in our fair city, my good man. Would you suppose that a school was intended, for example?'

Sutherland blinked. 'Wouldn't be my first guess, sir. Given what else this Price-Babbington chap writes about—' he broke off, glancing about. 'Are these the... children?' He gestured at Sarah and Kate.

'They are.'

'Right.' His expression became pugnacious. 'I'd say he meant an orphanage, your honour.' He flushed. 'Calls them *pauper brats*. Says he prefers not to have them raised with his sons—'

'I meant only that—boys of an impressionable age, you know. They...they might fancy themselves in love or some such nonsense! It seemed safer for the girls if—'

'Are you telling us, Wilfrid, that your sons are not to be trusted around young ladies?' Althea enquired, her tone dripping sweetness. 'That says a great deal about their upbringing. And none of it good!'

'Thank you, Sutherland. That will be all for now. You've been very helpful.'

The clerk withdrew.

Sir Richard turned to Sarah. 'Miss Price.'

'Sir?'

'How did you and your sister reach London?'

'On the stagecoach, sir.'

'I assume that your cousin sent a servant to take care of you?'

'No, sir. The gig took us to the coaching inn. Vickers was supposed to go straight back, but he said the horse had a loose shoe and he took it over to the smithy and came back to wait with us for the coach.'

'I see. How old is your sister?'

'I'm eight, sir.' Kate clung to Sarah's hand. 'And Sarah is nearly fourteen.'

'Thank you, my dear. What happened when you reached London?'

'Why, Mr Guthrie met us. He said it was too late to make decisions that day so we dined at the inn, and then he took us back to his lodgings and slept on the sofa so we could have his bed.'

Sir Richard looked at Hugo. 'Did your reading of that letter concur with Sutherland's opinion?'

'Yes, your honour. I understood my instructions were to enter both girls in an orphanage.'

'And they remained in your lodgings while you made enquiries?'

'Yes.' He was going to have to tell the truth, and nothing but the truth. He hoped he could avoid the whole truth about *why* he had been unable to send the girls to an orphanage.

'But you took them to Lady Hartleigh instead.'

'Not immediately, sir. Since my father had acted

for the family for many years, I knew a number of the girls' relatives. I wrote to everyone I could think of, even Lady Hartleigh.'

'Why *even* Lady Hartleigh?'

'I knew her to be estranged from the entire family, especially her brother, and thought there was little likelihood on those grounds of her being willing to house the girls. Also, I knew her finances to be straitened.'

'But she did!' Kate protested.

Unthinking, Hugo smiled down at her. 'Yes, she did, sweetheart. I was completely wrong.'

'Hmm. So you ignored your instructions from the girls' lawful guardian to enter them in an orphanage.'

'Yes.'

'Why was that?'

'I thought they would be happier with a family member. Even one in straitened circumstances.'

'Yet you failed to inform Mr Price-Babbington of your actions.'

Hugo frowned. 'On the contrary. I wrote again to each member of the family I had previously written to on behalf of the girls, *and* Price-Babbington, informing them that Lady Hartleigh had offered the girls a home.'

Sir Richard raised his brows. 'Naturally you wished them to know the girls were safe.'

Hugo hid a grin.

Do be sure to stress my Christian charity, won't you? Especially to that insufferable prig Wilfrid!

He took refuge in a half truth. 'Something like that. The only member of the Price family to respond in any way was Miss Elinor Price, but I assume that Mr Price-Babbington received his letter.'

Whittenstall drummed his fingers on the desk. 'That rather brings us to the nub of the matter. The girls' inheritances.'

'But we haven't *got* inheritances, sir,' Sarah told him.

Whittenstall frowned. 'Your cousin didn't tell you? I understood that he took you into his care yesterday.'

'I wouldn't call it *care*,' Sarah muttered.

'Leaving that aside, Miss Price, did your cousin not inform you of your inheritance?'

'No.'

'I felt it was better,' Price-Babbington said, 'given that Sarah was quite intransigent, to defer any mention of her good fortune until she was more amenable to her new situation.'

'I see.' Whittenstall's tone suggested he was seeing all sorts of things to which Price-Babbington might have preferred he remained blind.

'It falls to me then, Miss Price, to inform you that your Great-Aunt Elinor Price—'

'She called on us,' said Kate. 'And Aunt Althea said she was our great-*great*-aunt, and that she was surprised she was still alive. And Great-Great-Aunt

Elinor heard her and said she was still alive because the devil wouldn't have her.'

From Whittenstall's face it was clear that he'd found his way through the morass of pronouns. Hugo didn't dare look at Birnie.

'Whether or not the devil changed his mind, Miss Kate, I'm sorry to tell you that your Great-Aunt Elinor died very recently. She has left you and your sister very handsome fortunes.'

'*Did* she?' Sarah stared at him. 'I didn't think she liked us. And Aunt Althea threw her out for being nasty.'

'Be that as it may, Miss Price, she left you and your sister ten thousand pounds each.'

Althea felt her jaw drop in unison with Sarah and Kate's gasps. *Dear God!* Even if they could stop Wilfrid's claim, all the girls' relatives would be offering them a home now. She swallowed hard. She ought to be glad for the girls—she was—not fighting back tears because she was going to lose them regardless.

She took a steadying breath, drew on the memory of Hugo's deep voice reciting a fairytale, and smiled. 'That was very kind of Elinor. You can thank her in your prayers tonight, girls.'

'Which brings us back to the question of guardianship.' Wilfrid looked smug. 'I am sure Althea must agree that a widow of straitened means is far from the best person to have charge of two wealthy orphans.'

'Must I, Wilfrid?' Althea kept her voice polite. 'I note you have not lost that irritating habit of telling everyone else what they must think.'

Whittenstall cleared his throat. 'That is a point, however. Guthrie, have you anything to say?'

Hugo rose. 'Yes. I would ask you to consider whether or not a man who put two unprotected young girls on a stagecoach bound for London, without making quite sure they would be met, is a fit and proper person to have charge of them. I will not go into detail about the dangers they faced had I been out of town or somehow not received that letter.'

'A…a mere oversight,' Wilfrid managed. 'Naturally I was expecting you to meet them or arrange for a substitute.'

Hugo looked him up and down. 'An oversight. I must also query the fitness of a guardian who declined to act for two orphaned children when they were destitute, sent them away from the only home they knew, lest they corrupt his impressionable sons, and snatched them back when they inherited a fortune. I would argue that he has not their best interests at heart and has thus disqualified himself as a suitable guardian.'

'And are you suggesting that *Althea*, with her tarnished reputation—' Wilfrid broke off, affecting a pious expression. 'I am grieved to raise this subject in front of innocent ears—perhaps the girls might be removed temporarily?'

'We're not going anywhere.' Sarah's mouth was a

flat line and Kate's hand was tucked firmly in hers. 'Aunt Althea took us in when we had nothing, and she's not so frightfully well-off herself. She was the only one who wanted us. We're staying.'

Whittenstall glanced at Sir Richard, who nodded.

'Agreed.' The magistrate gestured to Wilfrid. 'If you have something to say, say it.'

Wilfrid shot Althea a vicious look. 'My cousin has been ostracised by the family since Lord Hartleigh's death. Not only did it transpire that she had managed to run through her own fortune, coercing her trustees to hand over capital sums, but she attempted to recoup her fortune by engaging in liaisons of an unsavoury nature with an uncounted number of wealthy gentlemen!'

She sat very still and straight, chin up. 'Are you implying, Wilfrid, that you can't count to *two*? Because that is the number. I had affairs with precisely two gentlemen. Both of whom were unmarried, as was I.'

'The number, my dear Althea, is irrelevant.' Wilfrid adopted a pious expression. 'A woman's reputation is a very lovely and fragile thing. Once gone, it is gone for ever.'

Althea shrugged. 'Unlike gentlemen? Who can wade through the muck, tell lies and whore as much as they please without consequence?'

Sir Richard leaned forward. 'You admit the affairs then, Lady Hartleigh?'

She snorted. 'Since I'm not a hypocrite, yes. However, for the past six years I have lived very privately and, believe it or not, chastely.'

Wilfrid sniggered. 'Not so chastely that Guthrie here hasn't been seen visiting your house at all hours. And last night he did not go home at all!' He turned to the magistrates. 'This is a plot! A plot to steal the money of two defenceless girls!'

'You can't have thought they were so very defence-less when you put them on that stagecoach,' Whitten-stall remarked.

Sir Richard spoke. 'Guthrie, did you indeed remain at Lady Hartleigh's home last night?'

Hugo looked disgusted. 'I did. Your magistrate, Wilcox, had released Lady Hartleigh into my custody. I took that to mean that I should remain with her. In fact, he stipulated that I must do so. In addition,' he added, 'there had been an attempt by Price-Babbing-ton to snatch Kate the day before. The child was—'

'I had nothing to do with those men!'

'What *men*, Cousin?' Althea's voice dripped malice.

'Thank you, Guthrie.' Sir Richard gave Wilfrid an icy glare. 'I think we can dispense with any further accusations of impropriety, sir.'

'Well, it's…it's all very fishy if you ask me,' said Wilfrid.

'No one did,' muttered Sarah.

Whittenstall cleared his throat. 'Ah, Miss Price, you are very nearly fourteen, I believe.'

'Yes, sir. Next month.'

'Fourteen is the age at which we consider a potential ward in Chancery old enough to have a say in who their guardian should be.'

Kate spoke up. 'Mr Guthrie said that last night. He found it in a law book with Aunt Althea.'

Whittenstall smiled. 'Did he now? That's good to know.' He looked back at Sarah. 'If I were to ask you next month whom you would prefer as your guardian, what would your answer be?'

'Aunt Althea,' Sarah said. 'She gave us a home rather than sending us to an orphanage. We'd rather stay with her. Are you going to make us go with *him* for a month until I turn fourteen?' She paled. 'You… you wouldn't separate us!'

'No.' Whittenstall shook his head. 'As your friend Mr Guthrie pointed out, we must have your best interests at heart. Separating you and your sister would clearly not be in your best interests. So you would prefer to remain with your aunt, despite her straitened circumstances, rather than live in your old home in comparative wealth and luxury?'

Sarah looked down at Kate, who nodded. 'Yes, sir.'

'Very well.' He looked at Althea. 'If—I repeat *if*—I award you guardianship of these girls—Did you say something, Price-Babbington?—then you must understand that there can be no allowance made from their fortunes to reimburse you.'

'That will not be necessary, sir. I am perfectly beforehand with the world these days.' Please God, he wasn't going to ask how she had achieved that.

'I am more than a little concerned about that fortune you ran through,' Whittenstall admitted. 'While you will not have control of the girls' money, you must be able to teach them prudence. That you dissipated your own fortune...' He shook his head, frowning.

Althea shut her eyes briefly. She *couldn't* say this in front of the girls. She glanced at them. 'Will you trust me?'

They stared, then nodded.

'I... I must ask you to leave the room briefly. Perhaps you could take Puck out for a stroll with Mr Guthrie?'

Chapter Twenty-Two

Hugo made a protesting sound, but she turned to him, begging with her eyes. He was not proof against that, no matter that he wanted to take her into his arms and shelter her from everything. If she wanted the girls out, whatever she had to say must be bad.

He scowled. 'I don't like it, but if you ask it. Come, girls.'

They followed him out.

'Why did we have to leave, Uncle Hugo?' Kate demanded. 'And what's an *affair*?'

'Don't be silly, Kate.' Sarah scowled down at her. 'There's probably something about Papa that she doesn't want to talk about in front of us. Something awful he did.'

Hugo stared. How much else did the child know?

She met his startled, questioning gaze. 'Cousin Wilfrid wasn't exactly discreet about anything. He was furious that Papa left the estate so heavily mortgaged. I would have felt sorry for him if he hadn't been so horrid to us.' She touched Hugo's wrist. 'You should go back in.'

'And leave the pair of you to get yourselves arrested?'

The clerk, Sutherland, looked up from his desk. 'They'll be safe enough with me, sir. Got a lass of my own.'

'There. See?' Sarah grinned at him. 'We're perfectly safe. Kate?'

Kate held out the dog's leash. 'Take Puck. He growled at Cousin Wilfrid before. He might do it again.'

Somehow Hugo found himself with the dog leash in one hand and the other reaching for the doorknob.

'Well! I like *that*!' Wilfrid glared at Althea as the door closed behind Hugo and the girls. 'When I wanted them removed—'

'Oh, do hold your tongue, Wilfrid.' Ignoring him, she spoke directly to Sir Richard and Whittenstall. 'You must understand that my brother Frederick, the girls' father, was my principal trustee after our father's death. My godfather, our mother's uncle, had made me his heiress, and Frederick, as the boy, believed the money ought to have been left to him. Our father encouraged him in this belief. Both of them resented my inheritance bitterly.'

Wilfrid snorted. 'I hardly see how this—'

'Does Price-Babbington have anything to do with this, Lady Hartleigh?' asked Whittenstall.

She blinked. 'Nothing whatsoever, sir. He may already know the truth. I hardly care.'

Whittenstall nodded. 'May I ask why you wished the girls to leave? You did not scruple to speak of your past affairs in front of them.'

Althea swallowed. 'I did not wish them to hear what I must reveal about their father. They don't deserve that.'

Sir Richard looked at Wilfrid. 'You will remain silent, or you will be removed. And you will remember that anything said here in my court is confidential.'

He raised his brows as the door opened. 'Guthrie. What have you done with your charges?'

Althea's heart and stomach tangled into a vicious knot. 'Sir—'

Hugo let go of Puck's leash and the dog trotted straight to her, then leapt into her lap.

'The girls are in the outer office with your clerk, Sir Richard.'

He nodded. 'Continue, ma'am.'

Her arms closing around Puck, Althea groped for her thread of thought. She didn't want Hugo to hear any of this either. To know what a fool she had been! And yet... She met his eyes across the dog. Saw the unfathomable kindness that had found two young girls a home, saw the man who refused to judge.

In the face of that, she couldn't refuse to trust. She swallowed, and trampled down all her misgivings. 'After our father's death, Frederick was my trustee along with my godfather's solicitors. In time Frederick introduced me to his friend, Lord Hartleigh, who…courted me.' She swallowed. That was all any of them needed to know. 'We…married when I was just eighteen. I was encouraged to take some of the income from my fortune as extra pin money, and discouraged, indeed, forbidden by Hartleigh from taking any interest in the management of the capital. He considered it unbecoming in a female to interest herself in money matters beyond the household accounts. We lived in London much of the time, unless he wished to hunt or shoot. When he died in a riding accident I assumed that I would have more than enough to live on. I was amazed to learn that the capital was nearly gone. Apparently I had been requesting large sums for several years, and my trustees had acquiesced.'

Would they understand? Could they?

'But you had not requested those sums?' Hugo's swift understanding steadied her. His matter-of-fact tone suggested this might even be something that did not surprise him.

'No.' She fought to keep her own voice level, not to reveal the rage, the *hurt*, that seared at the memory of her brother's betrayal. 'Each time my brother informed the other trustees—'

'Who were they, Lady Hartleigh?' asked Sir Richard.

'What? Oh, my godfather's solicitors. Dunstable & Frome.'

Sir Richard made a note. 'Please continue.'

'Frederick gave them a letter supposedly from me, and they acquiesced. Eventually I discovered that these sums had been given to Lord Hartleigh who used them to pay off gambling debts.'

'So not only did *you* not run through your fortune, your brother assisted your husband in defrauding you?' Sir Richard's fist was clenched on the desk.

Althea fought to control her trembling hands. 'Yes. In fact, he was one of Hartleigh's creditors. I wrote to Frederick when I found out what had happened. I... I demanded that he restore my inheritance. He refused.'

'What a tarradiddle!' scoffed Wilfrid. 'This is to avenge herself on a dead man because he cast her off when she created a scandal!'

'That scandal was created by Frederick to discredit me when I threatened to tell the entire family what he had done.' She took a deep breath. 'I have the letters that I supposedly wrote requesting the release of the money. They are not in my handwriting, but Frederick's. I have Hartleigh's accounts, noting the amounts and their source, and to whom he owed gaming debts.' The bulk had been to Frederick, but he had not been the only one. That no longer mattered. All that mattered now—

'I did *not* fritter away my fortune, and you may be sure that I will do my very best to ensure that Sarah and Kate are taught to live within their means, and to ensure that they are not foolish enough to permit themselves to be cheated as I was.'

'Oh, *bollocks*, Althea!' Hugo erupted.

'Perhaps, Guthrie,' said Sir Richard, 'you might express your very understandable sentiments in more seemly terms.'

'Your pardon, Sir Richard.' Hugo turned to Althea, annoyance clear on his face. 'Don't you dare blame yourself for trusting your husband and your brother! *They* were the cheats. You said Hartleigh *forbade* you to take any interest in the management of your money?'

'Yes.'

Hugo turned to Wilfrid. 'Were you acquainted with Hartleigh?'

Wilfrid nodded, looking as though he would rather have been anywhere else. 'I... I was.'

'And was he the man to brook any disobedience from his wife?'

Wilfrid's smirk said it all. 'I should say *not*! Hartleigh had very proper ideas in that regard. Very proper.'

'I daresay.' Whittenstall's voice could have dried the Monday washing. 'Birnie, may I assume you are satisfied there is no charge of abduction for Lady Hartleigh to answer?'

'You may.'

Whittenstall nodded. 'Very well. Lady Hartleigh, the Court of Chancery is satisfied that you have acted in all ways in your nieces' best interests. The girls themselves wish to remain with you. So be it. You will continue as their guardian of nurture. The court will consider and appoint *suitable* trustees for their fortunes.' He looked at Hugo. 'Perhaps you might consider—'

'No.'

Althea stared. 'Why ever not? You didn't refuse when I appointed you as one of their trustees if something were to happen to me.'

'You have made a will in favour of your nieces, Lady Hartleigh? Appointed trustees?'

She flung Sir Richard an impatient glance. 'Of course I did. I had to ensure their safety as my idiot brother did not. Why not, Hugo?'

'I'm already trustee for part of their inheritance—'

She waved that aside. 'Not a very large part. I've little enough to leave them in comparison to Elinor's fortune, so—'

'Not quite true, ma'am.' Sir Richard rifled through the papers on his desk. 'Ah, here we are. Miss Elinor Price remembered you in her will also. I wondered at the wording when I read it, but it makes perfect sense now.'

He cleared his throat. '"*To my great-niece, Althea, Lady Hartleigh, née Price, only daughter of James Thurston Price and his wife, Anna, both deceased, having been defrauded by her husband and brother, the sum of fifteen thousand pounds to her absolute use and—"'*

'She knew?' Althea could barely breathe, her knees wobbled, and she was grateful for Hugo's steady hand under her elbow.

'I think so, Lady Hartleigh.' Sir Richard looked at her kindly. 'And you should know that she left it to your absolute use *if* you were still a widow when you inherited. Had you remarried the money was tied up so tightly that an ant couldn't have found a way to get near the capital.'

Althea didn't know if she was laughing or crying. 'She found out, and she trusted me.' It meant everything. After leaving her that day, Elinor had set to find out the truth and, finding it, had done her best to set things right.

'This is not *fair*!' Wilfrid glared around the room. '*I* was supposed to be Elinor Price's heir! She intended the money for my cousin Frederick, and after he died—'

'She found out that the fool had stolen his sister's fortune, gambled his own fortune away leaving his daughters destitute, and so she attempted to set things right.' Sir Richard Birnie leaned forward on his desk.

'None of that was *my* fault!'

'Cousin—' Althea felt a little bit sorry for him. 'If a loan would—'

'Lady Hartleigh,' Sir Richard interrupted, 'before you make that very generous offer, you should know that your great-aunt did not entirely disinherit your cousin. The residue of her fortune, some thirty thousand pounds, I believe, goes to him.' He smiled at her. 'He won't be a pauper.'

Althea looked at Wilfrid. 'You really are a toad, Cousin. You only wanted the girls back so you could ensure one of them married your heir.'

Wilfrid flushed. 'There's nothing wrong with keeping money in the family!'

'No? What about when it involves defrauding your sister?' Hugo rose from his seat beside Althea. 'Thank you for your time today, Sir Richard, Whittenstall. With your permission I will see Lady Hartleigh and *her wards* safely home.'

They walked. A breeze had sprung up, taking some of the heat from the air, and the day had cooled. The girls walked hand in hand, slightly ahead, with Puck trotting beside them.

'I'm rich again.'

Hugo smiled. 'Yes.' She'd said it a few times, as if she couldn't quite believe it. Her hand was safely tucked on his arm, and he hoped, he prayed, he was going to be able to keep it there.

'Not…not disgustingly rich, but *comfortable*.'

'Yes.'

'I shall stop at Mr Gifford's shop and see about that pianoforte for Kate,' she said.

'And what about something for yourself?' he asked.

For a beautiful woman who had lived in fashionable society, she had the least acquisitive nature of anyone he knew.

'Me?' She shrugged. 'I have nearly everything I really need. I'm not going out to buy things for fun. I'm not *that* wealthy.'

He latched onto that first sentence. 'Nearly everything? Then there is something you want?'

They walked on a little way, crossed Denmark Street.

'It's not something I can buy,' she said at last. 'Hugo, may I ask you a question?'

'Certainly.'

'What did you wish to talk about that last morning at Petersham? Because there was something I wished to say to you, as well. And I... I wondered if we wished to say the same sort of thing to each other.'

He glanced down at her, saw the slight smile. 'Very likely. You understand why I couldn't say anything before I left?'

She scowled then. 'Yes. Your wretched professional ethics. I might love you for having them, but—'

'You love me?'

'Yes, of course, but they're still a damn nuisance.'

She loved him. His heart danced, and for a moment he floated along the pavement, his head somewhere on a level with the dome of St Paul's.

'You love me.' He said it again, scarcely able to believe it.

'Yes…' She sounded rather as though she were waiting for something.

'Ah. I love you, too, you know.'

She chuckled. 'Very well. When are you going to ask me to marry you?'

His head threatened to annoy St Paul's again, but he forced his brain to clear. 'When you have all your new financial affairs in order, and everything tied up in a trust. With proper trustees who can be trusted.'

'What?' She stared at him. 'Do you think I don't trust you?'

He looked down at her. 'I know you do. And because I'm such a trustworthy fellow, we aren't going to so much as be betrothed until you have all that tidied up.'

'But—'

'I would have spoken months ago if not for believing the girls were going to become heiresses. If you think I'm going to take advantage of you when *you* have inherited a fortune, think again. Once we are officially betrothed you can't do anything with any of your property without my consent. Which I would give, but we aren't going down that road. You'll have this done before we're betrothed.'

She sighed. 'And, of course, neither you nor your partner can draw this up. I don't *know* any other solicitors!'

He grinned. 'Use that chap, Kentham, who drew up your aunt's will. At least we know he can be trusted to follow a lady's instructions. And I spoke to Lacy this morning very briefly when I saw him out, about him replacing me as the girls' trustee.'

'What? Why?'

'Because I can't be one of their financial trustees and be a guardian of nurture. Which I will be when we marry.' He laid his hand over hers. 'I'm sorry, sweetheart. More professional ethics.'

'Are we going to tell the girls now? Or does that have to wait, too?'

He chuckled. 'Kate already told me I should be buying you a ring when I bought the watch. I thought I'd ask their permission.'

She laughed. 'That sounds exactly right. When we reach home, Hugo, I'm going to kiss you. Will that be acceptable to your professional ethics?'

His fingers tightened on hers. 'That will be more than acceptable, sweetheart.'

Epilogue

Hugo held Althea's hand as they walked towards the river in the deepening twilight. Under the sheltering trees the evening breathed the scents of night. The lantern he held in his other hand surrounded them in a little pool of light.

'This,' he said, 'has been the longest month of my entire life.'

They had married at St Anne's, Soho, that morning. A wedding breakfast had followed in their new home on the corner of Soho Square. Aunt Sue, having come up to town for the wedding, had remained there to look after the girls.

'Take Althea away for a few days. Brighton or some such.'

But when he had asked Althea if she might like to go to Brighton for their honeymoon, she had looked a little surprised.

'Brighton? Well, it's fun, of course. And if you would like that, then—'

'Where would *you* like to go?' he had interrupted.

'I thought your house at Petersham?'

'That would be *our* house,' he corrected. 'Are you sure you aren't saying that to please me?'

Now, turning onto the path along the river, with Althea's hand secure in his, and their wedding night before them, he smiled to himself, remembering her snort of laughter.

As she was laughing now. 'A long month?' she quizzed him. 'I admit that it surprised me that you suggested a walk after supper instead of going straight upstairs.'

He slipped his arm around her and his heart leapt as she snuggled closer. He felt the press of her cheek on his shoulder.

'Sweetheart, I've been waiting to be married to you, not merely to take you to bed. I've missed these evening walks.' He dropped a kiss on her hair, smiling at the soft laughter that shook her. 'Although,' he added, 'I've every intention of taking you to bed as well. Or letting you take me. And we won't be needing my new watch, either!'

* * * * *

COMING SOON!

We really hope you enjoyed reading this book.
If you're looking for more romance
be sure to head to the shops when
new books are available on

Thursday 21st November

To see which titles are coming soon, please visit
millsandboon.co.uk/nextmonth

MILLS & BOON

MILLS & BOON ®

Coming next month

THE LADY'S SNOWBOUND SCANDAL
Paulia Belgado

She hesitated, then straightened her shoulders. 'I've come to ask you not to evict the residents at number fifty-five Boyle Street.'

'Boyle Street?' He rubbed at his chin. 'Ah, yes. I purchased that building from a Mr Andrews...no, Atkinson.'

And it had been a fine deal as well, as Atkinson had been eager to sell to stave off his creditors. Desperate sellers always offered the best bargains.

'But why would I need to evict the residents? Isn't it some shop or factory?'

Lady Georgina's mouth pursed. 'I'm afraid it is not, Mr Smith. Number fifty-five Boyle Street happens to be St Agnes's Orphanage for Girls.'

'An orphanage? In the middle of a busy commercial district?'

She let out an exasperated sigh. 'You bought it, didn't you? You didn't know it was an orphanage?'

'I did not.' He frowned. While he had instructed Morgan to clear the building, Atkinson definitely hadn't mentioned there were any occupants, nor that they were orphans.

Damn.

'Oh, now I see!' She clapped her hands together. 'There was a mix-up then? And you really aren't evicting the girls?'

'I didn't say that.'

She blinked. 'You mean to throw over two dozen orphaned girls onto the street?'

Elliot ignored the knot forming in his gut and erased the vision of shivering waifs out in the cold her words had conjured in his mind. He'd made many cutthroat decisions in business before, and this one would be no different.

But his next move would no doubt be the most ruthless one he would ever make.

'I could change my mind. I mean, *you* could change my mind.'

'Me?' Her delicate brows slashed downwards. 'And what is it I can do to change your mind?'

'Marry me.'

Her bright coppery eyes grew to the size of saucers. 'I—I b-beg your pardon?'

'You heard me. Marry me and I will rescind the eviction notice.'

'You can't be serious.'

He was deadly serious.

Continue reading
THE LADY'S SNOWBOUND SCANDAL
Paulia Belgado

Available next month
millsandboon.co.uk

LET'S TALK

Romance

For exclusive extracts, competitions and special offers, find us online:

f MillsandBoon

𝕏 @MillsandBoon

◎ @MillsandBoonUK

♪ @MillsandBoonUK

Get in touch on 01413 063 232

For all the latest titles coming soon, visit
millsandboon.co.uk/nextmonth

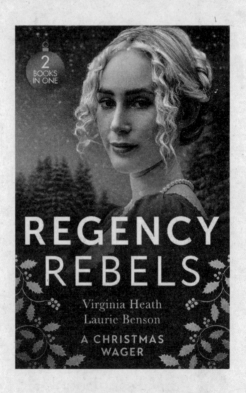